Just as they turned to go, a CSU, who had obviously been processing the car, jogged toward them.

"Excuse me, but I think you might want to see this."

He had a digital camera, the screen turned toward them.

"Shit," Mancusi said as she took a look.

Rachel wanted to feel vindicated, but all she felt was that spreading cold—it was everywhere now. "It's him," she said, her jaw tight. "He's Gemini."

She didn't care what Trick or Mancusi said. It could not be a coincidence that Sydney Cole had left a one-word message on the back of one of the pale leather seats. She'd written it in her own blood.

RACHEL.

By Kate Kessler

Dead Ringer

AUDREY HARTE NOVELS

It Takes One
Two Can Play
Three Strikes
Four of a Kind
Zero Hour (novella)

DEAD RINGER

KATE KESSLER

www.redhookbooks.com

Copyright © 2018 by Kathryn Smith
Excerpt from *It Takes One* © 2016 by Kathryn Smith

Author photograph by Kathryn Smith
Cover design by Lisa Marie Pompilio
Cover photographs by Arcangel Images
Cover copyright © 2018 by Hachette Book Group, Inc.

Redhook Books/Orbit
Hachette Book Group
1290 Avenue of the Americas
New York, NY 10104
hachettebookgroup.com

First Edition: October 2018

Redhook is an imprint of Orbit, a division of Hachette Book Group.
The Redhook name and logo are trademarks of Hachette Book Group, Inc.

The publisher is not responsible for websites (or their content) that are not owned by the publisher.

The Hachette Speakers Bureau provides a wide range of authors for speaking events. To find out more, go to www.hachettespeakersbureau.com or call (866) 376-6591.

Library of Congress Cataloging-in-Publication Data:

Names: Kessler, Kate, author.Title: Dead ringer / Kate Kessler.Description: First edition. | New York : Redhook Books/Orbit, 2018.Identifiers: LCCN 2018038236| ISBN 9780316439053 (trade pbk.) | ISBN 9780316439039 (ebook) | ISBN 9781549147838 (audio book (cd)) | ISBN 9781549171185 (audio book (downloadable))Subjects: | GSAFD: Suspense fiction. | Mystery fiction.Classification: LCC PS3611.E8456 D43 2018 | DDC 813/.6—dc23LC record available at https://lccn.loc.gov/2018038236

ISBNs: 978-0-316-43905-3 (trade paperback), 978-0-316-43903-9 (ebook)

Printed in the United States of America
LSC-C
10 9 8 7 6 5 4 3 2 1

DEAD
RINGER

REAL CRIME

GEMINI KILLER STILL AT LARGE

A madman whose signature includes rape, psychological torture and drugs. He's kidnapped and killed one twin while tormenting the other with images of her sister's abuse for more than two decades. With a body count of at least nine, he has managed to continually elude capture. Several of his victims remain unfound.

Suki Carlton was seventeen years old and new to New York City in the fall of 1994 when she moved to Manhattan to pursue a career in magazine writing. Christmas that year was the last time her family heard from her. Her identical-twin sister, Zoe, woke up early New Year's Day convinced something horrible had happened to her sister. The next day the first photograph was delivered. A new photo was delivered every month for six months, until Suki's body was found in an alley near the Chelsea Hotel. Her death was made to look like a heroin overdose. Police believed it had been accidental until Carlton got yet another photo of her sister—this time depicting Suki dying.

In April 1996, eighteen-year-old Grace O'Brien went to a Backstreet Boys concert in Hartford, Connecticut. She was supposed to meet up with friends afterward, but never arrived. Two days later, her twin sister, Marley, received a photograph of her sister. The photos continued to arrive on a semiregular basis for the next four years, when they stopped. O'Brien's remains have never been found.

During the period while O'Brien's twin received photos, three more girls went missing—Asia Newton from New Jersey, and Megan White and Hannah Ward, both from Connecticut. Asia was found one month after she had been taken, also dead of an apparent overdose. Her sister received two photographs. Megan's body was found four months after she was taken, killed in the same manner. Her sister received five photographs.

CHAPTER ONE

Wednesday

*B*etter wake up, Ray Ray. You know what day it is."

Some days, like people, were assholes. For Agent Rachel Ward, the eighteenth of May was the biggest asshole of them all. She didn't need that familiar phantom voice in her head to remind her.

She stretched in bed, wishing she'd had just a little more to drink the night before so she didn't remember it so clearly, but glad, from a hangover perspective, that she'd stopped when she had. Spending the day worshiping the porcelain god would be an even bigger mistake than the one lying next to her.

Rachel turned her head. Dason Patrick—Trick to his friends—certainly qualified as a big mistake, but he was currently her favorite. Having sex with coworkers was not a good idea, but the FBI kept her busy enough that there was little time for socializing, so it was either the devil she knew or trolling for strangers. Strangers often required flirting, and she didn't have the patience for that.

She didn't have patience for much of anything.

Trick opened his eyes and smiled. His mother was Korean, his father Irish. It made for incredible offspring. "You're feeding me before you kick me out," he informed her as he scrubbed a hand over his face.

"Pizza?" she offered. He'd shown up at her door the night before with a large pie heaped with her favorite toppings. Maika, another coworker of theirs, had arrived shortly thereafter with what seemed to be a water tower of rum. She ought to resent the two of them for rallying around her, but she couldn't. They had cheered Rachel's younger sister, Naomi, as well, but today there'd be no consoling either of them. Today there'd be only regret and sadness, the same as there had been for almost two decades.

Trick watched her, his smile fading. He knew what day it was. He wisely—kindly—didn't acknowledge it by asking how she was. "I'll cook. You grab a shower."

She didn't want him to be there when she checked the mailbox, because she wouldn't be able to hide her reaction when she saw that familiar envelope. It was her private pain, but she couldn't make herself tell him to go. She lay there, silent as he swung back the blankets and slipped out of her bed. She was able to ogle his lean, naked body for all of fifteen seconds before he partially covered it with the jeans he'd tossed on the floor the night before. They hung low on his lips, the cut of his obliques on brazen display. He didn't even seem to notice, just fastened his belt and padded barefoot to the kitchen.

Rachel lay back against the pillows, her hand sliding over the warmth his body had left behind on the sheets. This thing with Trick was becoming more frequent. More comfortable. It couldn't go on. It was too convenient.

But they knew each other, had the same job. He understood that her life was busy and sometimes dangerous. She didn't have to pretend with him, or watch what she said. They could talk about the tough cases, be honest about their shitty days. It was nice.

And last night she had needed him. Not just anyone, but him. She'd needed his dependable strength, his silence. She could trust him enough to be vulnerable with him.

Which was why she was going to have to end it. Just not that morning. Not when she might be able to persuade him into one more go-around before she really did kick him out. They had yet to invent a better way of avoiding reality than sex.

She got out of bed, grabbed her robe, and headed for the bathroom. Her left hand tingled as though it had been partially asleep. She must have slept on it again. She gave it a shake and wrapped her hair in an elastic on top of her head as she went. Five minutes under the cool spray woke her up, cleared the fog from her brain, and rinsed the cotton from her mouth. She shaved her legs and under her arms and then turned off the water. She toweled off, moisturized, and slipped into her robe. After breakfast, she'd spritz her hair with some dry shampoo and put on a little makeup to make herself presentable for work. Normally, she took the day off, but they were still looking for Sydney Cole, who'd gone missing three days ago, and she couldn't bring herself to take the time—not when she believed Gemini had taken the teenager.

Normally she didn't use nicknames for unsubs—it was frowned upon by most at the Bureau, but sometimes one caught on. She used the moniker because it gave focus to her rage and her hate. Her frustration and pain. She needed to call him *something*.

She was getting close to catching the son of a bitch, she could feel it.

Her bedroom was on the main floor, giving both her and Naomi privacy. They shared the brownstone that had been their grandparents' house in New Haven. It was convenient for Rachel for work, and for Naomi because of its proximity to Yale, where she both studied and worked.

The smell of bacon and coffee wafted toward her as she entered the kitchen. Naomi drifted down a few seconds later. She didn't seem surprised to find Trick in their kitchen—another reason to end things, Rachel supposed. Or a reason to keep going.

Naomi and Rachel shared their mother's red hair, but Rachel had their father's gray eyes, while Naomi's were bluer. Rachel was also several inches taller, at about five-eleven in her bare feet. Trick was still a few inches taller than that, which made her appreciate him that much more.

"Morning, you two." Naomi said with a smug smile. The brat didn't look the least bit hungover either.

Trick flashed her that killer smile. "Good morning, Sunshine. Breakfast?"

"Please." Then she turned to Rachel.

Rachel smiled a little sadly as her sister came in for a hug, and gave her a hard squeeze. And then, close to her ear so Trick wouldn't hear, "Check the mail, will you?"

Naomi's eyes widened. "Really?" Like she couldn't believe she'd ask. Not because it was such a secret, but because Rachel was always the one to check.

She nodded. "Please."

They didn't get mail delivery that early in the morning, but every year since that fateful day there'd been an envelope left for her sometime during the night before. They'd been more frequent in the early years, sometimes coming every month. Now it was only on the anniversary, and sometimes special occasions. Her parents had installed security cameras after the first delivery, but somehow the photos still got there. Once, they'd actually found one of the homeless people hired to deliver it, but he couldn't remember who had paid him to drop off the "gift." That's what the bastard called it on the notes he left.

Rachel went back into the kitchen, admiring Trick's naked back as she entered the room. He was all tanned skin with muscles rippling just below the surface. "Need help?"

"You can start on toast," he suggested. He never used to trust her to do even that, despite the fact that she was a decent cook, and proficient with a toaster. She glanced over her shoulder as Naomi walked in. Her younger sister shook her head. Rachel frowned. Nothing? That couldn't be right.

"Just a sec. I need to check something."

Both of them looked at her as she practically bolted from the room, but neither said a word. She opened the front door and stuck her head out—the neighbors didn't need to see her in her robe. It was a beautiful spring morning and she barely noticed, or cared. The mailbox was bolted to the side of the house. She lifted the lid and stuck her hand inside, groping around for what she was sure her sister had missed.

Nothing.

Her heart gave a bewildered and hard thump. What did it mean? She'd gotten an envelope on this date for the past seventeen years, without fail. She craned her neck, checking the porch, the steps, even the front lawn. Nothing.

Her fingers shook as she closed and locked the door. She turned, pressed her back against the heavy wood.

Eighteen years ago, Rachel's sister Hannah had gone into New York on a school trip and never returned. Police in both New York and Connecticut looked for her. Then the FBI showed up, because when they learned that Hannah was one half of a set of identical twins, they realized what had happened: Hannah had been taken by the serial killer they referred to as "Gemini" because he had a thing for twins.

The "good news," they said, was that Hannah was probably still alive, because Gemini liked to keep his victims for a while—as if that was a comfort. What they didn't tell them—not until they had to—was that Gemini also liked to send "presents" to his victim's twin. Rachel had already begun to think her sister was lost forever when that first envelope arrived just a few days later. She'd been horrified to open it and see a photo of Hannah, sitting on a bed in a tank top and panties.

She'd had bruises on her thighs. That's what Rachel remembered most clearly. Those, and the breakdown her mother had when she saw the photo. She tried to hide them after that—

sometimes she succeeded. The only person with whom she shared them was Agent Crouse at the FBI. Lauren Crouse, who was now her boss.

"Rach?"

She opened her eyes. Naomi stood there, at the far end of the foyer, her pale face stricken.

Rachel shook her head. They couldn't talk about it now.

Trick was at the toaster when she reentered the kitchen. He glanced over his shoulder at her. "What's wrong?"

She shook her head. "Nothing."

He regarded her a little while longer with his shrewd dark gaze. "Okay." He wasn't stupid. He knew what day it was. He knew the case, but he didn't push.

Rachel didn't release her breath until he turned back to the toaster, which was supposed to have been her job. She swallowed. What was that feeling in the pit of her stomach? Despair? Relief? Whatever it was, it didn't stop the damn thing from growling. And it wasn't going to help, so she ignored it and pushed Trick out of the way. "I'll take care of this. You concentrate on the eggs."

He glanced at her—she could feel it—but she hid behind her hair. When the toast popped, she grabbed it and started scraping butter across it like her life hung in the balance.

What did it mean that she hadn't gotten an envelope? Was he done with her? God, she'd just left Naomi standing there, wondering what it meant. Maybe there would be something in the box later. All these years that annual delivery had been a knife to her heart, but she'd also begun to look forward to it, in a macabre kind of way. The fact that it was not there made the ground feel unsteady beneath her feet.

"Do you want me to go?" Trick asked, his voice low, for her ears only. He was so respectful and considerate, she used to wonder if it was an act. It wasn't.

She forced a smile—that wasn't too hard to do with him. "Who will feed me if you leave?"

His lips curved. God, he really was gorgeous. "I'm sure you'd find someone."

It was meant as a joke, she knew that, but there was an edge to his words. She really was going to have to end this thing between them. Or at least put a little distance there. Using each other to scratch an itch wasn't doing it for him anymore. He wanted more, and she was inexplicably terrified to give it to him. Still, she couldn't bring herself to be a decent person and cut him loose.

"I've been without her for as long as I was with her," she blurted. "It's been so long that sometimes I actually forget, and then May eighteenth comes around."

"There are some wounds time can't heal," he said. "It just makes them deeper."

His words struck her, resonating behind her ribs. She couldn't even make her mouth open to agree.

Trick's phone rang. He turned the burner off before grabbing it out of his jeans pocket. "Patrick." Rachel watched as his lean face registered surprise. His gaze locked with hers. "I'll get her. We'll be right there." He disconnected. "Get dressed."

Rachel's heart rate kicked it up a notch. "What is it?"

"They found Sydney Cole. She's alive."

Rachel ran to the bedroom.

They pulled into one of the parking lots at the Westport train station a half hour later, after a very fast trip on I-95 with lights flashing. Emergency vehicles had come and gone, the victim having been taken to the hospital, but police were still on the scene, as were evidence-gathering teams.

When Hannah disappeared, similar teams practically gutted their house. Never mind that Hannah hadn't been taken from there, they still tore the place apart looking for evidence. Her mother had lost her shit. Rachel had just watched them, silently, guiltily, hoping they'd find something. Anything.

They found nothing.

It was just past eight, and commuter traffic was dying down a bit, but the lot was busy and fairly full. Police had cordoned off a large section to keep travelers from corrupting the immediate scene—and to minimize the chances of nosy onlookers, or reporters getting a good look.

Rachel remembered what it was like to be a cop and in the thick of a crime scene—that sense of determination, wanting to put the puzzle together and catch the bad guys. Since joining the Bureau she sometimes felt more like an observer than an active crime solver. The Connecticut police were the ones working this crime; they were just...backup. That's how it felt. Obviously, the FBI had been instrumental in the apprehension of many of the country's serial killers, but at that moment it felt like they were late to the party.

They showed their credentials to the cop who approached. "Are you alright, man?" Trick asked.

The uni nodded. He looked young and pale in the bright sunlight as he gestured for them to follow him. "Young white female found stabbed in a car parked toward the back of the lot. A commuter who parked nearby noticed her in the vehicle, went to check on her, and called nine-one-one. She thought the kid was sleeping it off."

"Does that happen a lot around here?" Rachel asked. "Drunken teenagers passing out in cars?"

The cop caught her sarcasm. "Occasionally. I think it was more wishful thinking on her part."

Trick ducked under the police tape. Just ahead, in a row of cars, a group of cops looked on as CSU did their job. "The ID on Sydney Cole, is it good?"

"It is," came another voice. A woman in a dark suit approached them with a no-nonsense gait. A little shorter than Rachel, she had shoulder-length brown hair, a sharp jaw, and dark eyes. It was Jordan Mancusi, a Connecticut State Police detective Rachel had partnered with before joining the Bureau. Rachel knew for a fact that under that well-cut blazer there was the body of an MMA fighter. She'd made the mistake of sparring with her in the past and had been bruised and sore for days.

"Her purse was with her." Mancusi nodded at the uniform, who then walked away.

"I don't have to tell you guys how surprised I was to find the girl alive," the detective said as she led them toward a black

Audi surrounded by cops. The doors were open, and the cream leather interior was covered in blood. "I thought for sure Gemini took her, but nothing about this points to him."

No. Only one girl—that they knew of—had ever escaped becoming a Gemini victim. He didn't let people go. And he didn't make a mess like what was smeared all over the interior of the Audi.

Rachel jerked her chin toward the vehicle, which unsurprisingly cost more than her annual salary. "Who owns the car?"

Mancusi hesitated, then straightened her shoulders. Bracing herself? "Alex Carnegie."

Sensation—like an ice pick under her ribs—jolted Rachel's body. "You're fucking kidding me," she growled.

Alexander motherfucking Carnegie? The man who for the last three years had been at the top of Rachel's Gemini suspect list? *That* Alex Carnegie?

Her former partner held up a hand. "Rachel, he reported it stolen."

"When?" she demanded. "This morning?"

"Well, yes. He says the car was missing from the garage when he arrived at his house here this morning."

"Quite a coincidence, don't you think?" Rachel challenged. "A Gemini suspect's car turning up with a Gemini victim in it?"

"There's no conclusive evidence against Carnegie."

She opened her mouth to fight, but quickly snapped her jaw shut. Both Mancusi and Trick thought she was irrationally obsessed with Carnegie—and they weren't all that wrong. Going on about him wouldn't convince them of his guilt, only of her own inability to look past him. The only way to show them the truth was to prove it.

Rachel cleared her throat. "CSU get anything off the car yet?"

"A bloody fingerprint on the passenger door, obviously a lot of blood in the car itself. They're checking for hairs, fibers—the usual. If our guy left anything behind, they'll find it."

And if that guy was Carnegie, he could dismiss all the evidence because the car was his to begin with.

"Someone should talk to Mr. Carnegie," she said.

Trick laughed. "Yeah, that won't be you."

The photographer had threatened her with a restraining order about a year ago, when she'd discovered that he'd done a photo shoot in Central Park around the time her sister went missing from the Met. That couldn't be a coincidence. She didn't care how many other people could have been in the park or museum that day. He fit the description witnesses gave of the man Grace O'Brien was seen with before her abduction.

She didn't care that he had an alibi for the night Heather Montgomery disappeared. Alibis could be manufactured. He was a photographer; he had property in all three states where the killings took place. And he was creepy as hell, though she seemed to be the only one who saw it. Every time she looked at one of his photographs, it reminded her of the ones Gemini sent her. It was him, she knew it.

Hannah would have been naive enough to trust someone like him. She would have jumped at the opportunity to tell her absent twin that she missed out on hanging out with a fashion icon. She wouldn't do it to be mean. She'd do it so she could share it with Rachel, and someone—Carnegie—had taken advantage of that.

"I'll be paying a visit to Mr. Carnegie," Mancusi informed them. Her expression softened when she looked at Rachel. "I'm not dismissing him, Rach. Not at all."

Rachel hated when she used her first name. It made everything more personal. She nodded. "I know you're not."

"Should you even be working today?"

"Oh, shit," Trick muttered. "I'm going to talk to the techs."

Rachel's nostrils flared as she watched him walking away, trying to find the right words. "Should I be home in bed? Or maybe on my shrink's couch? Neither of those things is going to bring Hannah back."

"Neither is crucifying Alex Carnegie—guilty or not."

"Yeah, well, we can talk about all that shit when *your* sister gets taken by a serial killer." She closed her eyes and sucked in a breath. "Does Carnegie have a connection with Sydney Cole?" Rachel asked.

"Not sure yet, but her mother was a model—she might know him. You'd think they wouldn't have reported her missing if she was with a family friend."

Rachel adjusted her sunglasses against the glare. "Unless there was something going on between them."

Mancusi stared at her. "Seriously?"

She shrugged. "Teenage girl, older man, it's an old story. Maybe she threatened to tell." After Hannah's disappearance she had gone through a bit of a wild period and had an affair with the father of a friend. Not one of her proudest moments, but the sex had been amazing. He hadn't been pleased when she ended things.

Mancusi didn't agree, but she didn't argue either. "She was definitely attacked in the car, given the amount of blood splatter. So whatever the circumstances, the attacker was in there with her at some point."

"Any sign of the knife?"

"Nope. We're searching for it, but as you can see, there's a lot of area to cover."

Rachel nodded absently. Nothing about this felt like Gemini, yet she'd been certain Sydney had been taken by him. By Carnegie. She glanced around, looking for cameras. "Did you get security footage?"

"Working on it," Mancusi informed her. "EMTs said that from the amount of blood, they guessed the girl had been here for about an hour, which means she would have been attacked between six and six thirty."

"Is that a heavy travel time here?" Rachel asked. She normally took the train into the city from New Haven, and rarely during rush hour.

"Sure," the detective replied. "It's an hour commute to the city, and taxes aren't too bad. Lots of people travel this route into New York every day—more than one hundred thousand, I'm told."

They could kiss evidence good-bye, Rachel thought. With that kind of traffic the entire scene was already completely contaminated.

"So, our stabber could have come here to catch a train, but why bring her along?" Rachel wondered out loud.

"Yeah," Mancusi agreed. "Maybe they figured Carnegie would report the car stolen. We're checking with MTA regarding trains going to and from Grand Central in that block."

Rachel doubted they'd come up with much. Like the detective had already stated, a lot of people made the trek from Connecticut to New York every morning. Though not normally splattered with blood.

But no one had reported seeing anything? A girl gets stabbed in a car and no one heard her scream?

"I don't think she was stabbed here," Rachel said, giving voice to her thoughts. "Unless Westport commuters see something but don't say anything."

Mancusi's lips twisted at her misuse of the slogan posted all over MTA trains and most public places in the state.

"So he drove to the train station with a bleeding girl in the back seat, but not to his final destination." Mancusi shrugged. "Less chance of getting pulled over, I suppose. Hard to explain that to highway patrol."

"How is the girl?" Trick asked as he rejoined them. Rachel kicked herself for not having asked the question earlier. She was just so used to not finding the people she was looking for alive. Today of all days, she ought to have been focused on the miracle of Sydney Cole. Instead, she was numb. No, not numb. She was cold with rage.

"Not sure. She was in pretty rough shape. They've taken her to the hospital."

"Parents been notified?" Rachel asked.

Mancusi shot her a wry gaze. "Not my first rodeo, *Agent Ward*."

Duly chastised, Rachel offered a sheepish grin. "Habit. Gotta ask. Okay, we'll leave the crime scene in your capable hands and head to the hospital. Let us know what you find out from Carnegie." The Connecticut police and the FBI had been working together for years to find the Gemini Killer, and both agencies would be painfully thorough in their investigation. They'd also be forthcoming with information—contrary to popular belief, cops and feds generally worked well together.

Just as they turned to go, a CSU, who had obviously been processing the car, jogged toward them. "Excuse me, but I think you might want to see this."

He held a digital camera, the screen turned toward them.

"Shit," Mancusi said as she took a look.

Rachel wanted to feel vindicated, but all she felt was that spreading cold—it was everywhere now. "It's him," she said, her jaw tight. "He's Gemini."

She didn't care what Trick or Mancusi said. It could not be a coincidence that Sydney Cole had left a one-word message on the back of one of the pale leather seats. She'd written it in her own blood.

RACHEL.

CHAPTER TWO

She ought to have become a photographer, Jordan thought as she pulled through the gates of Alex Carnegie's Westport home. Immaculate white stucco, gleaming windows, Corinthian columns, and beautifully sculpted landscaping lay displayed in front of her like some kind of offering. *Here, mere mortal, enjoy this splendor for a little bit before you crawl back to your hovel.*

She'd cranked the AC on the drive there, lifting her elbows out straight to cool the heated dampness under her arms. By the time she turned off the engine, she was chilled, and slipping on her jacket was a welcome reprieve. She stepped out into the afternoon sunshine, the May heat slamming into her like a brick. Typical Connecticut weather—a brief, wet spring followed by full-on summer. It had to be ninety-five. It was like someone held an iron against her back as she climbed the front steps and rang the bell.

A small Hispanic woman opened the door with a serene smile. "Hello," she said in richly accented English.

Jordan smiled. How very white of Carnegie to employee brown help. She showed her badge. "Good morning. Detective Mancusi. Is Mr. Carnegie at home?"

"Yes, of course. Please come in." The woman stepped back to allow her entry, then closed the door. "Follow me."

The inside of the house was exactly what Jordan had expected—large and spacious, cool and somewhat like walking through a museum. The clicks of her boot heels echoed slightly as she followed the housekeeper through the hall.

"Mr. Alex is in his studio," the woman said over her shoulder. "Would you prefer to talk in his study?"

"His studio is fine," Jordan replied. It occurred to her, and not for the first time, that it would be exceedingly easy to make Carnegie Gemini. Too easy. That was part of the reason she didn't believe it was him. He'd have to be incredibly talented to keep his professional life and his "hobby" separate. There would be rumors about him, wouldn't there? Something about him that made his peers uncomfortable? Serial killers could fake being normal, but not all the time. Someone with a high-profile job like his was bound to show his true colors once or twice, wouldn't they? Even his exes had nothing but nice things to say about him.

Though...did someone he dated for three months really count as an ex? None of his personal relationships had lasted longer than that. Maybe it was the hectic lifestyle. Maybe he was just a dog.

Or maybe he could really only give his heart to a girl who was chained up in his basement.

Carnegie's studio was at the far end of the house. Large double doors opened up into a two-story space with a spiral staircase at the far end. Three of the four walls were mostly windows, letting in the full light of day, yet it was comfortably cool. The walls were stark white. The ceiling was white. The furniture was white and black, and the floor was gleaming marble.

Just how rich was this guy?

"Mr. Alex, Detective Mancusi is here to see you."

Jordan saw him then—standing at a table on the left side of the room. He held a digital SLR camera in his hands and was looking intently at the screen. When he lifted his head, his expression was confused—the look of someone being yanked out of his head into the real world.

"What?" he asked. "Oh, of course. Come in, Detective."

Alex Carnegie was in his early to midfifties, Jordan guessed. He was tall—six feet at least—with a build that was somewhere between swimmer and cowboy—good shoulders, lean hips. He had thick, wavy blondish hair and bright blue eyes made even bluer by his tan. He looked like he should be in front of the camera, not behind it, selling cigarettes or cologne. That image was aided by the fact that he was wearing a white button-down with faded jeans.

He set the camera down and came toward her with an outstretched hand. Jordan accepted the handshake—his grip was firm but not dominating. "I won't keep you long, Mr. Carnegie," she said, glancing at the door as the housekeeper closed it behind her.

"I'm at your disposal," he told her. "I just got a call from Vic. She said you found Sydney? I can't tell you how happy I am that she's alive."

Right. Victoria Cole used to be a fashion model. Looked like Carnegie did indeed know the family. "We did find her, and that's why I'm here, Mr. Carnegie. She was found in your car."

He blinked. "My car? I'm afraid I don't understand how that's possible."

"The car you reported stolen. The Audi." She paused for a moment—for gravitas. "Can you think of any way that could have happened? We're at a loss."

He leaned against a nearby tripod. "Jesus." And then, "Does Rachel Ward know about that?"

That's the question he chose to ask? "She does."

He closed his eyes. Faint lines fanned out toward his temples. "She's going to come after me again because of this."

"It does look suspicious." Mancusi shifted her stance. "But that's why I'm here talking to you. Can you think of any way Sydney might have ended up in your car?"

He shrugged. "I suppose she could have been the one to steal it. They've been here on several occasions, and I've always treated them like family. They know where I keep my keys. I wouldn't be surprised if she knew my security codes as well."

"You don't seem particularly upset that someone you know might have robbed you."

"I'm not," he replied honestly. "Cars are replaceable. Human beings, as you know, are not. I would have lent her the car if she'd only asked. I can only suppose she had some romantic plan to run away."

Jordan's gaze narrowed. "Why would you say that?"

He smiled. "Sydney and Morgan are identical twins, but they're as different as you can get. Syd's always been the wilder of the two—fancies herself something of a rebel. I can see her wanting to impress some guy by doing something badass." His smile melted into a frown. "Though I don't understand why she'd take the Audi and not the Porsche."

First World problems. "Do you have security cameras on the property?"

He nodded. "I do, but the footage from last night is missing a chunk of time. My security company tells me the system got reset." He arched a brow. "Quite the coincidence, wouldn't you agree?"

Yes, it was. "So you think someone tampered with your system on purpose?"

"Detective Mancusi, what else am I to think? There's no way any of this just 'happened.' I wish to God I had that footage so I could prove that the car was indeed stolen, just to keep that lunatic away from me."

The lunatic was Rachel, of course. Jordan didn't know exactly what had happened between Rachel and Carnegie. Her former partner's obsession with finding the man who took her sister made her fixate on the photographer. She was convinced he was Gemini, and she'd set out to prove it—even going so far as to confront Carnegie. Jordan had heard that Rachel was lucky she hadn't lost her job over it. Carnegie didn't press charges, which only seemed to make Rachel all the more convinced he was the one.

"Agent Ward is well aware of the trouble she can get into if she harasses you, sir. Did any of your staff hear anything last night?"

He shook his head. "I don't have overnight staff. That's just too...pretentious." He smiled. She appreciated the self-deprecation, but it also made her aware that a man like Carnegie wouldn't have to try too hard to seduce a young woman away from her friends or family. "I divide my time between here and Manhattan, so the house is never empty for long, but Sydney would also know my schedule—I often speak to her and Morgan."

"Oh?" Jordan thought that was interesting. "About what?"

Carnegie shrugged. "School, life. Boys." He chuckled. "Both girls have expressed interest in the industry. Sydney wants to be a makeup artist, and Morgan is more interested in the editorial world. They're exceptionally intelligent girls. I have no doubt they'll succeed in whatever they choose."

"So, you're something of a mentor to them?"

He seemed surprised by the suggestion, as though it hadn't occurred to him. "Yes. I suppose I am. God, that makes me feel unbearably old." He chuckled again, a little rougher this time. "Is there anything else you need from me, Detective? I'd like to go to the hospital and check in on Sydney. Vic asked me to come by."

A not-so-subtle reminder that the mother didn't think he was a threat to her girls. Yeah, there was a lot of "coincidence" linking him to this case, but she had yet to find anything concrete.

"Who else has access to your security codes, Mr. Carnegie? Your staff?" The people who would know when he was going to be gone. Maybe even someone who knew how to meddle with the security system. Someone who could have seen the Cole twins at the house...

"Well..." He thought for a moment. "Yolanda, whom you met, of course. And Pete, who takes care of the grounds."

"Does Pete have a last name?"

"Gallagher."

"Is he working today?"

Carnegie gave her a confused look. "Pete has worked with me for years. He'd never steal from me. He's the one who called me to tell me the car was gone."

"I didn't mean to insinuate that he would." Jordan offered a friendly smile. "I just want to ask him a few questions. Maybe he noticed something and didn't realize it."

That seemed to mollify him. "He was here very early this morning to deal with the police, so I sent him home. I can give you his information if you'd like."

"I would, yes. Thank you. What time did Yolanda come to work this morning?"

"Seven thirty. Her usual. The car was already gone at that point, I'm afraid."

Yeah, she knew that. "Thank you for your time, Mr. Carnegie. If there's anything else, I'll be in touch. Meanwhile, here's my card." She took one from her jacket pocket and offered it to him. "If you think of anything that might be helpful, please don't hesitate to give me a call."

"Of course," he replied, putting the card in the back pocket of his jeans. "I'll walk you out."

At the main entrance to the house he pulled out his cell and sent her both Pete and Yolanda's information. Jordan would do background checks on both, just to be thorough. She was biased against Pete, of course, him being the male of the two. She was also going to dig a little deeper into Carnegie's own alibi. She didn't think he was Gemini, but that didn't mean someone close to him wasn't.

"One more thing, Mr. Carnegie. Do you have an assistant, or anyone else who would have access to your house and properties?"

"Why, yes. Blake Kelly has worked with me for the last...oh, twenty years, I suppose. I didn't mention him earlier because he's been away on business."

"Have you spoken to him recently?"

"I saw him two days ago in New York." Carnegie frowned. "Why?"

"Does he know your schedule?"

"Of course he does. Detective Mancusi, I trust Blake Kelly with my life."

"Just covering all our bases, Mr. Carnegie. Please call me if you think of anything else."

She shrugged off her jacket before getting into her car. She sat in the driver's seat and sent the information Carnegie had given her to Carl at the troop office to begin checking it. God, she hoped CSU got something useful out of that bloody print from the scene. Maybe they'd find the knife. There was security footage to comb through as well.

She'd just hit Send when a black Porsche drove out from behind the house and sped down the drive. Nice car. Again, she reconsidered her career choices. Then, she remembered that Carnegie was headed to the hospital.

Rachel was at the hospital.

"Fuck," she lamented, and reached again for her phone.

On the evening of their twelfth birthday, Rachel had wandered into Hannah's room to see if she was ready to go out. Their parents were taking them to get their ears pierced and then to dinner at the girls' favorite restaurant. Rachel had been counting down the days until she could get her ears pierced—she even had a pair of earrings on her dresser that she couldn't wait to wear.

Hannah was in bed. She looked sick. Rachel's stomach sank. "What's wrong?" she asked.

"I got my period," her twin replied.

"Your period?" Rachel stared at her. Why did Hannah always get things first? She lost a tooth before Rachel had, walked before Rachel had. She'd even been born first. Just once, Rachel would like to experience something before her twin did. "When?"

Hannah looked at her like she was stupid. "Today. After we got home from school."

Mom hadn't said anything to Rachel about it. "Well, get out of bed. We've got to go soon."

"I can't. It hurts."

"But we're getting our ears pierced," Rachel told her.

"Not tonight, I'm afraid," came their mother's voice from the doorway. Rachel turned to face her, stricken.

"But you promised! You said we could get our ears pierced!"

"And you will," her mother replied sharply. "But right now, your sister is unwell. You could at least have a little sympathy for her."

Sympathy! Why would she feel sorry for Hannah for becoming a woman before she did? "She ruins everything," Rachel said. "And I'm the one who pays for it."

"That is not true," her mother scolded. "You're being unfair. I'll take you tomorrow to get your ears pierced."

That wasn't the point. "*You're* unfair. *She's* unfair. My *life* is unfair!" With that, Rachel stomped back to her own room and slammed the door. She stood at her dresser and stared at the earrings she'd bought months ago. She'd probably never get her ears done now. Every day she waited to get them done was another day longer she had to wait to wear the pair that taunted her from her jewelry box. All of her friends already had their ears done. And now she was going to have to go to school tomorrow with naked lobes after telling everyone she was going to get them pierced. It was Hannah's fault. There was no reason why Mom couldn't still take her to get them done, and then take Hannah another day. Why did they always have to do everything together?

Together, or Hannah first. It was always Rachel last.

Though their rooms were separated by a bathroom they shared, Rachel heard her sister sob. Hannah was a loud crier. The sound of it echoed in her head. Her mother was right— she hadn't been fair. It wasn't just her birthday ruined by the arrival of Hannah's period.

She opened the door and crept back to Hannah's room. Her sister was curled into a ball, crying.

"You okay?" she asked.

"Cramps," her sister tearfully replied. "And you're mad at me."

"I'm not mad," Rachel replied. And she wasn't. Not anymore. It was gone as quickly as it had come. Silently, she crawled into her sister's bed, curving herself against her back as she wrapped her arm around her. She put her hand on top of the one Hannah pressed against her stomach. "Better?"

Hannah nodded. "I'm sorry I ruined everything."

"You didn't. We'll go tomorrow." She was silent for a moment. And then, "Do you feel like a woman?"

"I feel like shit," Hannah replied. Then the two of them started laughing. Rachel hugged her sister and closed her eyes. So what if she had to wait to get her ears pierced? What did it matter if they went out to dinner tomorrow night? She was exactly where she wanted to be. She didn't mind having to wait, or being second, so long as she and Hannah were together.

"She's alive. That's about all I can tell you at this point," the doctor said.

Rachel, standing with Trick and the doctor in the corridor, glanced at the couple sitting together in the waiting room. They leaned toward each other, knees touching, hands clasped. Their daughter—their *other* daughter—sat two chairs down from her mother and stared at the screen of her phone.

She knew the feeling of that isolation, that distance. She and Hannah had been closer to each other than to any one, or even both, of their parents. Morgan Cole couldn't console her parents, and she couldn't be consoled by them.

Rachel's parents hadn't wanted to console her. They blamed her.

"She's lost a lot of blood," Dr. Kullar continued. She was a little woman with a dark bob and a direct gaze. "Fortunately, we just had a blood drive. You're lucky your guy didn't have a better understanding of human anatomy, or you'd be talking to someone in the morgue right now."

Rachel hoped the woman's bedside manner was better than this. "When can we talk to her?"

"When— If she wakes up, we'll have to assess how strong she is and go from there. Excuse me. I have to get to the OR. I'm sorry. Here's my card. I'll answer any questions I can."

Trick thanked the doctor, then moved to Rachel's side once it was just the two of them in the hall.

"Let's hope she's better in surgery than she is in conversation," Trick quipped.

"We need to see the security footage from the lot," Rachel said, for his ears alone. Whoever had done this was on that feed, and she wanted to see his face. At that point she wouldn't even mind being wrong about Carnegie.

"Mancusi's going to send it over once she has it," Trick said, keeping his voice low. "You okay?"

She didn't look at him, but scowled her annoyance. "Of course." Just because her own sister hadn't been returned to them didn't mean she couldn't be happy someone else's daughter had. "Why wouldn't I be?"

He just looked at her.

Rachel scowled at him some more, straightening as Morgan Cole left the waiting room. "Go talk to the parents," she murmured, already moving toward the girl.

She was tall—just a couple inches shorter than Rachel. Her shoulder-length copper hair was pulled back into a loose ponytail, and her green eyes had a vaguely hollow look about them that Rachel recognized. She leaned her shoulder blades against the wall and looked down at her phone again.

"Waiting for a call?" she asked.

The girl's head snapped up. "Just checking the time."

"It's going pretty slow, huh?"

Morgan nodded. "Are you the FBI?"

Rachel smiled in what she hoped was a reassuring manner. "Yeah. My partner's in with your parents. Is it okay if I hang out with you for a bit?"

Slim shoulders shrugged. She had nothing better to do. The gesture made Rachel's smile more relaxed. "Sure. You lose a bet or something?"

Adopting a similar stance, Rachel frowned questioningly. "What makes you ask that?"

"Because you're stuck with me."

"I chose you. You know, I have a twin," she remarked casually. She refused to use past tense.

"You do?" There was real interest in those wide eyes. "Identical?"

Rachel nodded. "Mirror. You know what that is?"

The girl shook her head.

"It happens when the split takes place later in development.

My sister and I are identical, but we're mirror images of each other. I'm right-handed and she's a lefty."

"That's weird."

"You want to know what's even weirder?" Rachel showed her the Medic Alert bracelet she wore on her left wrist. "I got this when I was seventeen. I got hurt kickboxing and when they did an MRI at the hospital, they discovered that I had a broken rib and a condition called situs inversus. All of my organs are on the wrong side of my body."

The look on Morgan's face was either awe or horror. "For real?"

Rachel nodded. "Yep. My heart's on the right side. My appendix is on the left. It doesn't just happen in mirror twins, and it only affects about one in ten thousand. But everything works the way it should, so ninety-five percent of those who have it don't even realize it. Bizarre, huh?"

"Uh, yeah."

Rachel waited a second before dropping the bomb. "My sister was taken by the Gemini Killer the year we turned sixteen."

Morgan stared at her, pale and horrified. "You're shitting me."

"I wish I was. You can look it up. Her name is Hannah Ward, and she disappeared during a class trip to the Met." Not her own class, though. Rachel pushed the thought away.

"Is she...dead?"

"I don't know. She's never been found."

A heartbeat of silence.

"Is that why you're an FBI agent?"

A small smile curved Rachel's lips. Sometimes she loved

teenagers—they were just self-absorbed enough that they didn't offer unwanted sympathy. "Kind of transparent, huh?" At the girl's nod, she continued, "Yeah. I like trying to find other people who are lost. It helps." Except that sometimes it didn't help at all.

"We were at a concert," Morgan shared. Rachel knew this, but she didn't interrupt. "We were with friends. I don't know how someone managed to just walk out with her."

Training made her want to start asking questions, but she resisted. "I know. I don't know how my sister vanished either, but Sydney's back now." And someday this girl was going to realize just how much of a miracle that was.

"Is she?" The girl blinked back tears. "Even if she lives, we have no idea what he did to her. She'll never be the same again."

"Maybe not." She wasn't going to lie to the kid. "But with your help she might get pretty close. That's better than my sister will ever get."

Morgan had a gaze that threatened to see too much. "Do you ever wish it had been you instead?"

"All the time."

They stood there for a moment, gazes locked, understanding one another as only two people with such similar circumstances could. For those few seconds, the hospital and all the chaos of it ceased to exist.

"Did you know that scientists can now tell the DNA of identical twins apart?" Morgan asked suddenly.

Rachel shook her head. "I didn't."

"It takes a while, and it's hard to do with twins that share habits and environment, but still, it's pretty interesting. They have to melt the DNA."

"I'm not sure how I feel about that. When I was young, I hated people treating my sister and me like we were the same person, but after she was gone, I felt like part of me was missing." Half, to be exact.

"Do you ever feel her?"

Not *did*, but *do*. "Sometimes. I know it's not real, though."

The girl tilted her head. "I didn't feel anything the day she disappeared, but I woke up this morning with a pain in my chest. Do you think it was her?"

"Could have been. I don't know how it works, I just know that sometimes we know, and sometimes we don't. There's nothing you could have done either way."

Morgan turned her head to look at her. "Thanks."

Rachel nodded. Now if only she could believe that herself. But it was impossible, because she knew she could have done something that day. She could have changed everything.

But she hadn't.

"Do you know anyone named Rachel?" she asked, thinking of that bloody scrawl the CSU had shown her.

A shake of copper hair. "I don't think so."

"Can you think of any reason your sister would have had Alex Carnegie's car?"

"Alex?" The girl looked confused. "She was with him?"

"She was found in a car he reported stolen early this morning. Does that make any sense to you?"

Frowning, the girl glanced away. "No. It doesn't."

She was hiding something. "Have you and Sydney spent a lot of time with Mr. Carnegie?"

Morgan slowly looked at her, her green eyes narrowing. "Are you the agent that accused him of being a serial killer?"

Rachel opened her mouth, unsure of how to reply...

"Morgan." The voice was familiar—so familiar, Rachel stiffened at the sound of it. She heard it sometimes in her dreams, when she searched for Hannah and couldn't find her. Or worse, when she did.

Morgan's face brightened as she turned her face toward him. Rachel turned her head as well, interested to see his reaction.

Alex Carnegie stopped dead in his tracks, about five feet away. For a second, he looked as though he'd seen a ghost—maybe he had. He went pale beneath his tan. Then his expression hardened. "You," he said.

Rachel forced a smile. It wasn't much of one, she could tell. "Mr. Carnegie."

"You're not supposed to come anywhere near me."

"I'm here on FBI business, sir. And you are the one approaching me." She turned back to the bewildered Morgan, who watched their exchange with wide eyes. "If you ever want to talk, or if you remember anything, please give me a call." She handed the girl her card, then straightened away from the wall and began walking toward Carnegie.

He inched closer to the far wall, as though he thought she might bite. It was all for show, she was sure of it. He wasn't any more afraid of her than she was of him. She didn't even look at him as she slipped into the waiting room and sat down in a chair with the best view of the hall. She watched as Carnegie approached Morgan and the girl fell into his open arms. He rested his cheek on the top of her head.

Would he hurt someone he obviously cared so much about?

She shook her head. Now was not the time for doubts. She knew what he was—felt it every time he was near. Just the sight of him was enough to make her skin crawl. It was like something clawing at her stomach whenever he looked into her eyes. Something trying to climb out of her, like a scream.

He would tell Morgan to stay away from her, that she was certain of. Because he thought she was crazy, or because he was really guilty. It didn't matter. Whatever connection she'd made with the girl was probably now lost.

Carnegie and Morgan walked into the room. Trick and the Coles looked up. Instantly, Victoria was on her feet, her beautiful, Botoxed face barely crumpling as tears ran down her smooth cheeks. "Darling," she said, enveloping him in a hug.

Rachel met Trick's gaze and gave him a slight nod. Time to go. He said something to Mr. Cole as they both stood and then moved past the group to join her at the door.

"Did you speak to him?" Trick asked in the hall.

"He spoke first," she countered. "I didn't say anything nasty. I didn't even look at him if I could avoid it."

"He irons his jeans." This was said with such disdain that Rachel couldn't help but smile.

"*Someone* irons his jeans, but I doubt it's him." She began walking, and he easily fell into step beside her. "The parents give you anything?"

"Nothing useful. They don't believe Carnegie was involved."

"Of course not."

Trick sighed. "You have to at least allow for the possibility that it was someone else, Ward. It's how we're supposed to work."

She made a face. "Mm."

"Wanting it to be him isn't the same as it actually being him."

Rachel shot him the stink eye. "Tell me you don't look into his eyes and see how dead they are."

"I think he's a conceited asshole. Possibly a sociopath, but Gemini has been meticulously careful, and that mess we saw this morning? That was just sloppy."

He was right and they both knew it. Nothing about this suggested they could be dealing with the serial killer, except for the fact that Sydney Cole was an identical twin. And Rachel's name had been left at the scene. It wasn't enough to prove it was Gemini.

But that didn't mean Carnegie was innocent.

"Let's go back to the office," he suggested. "It will be hours before we hear anything about the girl's condition. "We can look over the crime scene photos and see if we missed anything. Maybe Mancusi's gotten the security footage by now."

"Not like I can stay here, what with Mr. Restraining Order in the building." Officially, there wasn't really a restraining order—Carnegie had been talked out of it, but he'd been assured that Rachel would stay away from him, and she risked her job if she didn't comply.

"Yeah, Mancusi texted me but I didn't see it right away."

"That was nice of her." Maybe her old partner didn't resent her as much as she thought.

"Is it true you threatened to kill him?" Trick asked.

"Of course not," she replied in disgust. "I'd never find my sister that way. I threatened to keep cutting off pieces until we got to one he decided he couldn't live without."

"Jesus." Trick's laugh sounded strangled. "Remind me never to piss you off."

"Don't worry. I like all your pieces." Her smile melted as the hair on the back of her neck stood on end. Rachel glanced over her shoulder just in time to see Carnegie duck back into the waiting room.

The son of a bitch had been watching them.

CHAPTER THREE

Eighteen years ago

Y ou so owe me."

Rachel arched a brow as she finished putting on her lip gloss. "Seriously? You love going to the Met—and into the city."

"True. But I hate having to dress like you to do it." She grimaced at the jeans and T-shirt Rachel had picked out for her. "Could I be any more repellent?"

"Fuck off. You think I like dressing like you?" She gestured to her own clothing—long, flowy skirt and camisole topped with delicate layers of crochet. "I feel like I'm a fly in a spiderweb."

"Well, you look fabulous," her twin teased. "I guess we can suck it up just for one day—especially since I get to go to the Met and you're finally going to get laid."

Rachel flushed. The day before her twin had confessed to her that she'd slept with Aaron Newman two weeks earlier at a house party. Hannah knowing what sex was all about when she didn't was *not* acceptable. So she told her boyfriend, Cal, that today was going to be his lucky day.

Hannah was going to go on the class trip Rachel was supposed to go on, and Rachel, disguised as Hannah, was going to meet Cal at his house after the history test she agreed to take for her sister.

She wasn't nervous about having sex. She wasn't excited either. She was determined. Determined to put herself and her "big" sister back on equal footing again.

They walked to school as normal.

"If he doesn't have a condom, don't do it," Hannah told her.

Rachel scowled at her twin. "I'm not stupid."

Hannah made a face. "Yeah, you are, if you think giving it up to Cal is going to make him the least bit interesting."

"You're just mad because you wanted to date him last year and he wasn't interested." It was a low blow, but Rachel hated it when Hannah acted like she was somehow smarter or more worldly than she was.

Her sister looked her right in the eye, her expression full of hurt. "I'm not the one who acts like we're competitors instead of sisters."

Having no suitable reply—or excuse—Rachel remained silent for the remainder of the walk.

They went their separate ways once they reached school. Rachel wanted to apologize, but she couldn't make herself do it.

A hand touched her arm before she walked away. "You sure you want to do this?" Hannah asked.

Rachel nodded, pulling her arm back because she was having second thoughts and didn't want to give in. "Yeah. Go have fun."

Her sister raised an eyebrow at the brush-off. "Yeah. You too."

Rachel watched her walk away, but only for a second. Then

she headed to Hannah's homeroom and began her day pretending to be someone else.

It wasn't that hard. In fact, it was kind of fun. It didn't matter if she got an answer wrong, because she wasn't Rachel. She was Hannah, the smarter twin. People would be surprised if she was wrong, but they wouldn't feel sorry for her for not being as smart as her sister. The only subject in which Rachel got higher grades was history, because she seemed to have a knack for remembering dates and trivial things that really didn't matter in the real world. Taking the test for Hannah later that day would secure her twin a higher mark and improve her overall average, which would score points with the parental units.

She got through the day, but had to remind herself numerous times that she wasn't herself. She and Hannah had never switched identities for that long. She thought she had done a pretty good job, but there was no way she could write with her left hand, so she could only hope no one noticed.

They didn't, and she managed to finish the history test in record time. Being Hannah gave her more confidence, and she answered every question with her sister's flair for story and drama. She knew she'd gotten all the questions right—she'd taken a similar test for the same teacher the day before.

After class she skipped the rest of the afternoon. It was easy to do, she just pretended to be her mother calling in and excusing her. Then she walked over to Cal's house. He was eighteen and in college and had the afternoon off.

He kissed her when she walked in and took her straight

upstairs to his bedroom, where they spent less time making out than normal, and he was a bit more insistent taking off her clothes.

So this was how guys behaved when they knew they were going to get some.

Whatever Rachel had expected or hoped for the first time she had sex, a few sloppy kisses, a half-assed tweak of one nipple, and then two minutes of discomfort while Cal panted and told her how tight she was, was not it.

Cal actually wanted her to stick around afterward. He was going to order pizza and they could watch a movie. He was hoping they'd do it again—it was obvious.

"I think I'm going to go home," she told him. It was almost the end of the school day anyway.

He looked surprised. His lean cheeks were flushed, his blond hair rumpled. When he first asked her out, it had been like everything she'd ever wanted in a boyfriend had been handed to her. His appeal was only sweetened by the fact that Hannah had once wanted him because it was so rare that she got something that Hannah didn't.

Competitors instead of sisters.

God, she was such a bitch.

"Oh," Cal said. "Okay."

She picked up her backpack and started for the door. It took a few steps for her to gather her courage, but then she stopped and turned to look at him.

"I think we should break up," she said. Then, before he could say anything, she let herself out of the house and walked away. There was a slight burning between her legs and a deep disappointment in her gut. Innocence, she realized at that moment, had nothing to do with sex and everything to do with optimism, and she had just lost some of hers.

She owed her sister an apology. And she wanted to talk to her about what had happened with Cal. She needed Hannah to tell her it was okay.

When she got home, she went straight to her room—then left and went to Hannah's. Just a few more hours and she'd be herself again. She took a shower, put on some of Hannah's pajamas, and lay on her twin's bed. She worked on a paper that was due the next week and fell asleep with her face on her research book.

Her mother's worried voice woke her up a few hours later. "Hannah, Rachel didn't come home from the trip to the city." Her face was pale, her mouth tight. "Do you know where she is?"

Groggy and confused, Rachel wiped drool from her mouth and squinted up at her mother. She wasn't quite sure what she was talking about, so she gave the only answer she could, "I'm not Hannah."

"I have something to tell you," Trick said to Rachel when they were in the SUV on their way back to the field office in New Haven.

She glanced at him. "The last time someone told me that, it was followed with 'I think we should see other people.'"

"That would be weird, considering we're not even seeing each other, wouldn't it?"

Her head turned, but he refused to regret saying it. For months he'd allowed her to dictate the pace and scope of their relationship, because he respected her and it was what good men did. And for the first while he had thought they were actually moving toward something, but then Rachel just stopped, and they'd been stuck in the same place for a long time.

He supposed he should consider himself lucky. He was in his midthirties—his prime—and he had a hot woman who was more than willing to keep their intimacy level at friends with benefits. He was an idiot to want more, especially after his last relationship self-destructed like it had, but...yeah. He was an idiot. That didn't mean he'd wait forever. He was an idiot with pride.

"I'm not looking for a husband, Trick."

"I wasn't offering," he shot back. That stung. What the fuck was she looking for?

"No, but you're looking for something more than what I can give."

"You don't know what I'm looking for. You've never shown any interest. The last question you asked me that was even the slightest bit personal was if I minded if you spit rather than swallow."

"Jesus," she muttered. The pale skin of her cheeks flushed dark. "Is this really what you wanted to talk about? Because I'm not up for it. Not today."

"You started it." What was he doing, then? "I wanted to tell you something else."

"What?"

"It doesn't matter now." After that exchange the fact that he wanted to tell her that his given name was supposed to be Dae-sung seemed trite and pointless. Why give her any personal information, or share the fact that his mother had made his name more English-sounding in the hopes her son wouldn't be bullied? It was obvious Rachel didn't want to know more about him than she already did.

She sighed, pressing the tips of her fingers to her forehead. "Can we just stop talking, please?"

He tightened his lips and said nothing. She wanted silence, she could have it. Let her wallow in memories of her sister and the tragedy of eighteen years ago. Every time he tried to get close, or offer anything of himself to her, she walled up. A sane man would take the fucking hint.

No more personal stuff, then. "We need to check out Blake Kelly, Carnegie's assistant."

"He's not Gemini."

"You fucking clairvoyant now? You don't need to do actual investigating anymore?" he demanded, jaw clenched.

She looked surprised, maybe even a little hurt. "I'll look into him again."

"You do that."

They didn't speak for the rest of the drive, or the walk through the parking garage. They didn't speak for the entire time it took them to get into their section of the building either. Still, Rachel never tried to get ahead of him or walk behind. She kept pace with him, as if she was bound and determined to make the silence as tense as possible.

"Agent Patrick," their boss, Lauren Crouse, called as soon as they walked in.

Trick glanced up. The Special Agent in Charge stood in the doorway to her office, an expectant look on her face— one that said he was not to keep her waiting any longer. He didn't even bother going to his desk, he simply turned toward her and kept walking, right into her office. She closed the door behind him.

"How's she doing?" was the first question out of her mouth. Crouse was in her late fifties, average height, with dark blond hair and piercing blue eyes. She smoothed the skirt of her black suit before taking a seat behind her desk.

"As can be expected," he replied, also sitting.

"We're not considering this a Gemini abduction as of this morning."

He nodded. "I've seen no evidence to argue that conclusion."

"What about Agent Ward? Does she still believe it was Gemini who took the Cole girl?"

"She hasn't said."

"You haven't asked her?"

He met her gaze. "No, ma'am."

His boss regarded him for a second. "Would you be surprised to hear that Alex Carnegie called me a few moments ago?"

Fuck. "No."

"He said Agent Ward approached him at the hospital."

"He lied. Ward was talking to Morgan Cole when Carnegie arrived and approached them. As soon as Ward realized it was him, she backed off."

"Did you see their encounter?"

"No. I was with the parents when he arrived."

"He went to speak to the daughter first?" Crouse asked, her brow puckering. "That seems a little odd, doesn't it? That he'd go to the sister before the mother?"

Trick shrugged. "Could be that he saw her first. She was in the corridor."

"Mm." That was all she said on that. "But based on what you witnessed, Agent Ward behaved professionally?"

"She did, yes."

"Good. I'll consider Carnegie's histrionics addressed. But if Agent Ward even sneezes in that man's direction, I want you to tell me, understood? The last thing we need is a lawsuit."

Trick nodded, but he wouldn't throw Rachel to the wolves unless she endangered herself, or him. "She wants to catch this guy."

Crouse arched a finely plucked brow. "Of course she does. The monster took her sister. In all the years Agent Ward has worked at this field office I've not had one complaint—until she got it into her head that Carnegie is Gemini. I'm worried her obsession has clouded her judgment."

"It hasn't." He wished he sounded a little more convincing. "Ra...Ward wants to put Gemini away. She won't do anything that will risk her not finding what happened to her sister."

"Good. Bring me up to speed."

He told her everything they knew and what they were hoping to find out in the immediate future.

"Did the Coles know anyone named Rachel?"

Trick shook his head. "They go way back with Carnegie, though."

"I don't like how close Carnegie is to all of this," Crouse said when he was done. "Either he's involved, or someone's making it look that way. Dig deeper into him—and don't let Rachel know you're doing it. The farther she is from him or any investigation into him, the better. I'd pull her off this, but I know she wouldn't stop looking."

"Son of a bitch took her sister. Can you blame her?"

Crouse's lips thinned. "No, I cannot, which is why I'm allowing her to stay on the case."

"Speaking of which, I'd like to get back to it. Mancusi is supposed to send some information over. Unless there was something else you wanted to discuss?"

His boss sighed. "No. I'll brief everyone once I've talked with the state police. Meanwhile, watch out for your partner. I don't want her to suffer more than she already has."

"I will." He rose to his feet and walked toward the door. It was good of Crouse to be so concerned about Rachel and her well-being, even if it was more of a covering-the-Bureau's-ass kind of thing. What Crouse didn't seem to understand was that Rachel wasn't the only one she ought to be concerned about. If Trick was there the day they caught the man who took Hannah Ward and tortured Rachel with photos of her, it would take a small army to keep him from killing the bastard with his bare hands.

"I think there was something going on between Carnegie and Sydney Cole."

Trick looked surprised that Rachel spoke to him as he sat down at the desk across from hers. "We're talking now?"

"We're at work," she reminded him—a little more sharply than she intended. She wasn't going to continue a personal argument at the office. It was stupid, not to mention unprofessional. And besides, she liked him. Regardless of the sex they had, he was her partner and she trusted him with her life.

"Alright," he conceded. "Why do you think something was going on between them?"

"Just the way Morgan reacted when I asked her if she knew why Sydney might have been in Alex's car."

"So now you think Carnegie was her lover, not her attacker?"

"He could be both. She's underage. She could have threatened to tell."

"He left her alive. In his stolen car."

Okay, so she was grasping at straws. "He's Gemini, Trick. Why else would my name be left in blood at the scene?" Even he couldn't talk his way around that.

"Okay," he allowed. "Let's say he is, what do you think is going to happen when you prove it?"

"He'll tell me where Hannah is."

"Do you still think Hannah's alive?"

She heard the doubt—the concern—in his voice. "Would you wish for your sister to be held by a monster for more than a decade? Jesus, Trick. No, I don't hope she's alive. I hope she's dead. I hope that she's been dead for years and that I'm the only one he's torturing." The oldest Hannah appeared to be in any of the photos was in her early twenties, which meant he'd kept her for at least six years. Bastard. It made her want to vomit whenever she thought of it. What Hannah must have suffered...

It was obvious he didn't know how best to respond. "I'm sorry."

His regret—his pity—wasn't something she wanted or needed. "I just want to know where she is. I want to know where all those missing girls are, and bring them home."

"You think he'll give them to you? You know odds are he'll hold them over you to cause you more pain."

"He will," she said, voice low. Trick opened his mouth, but she cut him off. "Did you talk to Crouse?"

Holding her gaze, he nodded. "I did."

Rachel wanted to look away, but she didn't. "About me?"

"Yes."

"What did you tell her?"

"That I thought you could work this case, and I agreed to let her know if that thought changed."

She couldn't ask for anything more fair than that, she supposed. "Thank you."

"You can't speak to Carnegie again," he warned her. "Just stay the hell away from him."

"I will," Rachel agreed. "But when that print comes back and it's his, I'm going to be the one to put him in cuffs."

Trick simply watched her, his expression unchanging. "Why are you so sure it's him?"

"I can't explain it. I just know it's him."

"That's really not going to stand up in court."

Rachel's phone dinged. "It's Mancusi. She's sent the security footage from the lot."

Rachel turned on her computer screen and logged in. A few moments later the message from Mancusi was in her inbox. Trick braced his hand on her desk and leaned over her shoulder to watch—uncomfortably close, but she couldn't edge away, because she liked it. She was so twisted. It would serve her right if he met some nice woman and married her, living happily ever after while Rachel collected cats and tattoos.

The footage wasn't great—very few public security cameras were high quality—but it clearly showed someone in a hooded jacket walking away from where they'd found Carnegie's car and at the probable time. Rachel squinted at the screen as she watched the person join others on the platform.

"Average height for a guy, you think?" she asked.

Trick nodded. "I'd guess between five-nine and six feet. Can't see his face."

"That coat's about four sizes too big for him. He doesn't look very muscular."

"Neither do half the Taekwondo practitioners I know, but they could still beat me snotless."

Rachel inclined her head, even though she had a hard time

imagining that. She'd seen Trick fight. "Fair enough. I think that's definitely who we're looking for. Head down, avoiding eye contact, hands in his pockets."

"You'd think he'd have blood on him."

"Maybe that's why he's wearing the jacket—to cover it."

"It's not Carnegie—too slim."

"I'm aware of that," she shot back. "Maybe this person stole the car to save themselves from the same fate. Maybe they're a witness, not a suspect."

"Mm" was all he said.

"Innocent until proven guilty," she reminded him.

"You did not just say that to me," he shot back. "You would have had Carnegie in front of a firing squad for less."

"Shut up," she muttered.

He didn't. "That's not the Grand Central track."

"No, it's the New Haven side." Her heart gave a thump. That made their POI closer than she thought—and kept the investigation in the state.

They watched until the train pulled up and their suspect got on it.

"Seven-oh-one," Trick said.

"Not the express train," Rachel commented. She massaged her left hand—those damn tingles were back. "How long does it take to get to New Haven?"

Trick checked the schedule on his phone. "Seventy-two minutes. That's assuming this was his final destination."

"We'll need to get footage for every stop in between if it wasn't."

Trick was already looking for a phone number. "What car is that? Can you tell?"

"The third, I think." Just as she said it, Crouse came out of her office.

"Alright, everyone, listen up."

Everyone in the bull pen stopped what they were doing and turned their attention to the Special Agent in Charge, who gave them each an encouraging smile before she spoke again. Rachel thought she lingered a little longer on her, but maybe she was just being paranoid.

"This morning, Sydney Cole was recovered, alive but injured, in a car near the Westport MTA station. While she does not appear to have been a victim of the unsub the press named 'Gemini,' we are still assisting police with this investigation."

Rachel tried not to bristle. Every eye in that room had taken a glance at her when Crouse said the "G" word, and she didn't want them to see her reaction to their boss casually rejecting the theory Rachel herself was certain was correct.

"That said, I don't have to tell any of you that the ongoing search for the person responsible for twin murders in Connecticut, New York, and New Jersey is a particularly important one to this office, so until we know for certain Sydney Cole was abducted by someone else, everything you uncover is to be turned over to Agent Patrick. This investigation is our top priority, and I trust each and every one of you will treat it with the diligence it warrants."

More glances—not so secretive this time. Each one crawled across Rachel's skin.

"The car in which Miss Cole was found was reported stolen by Alexander Carnegie, who has been a person of interest to law enforcement in the past. Miss Cole is also known to Mr. Carnegie. We're running blood and prints found on the scene. Also, we have security footage of the parking lot in which the car and Miss Cole were recovered. Carnegie wasn't in state when the car was stolen. State police are following up with Carnegie's household staff and will keep us informed. Agents Patrick and Ward, anything you'd like to add?"

Trick leaned against Rachel's desk, hands in his pockets. He looked like he'd just stepped out of a *Vogue* photo shoot. "We have security footage of a suspicious individual on the train platform in Westport that fits with our timeline, and are following up on that lead with state police. We're also looking into Carnegie's alibi, given his relationship to the victim."

"Which was?" Maika asked, twirling a pen in her long fingers.

"Family friend," Trick answered. "Which means she not only had access to his property but knows security codes as well."

"She didn't steal a car and stab herself," Maika pressed, no mockery in her faint Haitian accent. "Carnegie's closeness to this makes all kinds of alarms go off for me. Either he's involved or someone's doing a good job dragging him into it."

"We're also interested in Carnegie's assistant, Blake Kelly," Trick informed them. "He's five-ten, skinny, and has access to all of Carnegie's properties. He's also got a few complaints on file from various women he's worked with. Apparently, he's a bit of a stalker."

"Speaking of stalker, hey, Ward," came a male voice from behind Rachel. "Where were you when the car was stolen?"

There were a few chuckles. They all knew about her past altercations with Carnegie. She didn't take it personally—it was meant as a joke. Rachel turned and shot the agent a droll glance. "With your wife, Kowalski."

More laughter.

"Alright," Crouse said, her voice rising above the noise. "Enough of that. Back to work."

Trick's phone rang.

"It's Mancusi," he said. Rachel didn't wonder why her old partner didn't call her instead of Trick. She knew why. She didn't want Rachel keeping evidence to herself. She figured when it came to Gemini, Rachel couldn't be trusted not to go vigilante.

"Hey," he said, holding the phone so Rachel could hear as well. "We just watched the security footage."

"Get this." The cop's voice was a little muffled over the phone. "A passenger on that train this morning found a jacket in the restroom stained on the inside with blood. Description matches the one worn by the suspect at the train stop. I'm driving up to Bridgeport to take custody of it."

"That was luck."

"Yeah, well, after we saw the tape, we put out calls to all stations along the line with a description. When the jacket was brought into the station and the staff saw the blood, they called us instead of sending it through to Grand Central."

Trick frowned. "Why would they send it to GC?"

"That's where their Lost and Found Department is."

Rachel didn't really care. "We can get those results faster using the Bureau's lab." It could take weeks to get results using the state lab that the cops used, but the FBI had its own, and Rachel had a friend there.

"Okay," Mancusi agreed. "We'll collect the samples, you guys analyze them."

"Sounds good. Talk soon." He hung up. "Okay, so what makes you so sure when we catch this guy he's going to give his victims' whereabouts to you? You gonna threaten to cut parts off him? Bury him alive?"

"No," Rachel replied, watching the footage again. "I'm going to give him what he wants."

"What's that?"

"Me." She forced a sweet smile as she looked up at him and dropped the bomb. "I'm the one he originally wanted."

CHAPTER FOUR

Jordan chewed a piece of mint gum before getting out of her car at the Bridgeport train station. She had finished off a large coffee on the way there and hadn't eaten since breakfast. It was now early afternoon and she had that acrid taste in the back of her mouth that was mostly bile and caffeine. Not the kind of thing she wanted to inflict on anyone.

Bridgeport was the largest city in Connecticut, but it was a far cry from what most of the world imagined when they thought of the state. At one time it had been a thriving industrial city. P. T. Barnum once served as mayor and housed his circus there in the winter. But when industry faded, poverty swept in. It was a shadow of its former self, with high crime rates and run-down buildings. The view from the highway was hardly enticing, but Mancusi had heard that there was some gentrification going on, and new developments popping up. Maybe the city could reclaim some of its former glory.

She parked in the fire lane in case she had to leave quickly, and entered the building. She had to go upstairs to find the ticket booth. Thankfully, it wasn't a busy time of day, though there were still a number of people inside and on the platforms outside. Did people even use the booth anymore? Most probably bought their tickets from the machines or had passes.

She showed the woman at the window her badge. "I'm here for the coat that was found on the train to New Haven this morning."

The woman's dark eyes widened. "Oh, yeah. Come on back."

The Staff Only door opened as Jordan approached it. The ticket agent held it for her as she crossed the threshold.

"I didn't know what to do with it, so I put it in this Macy's bag. I hope that's okay. I thought leaving it sitting out might contaminate it or something."

Jordan smiled at her worried expression. "I doubt your shopping bag is any worse than an MTA bathroom at rush hour."

The woman actually shuddered. "You are so right. The girl who found it picked it up by the hood, and as soon as I saw the blood, I put on gloves before I took it from her."

"I appreciate that."

"Yeah, well, these days you never know what folks might have, do you? You can keep the bag, by the way. I don't need it back."

Jordan had to suck in her cheeks a bit to keep from laughing. It would never have occurred to her to return a paper shopping bag. "Thanks. Is the person who found it still here?"

"Mm-hm. I put her in the break room. I figured you'd want to talk to her. Honestly, I think she was glad for the excuse not to go to work. Follow me."

The woman sitting, drinking coffee in the break room, looked to be about thirty years old. She had a sweet, round face and blond hair. She swore under her breath as she checked e-mail on her phone.

"Hi," Jordan said.

The woman's head snapped up. Her fair cheeks flushed bright pink. "Oh, my God. I'm so sorry. Are you Detective Mancusi?"

"I am." Jordan offered her hand as the woman stood, almost as tall as Rachel. "And you are?"

"Lauren," the woman replied as she accepted the handshake. "Lauren Miller."

"Do you work in Bridgeport, Miss Miller?"

"'Mrs.,' actually, and no, I was on my way to a meeting in Milford. I'm an event planner."

Smiling, Jordan took a seat across the table from her. "Who were you meeting?"

"A woman named LeeAnne Albright. She's putting together a conference for professional women."

"And the name of your company?"

Lauren reached into her pale-mint briefcase—which matched her coat and shoes—and handed Jordan her business card. Jordan glanced at it before tucking it inside her jacket.

"I'm sorry to have messed up your day."

"No worries. They rescheduled. So, you want to ask me about the jacket?"

Jordan nodded. "What car were you in?"

Bright blue eyes looked upward in thought. "Third? Yeah, the third."

"Did you see the person wearing the coat in your car?"

"Not that I noticed," Lauren replied with a shake of her head. "I usually work on the train, so I'm afraid I don't notice much around me."

"When did you get up to go to the restroom?"

"It was right when we left Southport. I spilled coffee on myself and had to go clean it up and wash my hands." She gestured to a barely noticeable stain on her shirt. "The jacket was hanging on the hook."

That was a surprise. "Not on the floor?" Had the perp wanted it to be found?

The blonde wrinkled her nose. "I would *not* have picked it up if it was on the floor."

Jordan smiled. "I don't blame you. Why didn't you just leave it there?"

"You know, I asked myself that same question." Blue eyes widened. "I should have, right? I mean, someone could have come back looking for it, but I didn't even think that. I just thought, 'Oh, someone left their coat. I have to turn it in.' Weird, huh?"

"Not at all. When did you notice there was blood on it?"

"Around Fairfield. When I finally snagged the conductor, she told me to get off here and take it to the office."

"Did anyone speak to you or pay strangely close attention to you?"

"Not that I remember, no."

"Okay." Jordan gave the woman her card. "Thank you for your time. If you remember anything else, please let me know."

When she got back to her car, Jordan put the Macy's bag in the back seat along with her jacket. Had Mrs. Miller been a little taller and a little thinner, she might have wondered if she was the person they were looking for, but a quick call to her employer would undoubtedly prove she wasn't.

And it did. Jordan had just disconnected from that call when her phone rang.

"Mancusi," she answered, slipping the key into the ignition.

"Hey, it's Carl." He'd been at the scene that morning. "I might have something."

"Give it to me."

"So, your fed friends and I were talking about getting Union Station security footage. I've got a cousin who works there, so I called him up, and he told me that they had a woman come in a little while ago who had been on that exact same train claiming someone stole her jacket while she was asleep."

Jordan arched a brow. "Really? Did he say what car she was in?"

"The second."

She smiled grimly. Steal a jacket in the second car, put it on in the third when you ditch the old one? It wasn't much, but it was something. It also meant the person they were looking for was a woman—or a very slender man. "Send me her info."

"Would you die for me?" Rachel asked Hannah shortly after they turned fourteen. They were lying on a blanket outside, staring at the stars twinkling in the summer sky.

"You're so dramatic," Hannah replied. Then she sighed. "You know I would, loser. Would you die for me?"

Rachel glanced at her and smiled. "Nope."

Hannah punched her in the arm. Shit, it hurt. "Asshole."

Laughing, Rachel tried not to rub the tender spot. "Yes, I'd die for you, but I'd try to save you first."

"Dying for me would save me."

"Then I guess I'd try to find a way to save us both."

"Did they recover the weapon from the scene yet?" Rachel asked Trick. They were both at their desks. Rachel had been silently going through details of Sydney Cole's abduction, trying to find something—anything—they might have overlooked before.

He shook his head. "They're still searching. Mancusi has the coat, though, and she's going to drop it off. Also, it looks like our unsub might be a woman."

Rachel leaned back in her chair. She was hungry, but she couldn't bring herself to go get food. "Might have been another potential victim."

"You'd think she'd go to the police instead of running away."

"Not if she's afraid he'll find her." They both knew scared people didn't always do what they "should."

Maika appeared at that moment and set a sandwich wrapped in cellophane on the desk in front of her. She gave one to Trick as well. "What about a jealous lover?" she suggested, pushing dark curls behind her ear. "Trying to take out the competition?"

Rachel considered it. "It supports the theory that Sydney and Carnegie were involved."

"Mm," Maika agreed, perching herself on the corner of Rachel's desk. "But makes less sense if our twin-killer is actually involved."

Trick unwrapped the sandwich. "Maybe the girlfriend found out the truth." They were just throwing things around, trying to find something that made sense.

"But why not call the cops?" she asked. "Why stab her and run?"

"Maybe the girlfriend's part of it," Rachel suggested. "We've theorized that Gemini has used an accomplice in the past."

"There was that girl," Maika began, holding up a finger. "Cassandra Lennox. We wondered if she was almost a Gemini victim. She and her twin sister were at a mall with friends. Cassandra was approached by a woman who claimed to be in the fashion industry and asked if Cassandra had thought about doing makeup for a living. She said she knew someone who could help her out. Cassandra said the whole thing didn't feel right, so she didn't go."

Trick glanced at Rachel. "You want to look into that?"

She nodded, her mouth full of tuna. She appreciated him allowing her to run with the Gemini angle. Hell, she appreciated that he still considered Gemini a viable suspect. If not for her name left at the crime scene, no one but her would even think there was still a connection. And the mention of the fashion industry was another arrow pointing at Carnegie, the slimy prick.

Rachel's phone buzzed. When she looked at the screen, she saw—along with a list of missed calls from her mother—that

Crouse wanted to speak to her. Great. She was probably going to be pulled off the investigation. Her sandwich churning in her stomach, she wiped her mouth with a napkin, got up, and made her way to her superior's office.

Crouse smiled when she spied her in the doorway. "Come in, please. I'll only keep you a moment. Would you mind closing the door?"

"Am I about to be set down?" Rachel asked, doing as she was told.

"No, but I presume you don't want everyone out there to hear our conversation. Sit." When Rachel did, the senior agent asked, "How are you holding up? It's a rough enough day for you already without the Cole girl being found."

Rachel sighed. "I can't do my job with everyone watching me like they're waiting for me to break."

Her boss folded her manicured hands on the top of her desk. "Are you about to break?"

Instinct told her to indignantly defend herself, but she didn't give in. "Are you questioning my ability to do my job?"

"Yes." Crouse didn't hesitate. "I am concerned for your well-being, but I am also concerned that any evidence you gather might be questioned at a trial, given your personal connection with the twin abductions."

"So, I'll let Trick do all the heavy lifting and sign off on everything. Please, ma'am, don't bench me." God, she sounded so whiny.

"I just got off the phone with Alexander Carnegie. He said you approached him at the hospital."

"That's not true. I was talking to Morgan Cole when he approached us. As soon as he arrived, I left the area."

Crouse nodded. "Good. Dason will handle him. The less rope we give Carnegie, the less he'll have to try to hang you with."

"I won't do anything to endanger the investigation, I promise." Now she sounded like a little kid. "I won't give Carnegie any reason to trouble you."

Crouse's brow creased. "Rachel, you need to know that the investigation comes second to my concern for you. Carnegie be damned."

Rachel stared at her. "Oh."

Her boss didn't seem to notice how much she'd been thrown off balance. "We both know that there's an overwhelming chance your sister is no longer alive. Do you really want to be the one that finds her?"

"Yes." Her voice was a cracked whisper, but it was honest. "I do. I need to." She wasn't going to launch into how it was her fault—that would only get her a psych eval. She was already dangerously close. She knew almost everyone involved thought she was unhinged.

Crouse sat there, impassively studying her for what felt like forever. "Okay. So this is how this is going to work: I want you with Trick at all times. Anything you find goes through him. I don't want any case we might build against Carnegie to get tossed out of court because his lawyer convinces a jury you tampered with evidence. Keep your head down and do *not* allow your emotions to influence your ability to work this investigation. Most of all, don't make me regret keeping you on."

Rachel nodded. "Of course. I won't. Thank you."

"Don't thank me. You might still get pulled."

A few moments later, Rachel rose to her feet and left the office with a sense of relief. She was still on the investigation, though slightly neutered. That was fine. She'd rather be a tagalong than not know what was going on.

Out in the bull pen, her phone buzzed. It was her mother. Annoyed guilt tightened her chest as she let it go to voice mail. She couldn't deal with her mother right now, with her questions and her hopes. It was too much even on a good day.

"What did Crouse say?" Trick asked when she returned. Maika was on the phone at her own desk.

Rachel fell into her chair. "What you'd expect. You're lead on this. I don't touch anything or do anything that might mess things up and I can stay on board."

He looked relieved, and she could kiss him for it. Never mind that she was still slightly irritated with him for earlier. She supposed she ought to apologize, but pride wouldn't let her. Not yet.

"Are we good?" he asked.

She nodded. "You know we are." And they were, or at least they would be soon. It was just their way.

Her phone buzzed again. This time it was Naomi.

"Hey," she said when she picked up.

"Is it true? You found the Cole girl alive?"

Rachel closed her eyes. It was her mother. Son of a bitch.

She glanced at Trick. He took one look at her expression, and immediately busied himself with something on his computer. "Mom, I'm working." She kept her voice low.

"Just tell me if it's true."

She sighed. "Yes, it's true." She was going to kill Naomi for letting their mother anywhere near her phone.

"Her parents must be so relieved."

"I imagine they are, yeah."

"Naomi said you didn't get a photo this morning."

So going to kill her little sister. "No, I didn't. Look, Mom, I really need to get back to work."

"What does it mean?"

Rachel winced at the shrill pitch of her mother's voice at the end of the question. "I don't know. It might mean nothing."

"He's never missed a year! And now this girl is alive! It has to mean something, Rachel!"

"*Mom.*" Had her mother gone off her meds? She glanced around to see if anyone was looking in her direction, but no one was. "I don't know."

"Liar."

Rachel started. "What?" Her mother never sounded so ugly toward her before.

"You're lying. You do know and you're not telling me. You're lying, just like you did eighteen years ago. None of this would have happened if the two of you hadn't lied."

Anger rose up from the bottom of Rachel's stomach. "The only difference not lying would have made is you'd be talking to Hannah right now instead of me."

"I bet *she'd* tell me the truth."

Rachel hung up. The tingling in her left hand had turned into a tremor that ran up the entire length of her arm. She knew her mother was close to breaking, that she shouldn't take her words to heart, but...

But it was terrible to know not only that she ought to have been the one taken but that her own mother wished she had been.

Nineteen years ago

"Fucking bitch."

Hannah didn't have time to defend herself. One second she was getting a drink from the fountain and the next her face was slammed into the cold, wet metal. Water went up her nose as pain exploded in her head. She tasted blood, felt the impression of teeth in her lip with her tongue.

She tried to lift her head, but strong hands held her trapped. The fountain continued to run, water filling her nose and mouth. She couldn't breathe. Every attempt filled her with more cold water. It choked her.

Suddenly the water stopped. The force holding her down was gone. She heard shouting as she lifted her head. Water streamed from her nose. Blood poured from her mouth. She brought her hand up to her face as she turned to see what was going on.

Nicole Jones had been the one to attack her. Nicole wasn't as tall as Hannah, but she outweighed her by a good thirty pounds. The girl wasn't fat, but she was solid. And at that moment, Rachel had her by the hair. She watched in shock as her sister drove her fist into Nicole's face.

"Stop," she said, but it was a hoarse whisper no one heard. How could they, when everyone around her was shouting at the top of their lungs.

Nicole punched Rachel in the stomach, making her lose her grip on the other girl's hair. Free, Nicole grabbed at Rachel's shoulders and brought her knee up, but Rachel twisted—narrowly avoiding a knee to the face. She wrapped her arms around Nicole's waist and lifted her off her feet, slamming her back into the brick wall. There was a loud cracking sound as Nicole's head hit; then the larger girl slid down to the floor, dazed.

Rachel stood over her, fists clenched, breath coming in heaves. "Don't you touch my sister again," she warned.

Nicole stared up at her. "Bitch made out with my boyfriend."

Hannah swallowed blood as her sister crouched down. "*I* made out with your fucking boyfriend," Rachel said.

People in the crowd started laughing. Nicole scowled. "He said it was Hannah."

"I guess he was too drunk to tell the difference." Rachel shrugged. "To be honest, it wasn't that great."

More laughter. Rachel shot a glare at the spectators. "None of you got anything better to do?" she asked. Then she offered Nicole her hand. "We'd better get you to the nurse."

Once she had Nicole on her feet, Rachel turned to Hannah. "You alright?" she asked.

Hannah nodded. "I think so." Blood dribbled down her chin.

Rachel grimaced. "Shit. You'd better go to the nurse too. Come on." She pulled a packet of tissues from her bag and handed them to Hannah, who wasted no time soaking them with saliva and blood. "That shirt's ruined," Rachel commented.

Hannah didn't care. "You're going to get in trouble for this."

Her twin shrugged. At this point, one of Nicole's friends had her by the arm and was already leading her down the hall. The crowd around them dispersed as the bell for class rang. "I've been in trouble before."

The waiting room for the nurse was also the waiting room for the principal. Rachel held Hannah's arm as she sat down, then took the seat beside her. The receptionist arched an eyebrow at the sight of them, then shook her head.

"Why did you lie?" Hannah asked.

"You mean why did I tell her I was the one who made out with her lame-ass boyfriend?"

Hannah nodded, her cheeks warming. Nick wasn't that bad. He was cute, and he played the clarinet in the school band.

"Because you can't fight worth shit."

"I don't need you to protect me."

"Yeah, you do. Your teeth okay?"

Hannah probed around with her tongue. Nothing seemed loose. "I think so."

"Good. I wish I'd been with you when Nicole showed up. I think you need stitches."

She pressed the damp tissues to her mouth and nodded. It

could have been worse. It would have been if Rachel hadn't been there. And all because she thought it would be fun to swap spit with another girl's boyfriend. It had made her feel edgy and rebellious—the way she thought Rachel must feel most of the time.

Tears filled Hannah's eyes. "Mom—"

Rachel cut her off, "Let me worry about Mom."

"But she'll be so mad." A tear scalded her cheek.

Rachel wiped it away. "Don't."

In the end, Rachel got suspended for two days—the principal went easy on her because she'd been defending her sister—and Nicole was suspended for a week. Hannah came back to school the next day to sympathy and concern. When Rachel returned, she was branded a boyfriend stealer—a slut. She was grounded for a month—their mother's anger had filled the house—and she took her punishment without arguing.

Rachel did it to protect her sister. Hannah wasn't stupid. She knew Rachel thought her the more deserving of the two of them. Rachel thought Hannah was better than her. Smarter. And maybe weaker. It had gotten to the point where Hannah didn't know if she ought to be thankful or insulted. Thankfulness won out—it always did.

Someday, though, she'd show her sister that they were equals. She could be tough too, when she needed to be. After all, she'd gotten Rachel to take the blame for her, hadn't she?

CHAPTER FIVE

We got a hit on the fingerprint on the car door," Trick announced when Rachel returned from the restroom later that afternoon.

"Who?" she asked. *Please let it be Carnegie.*

"Peter Gallagher."

She frowned as she sat down at her desk. "Who the hell is that?"

Trick turned his chair to face her. "Carnegie's groundskeeper. Apparently he takes care of the cars."

Rachel tried not to roll her eyes. "Does he have a record?"

"Attempted sexual assault in college. Charges were dropped and he's been clean ever since."

"Worth following up on, though. What about the blood?"

"It's not Sydney Cole's on the door—they ruled that out pretty quickly. They're running it against Gallagher's now. They'll send me results as soon as they have them. Everything in the car matches the Cole girl."

Rachel leaned back in her chair and yawned. She checked her watch. It was after five. "I think I need to head out. I can't think straight anymore."

"It's been a long day."

She didn't want to see the sympathy in his expression, so she looked away. "Yeah. Twenty bucks says my mother's there waiting when I get in."

He moved his chair closer, wheels squeaking. "Do you want me to come over tonight?"

She did. She really did. And not just for the sex and distraction. "No. Naomi will have questions, and if Mom is there, you don't need to be a witness to that shit show."

Trick nodded. "You know where to find me."

She reached over and squeezed his forearm. "Thanks. I mean it. And I'm sorry about earlier."

He nodded. "Come on, I'll take you home."

Rachel yawned again. She was exhausted. It wasn't the most intense day she'd ever experienced at work, but all of it together—her emotional connection to the case, seeing Carnegie, and it being the anniversary of Hannah's abduction—had drained her. She collected her things and walked with Trick to the parking garage.

"Did you find Blake Kelly?" she asked.

"His roommate says he left last night for LA."

"Convenient."

"Isn't it? Maika's checking out his travel arrangements."

When Rachel arrived home, almost an hour later, Naomi was waiting for her as she walked through the door. Their house was on Livingston Street, a fairly old and respectable neighborhood in New Haven. It had belonged to their grandparents, and to their great-grandparents before that. They could sell it for a lot of money, but there were too many good memories there and they loved the old place. One day they'd have to decide who got to buy the other out, but for now the sisters still felt like the house belonged to all three of them, and it wouldn't be right to do anything until they knew for certain what had happened to Hannah.

"I'm sorry," Naomi blurted. "I went to the bathroom. I didn't know she'd get my phone out of my purse."

Rachel managed a smile as she set her bag on the small table by the door. "I'm not mad at you." She had been when it happened, but not now.

"It's all over the news that you found the Cole girl alive," Naomi said.

"I know."

"How is she?"

"Still unconscious." She unclipped her holster and put both it and gun in the safe concealed behind a wall panel in the hall.

"Was it him?"

She sighed and shook her head. "I don't know. I think so, but there are a lot of inconsistencies." It didn't matter if Rachel herself was convinced; she wasn't going to get Naomi's hopes up. They'd been close to catching the bastard before, and every time they lost him, her baby sister lost a little more hope.

"You want a glass of wine?"

"Sweet God, yes." She kicked off her shoes and shrugged out of her jacket. It had been a warm day and she was sure she smelled ripe, but a shower could wait just a little bit longer.

They sat in the living room, on either end of the couch,

legs tucked up. She tried not to look at the photo of the three of them on the mantle, taken a month before Hannah was abducted. It hurt too much to see their smiles. Naomi never smiled like that anymore.

"Are you okay?" Naomi asked.

Rachel ran a hand through her hair—it felt sticky and gritty. "For the most part. Scared we're going to find her one minute, scared we won't the next. Mostly I'm angry, with a side of numb." But what else was new? She'd felt that way since the day Hannah disappeared.

"Do you want to talk about it?"

"I can't, and my best advice would be not to answer if Mom calls."

"She's already called me twice. She thinks you're keeping the truth from her."

"Of course she does, because I lied all those years ago. Tell her I didn't say anything to you either. She'll call me, or get Dad to." She tried not to think about how mean her mother had been earlier.

"She always freaks out on you."

"That's because she blames me." She took a drink of wine. The crisp white was cold and tart on her tongue. Delicious. "She needs to blame someone."

"She should blame him."

"Yeah, well..." She was done with the conversation. Instead, she stretched out one leg and wiggled her toes. "God, I stink."

"Bet Trick doesn't think so."

A little smile curved Rachel's lips at her sister's teasing tone. "If he does, he's smart enough not to say anything."

"He likes you, you know."

"I know." She met Naomi's earnest gaze with one of her own. "I like him too."

"And that scares you."

Rachel swallowed another mouthful of wine. She didn't want to talk about Trick either. "How's your love life, Squirt?"

Naomi smiled smugly. "Classic deflection."

"But no less valid." Rolling her neck, Rachel glanced at the pile of mail on the coffee table. "What's that?" she asked, nudging a large envelope with her toe.

"Don't know. It's for you."

She leaned forward, stretching to reach it. The envelope was light, and slipped easily from the pile. Her name was typed on a label on the front. There was no return address.

There wasn't a stamp, or postmarks.

Rachel's heart skipped a beat. "Shit," she whispered.

Naomi sat up straight, her pale face turning even whiter. "Is it…?"

Rachel tore it open. There was no point in getting gloves and hoping for evidence—there was never anything on the envelope. Gemini was always so very careful. But if Gemini had delivered this today, then he couldn't be Carnegie. Could he? But then, he'd gotten other people to make his deliveries in the past. She made a mental note to check the security camera she'd had installed a few years ago.

From the envelope she pulled an eight-by-ten photograph.

It was of her and Hannah, taken a few days before the abduction. They were hanging out with friends at a coffee shop they'd loved to go to. Rachel had gone back once after Hannah disappeared, only to throw up her coffee in the bathroom. She'd never stepped foot in the place after that.

In the photo, they were smiling and laughing. A tear slipped down her cheek as she traced her finger over her twin's bright face.

There was something else in the envelope. She peered inside, blinking away the tears. It was a card. On the front it read, *Happy Anniversary.*

"Asshole," she whispered. Then she opened it. Her head spun, and it wasn't from the wine. "Get my phone," she commanded.

Naomi didn't have to be told twice. "What is it?" she asked, jumping off the couch.

But Rachel didn't respond. She couldn't. She stared at the words written inside the card. *All my love,* it read.

And she was pretty sure it was written in blood.

So Trick ended up coming over anyway. Of course Rachel called him after opening her "gift." She was combing through her security camera footage when he arrived. It wasn't difficult to view—there was only one camera, which showed the front steps, mailbox, and a good portion of the street in front of the house. She wasn't expecting to find Carnegie himself standing on her front step, but if they could find the delivery person, maybe they'd finally get a positive ID. She had to hope, even though it had never worked out that way in the past. Most of the people who'd delivered the photos were either drunk, stoned, mentally ill, or hired couriers. None of them ever seemed to give the same description of who hired them.

The footage wasn't perfect, but it was clear enough that she could make out the features of their mailman, Jim. It was also good enough that she could see that he hadn't placed the envelope in the mailbox. She fast-forwarded through another chunk. Quite a few people walked by during the next hour.

"There!" she exclaimed, finally. A tall, lean figure came out of the left side of the frame. They had an envelope in their hands as they climbed the steps. The shoes and jeans looked similar to what the person wore in the MTA video, but the jacket was different. This one fit better, and even though the hood was up, it couldn't hide the long hair that slipped out. Was it red, blond, or light brown, though? The black-and-white footage made it almost impossible to tell, though Rachel thought it looked more blond or red. She pressed a key to save the image.

"We need to show this to Mancusi," Trick said when he saw the screenshot. "Apparently a woman on the New Haven train had her coat stolen this morning. We'll see if this matches the description."

"I thought it was done," Naomi said from where she stood, a few feet away from the dining room table. "Why does he keep doing this?"

"Because he gets off on causing pain," Rachel replied before she could stop herself, glancing over. "It's his porn."

Her younger sister stared at her with an anguished gaze. "*Your* pain."

Rachel nodded. She didn't want to talk about it. If she talked about it, she'd fall apart, and that wasn't going to do anyone any good. But when she finally had the man who'd robbed her of her sister in custody, then she could let it out.

Trick put on gloves to handle the photograph, envelope, and card, which he then placed inside an evidence bag. "You're right about the writing looking like blood."

"Fuck," Naomi swore.

Rachel and Trick exchanged glances.

"Hey, Squirt," Rachel said. "You don't have to listen to this, you know."

"Is that a kind way of telling me to leave?" the younger of the two women asked, a bite of defiance in her tone.

"Nope. Just an option."

Naomi's chin jerked down in acknowledgment, but she didn't budge.

"The blood from the print matches Gallagher's," Trick informed her, stripping off the gloves. "And your name was written in Sydney's blood. No prints. We'll run the blood in the card against that of both Gallagher and the Cole girl."

"And Carnegie."

He looked at her for a long time, it seemed. She couldn't tell what he was thinking, but she could guess. "And Carnegie."

"I know you think I'm obsessed with him..."

"Because you are." His tone was soft, but no less cutting.

"Why can't you trust my instincts about him?"

"I do, but I don't trust them completely. You're too close to this, Rach. I wish you'd step back, but I know you won't."

"Would you stop looking for your sister?" she challenged.

He thought for a moment, still holding her gaze. He didn't look away until he shook his head. "No, I wouldn't. I just don't understand why you're so convinced it's him."

"Because she wanted to be a model," Naomi blurted.

Rachel closed her eyes. *Fuck.* She felt Trick's gaze on her as heavy as an anvil on her shoulders.

"Who did?" he asked.

"Me," Rachel whispered. "I wanted to be a model when I was a kid."

Naomi didn't seem to realize she'd revealed anything. "So did Hannah, but she wasn't into it like Rachel. She was always buying *Vogue* and other magazines. She knew all the top models, makeup artists, designers—"

"And photographers," Trick finished. He pulled out a chair and sat down. "So, why him?"

"He did several shoots with twins," Rachel replied. "And I tried to contact him once. I wanted to see if he'd help with my portfolio."

"Did he?" Trick asked.

She shook her head, shame keeping her gaze low. "He turned me down." She knew how it sounded, but she couldn't lie. Not to Trick.

"That must have been disappointing."

Her head jerked up. "I don't suspect him because he rejected me, Trick. I was fifteen for Christ's sake. I understood even then that he was a very busy man and that he probably heard from dozens of girls like me every week. He was shooting in the area where Hannah was taken. She knew who he was too—she wouldn't have been afraid to talk to him. He likes twins. He creeps me the fuck out!" She winced at the volume of her own voice.

"That's not enough." His gaze was kind, but there was a glimmer of exasperation he couldn't hide. He didn't believe her. Didn't trust her instincts. If he could only see the way Carnegie looked at her—like he knew her. Once, he'd actually grabbed her arm, and she could have sworn he had a hard-on. She'd had bruises in the shape of his fingers for a few days. But that was when he threatened the restraining order and called Crouse about her.

"I *know* it's not enough," she ground out. "And I'm fully aware that's not him." She pointed to the laptop screen. "But it could be a partner or submissive doing his dirty work for him."

"For the unsub, you mean. Gemini."

Her jaw was so tight she thought it might lock. "Yeah. For Gemini." God, she hated him at that moment. She wanted to close the laptop and brain him with it. Instead she pulled a thick file out of the computer bag on the floor and slid it across the table at him. "Here's all I have on Carnegie. You read it and then tell me you don't think it's him."

Trick stared at the dog-eared file like he thought it might bite. "You have a file on Carnegie."

It wasn't a question, but she answered regardless. "Damn straight." His expression was exactly why she hadn't told him about it before.

He raked his fingers hard through his hair. "Rach, do you know how this would look if Crouse saw this? It looks bad enough to me and I'm your partner."

"You think it's obsessive. I think it's thorough."

Trick's eyes glittered. "I think it's fucking dangerous."

Rachel turned to her sister, "Na, do me a favor and order some pizza, will you? I'm starving."

Her sister stared at her. "Seriously? You're this guy's victim as much as Hannah was. I would think your partner might treat you with the respect that deserves. I'm not leaving you alone to defend yourself when you shouldn't even have to."

Trick looked as surprised by the statement as Rachel was. "Please, Squirt. This is between me and Trick."

Naomi muttered something under her breath, but she left the room to do as Rachel asked. "You've pissed her off," Rachel remarked.

"You shouldn't be on this case," Trick murmured. "You can't see anyone but Carnegie as a suspect."

"Because it's him."

"Yeah, well, it's Peter Gallagher's print on that car, not Carnegie's. And Blake Kelly's the one with the record."

"Gallagher works for Carnegie. Maybe he's his partner. Maybe that's him in the security footage. Maybe he's skinny and has long hair."

"I think we both know that's a woman." He nodded at the screen, which had now gone black.

"He's hired homeless people before." She was grasping, and they both knew it. A homeless person would have no reason to stab Sydney Cole and write Rachel's name on the back of a seat.

Trick just looked at her. "You need to consider stepping back from this."

Rachel pushed the folder closer to him. "Just read it. Please."

He hesitated, but then picked it up. "Okay." He pushed back his chair and stood.

"You're not staying for pizza?"

He shook his head. "I don't think that's a good idea."

She stared at him. A bitter chuckle escaped when she realized the truth. "I need to distance myself from the case, and if I don't, that means you have to distance yourself from me, is that it? Don't want to get anything on you if I come apart, huh?"

"I care about you," he told her, his voice rough. "Maybe you want that and maybe you don't, but it's true. That's the only reason I'm taking this file home with me instead of turning it over to Crouse. I will go through it, and if I think there's any real evidence against Carnegie, I'll pursue it."

"And if you don't?" Suddenly she regretted giving him the file. It was all she had—— no copies, nothing. What if he destroyed it? Or worse, what if he did give it to Crouse?

Trick shook his head. "I don't know. I'm not going to throw you to the wolves, but I'm not going to let you destroy your career—or mine—with an obsession."

"Why don't you believe me?" she whispered, then hated herself for showing him her vulnerability.

He reached down and took her cold fingers in his much

warmer ones. "Because you feel guilty for what happened to your sister and you're desperate to find someone else to blame. Anyone else."

Rachel snatched her hand away as she struggled to breathe. Did he have any idea how much he'd just hurt her? Not because he didn't trust her, but because what he said was mostly true. The truth really was a bitch. She turned her head so he wouldn't see the tears in her eyes.

"I'll see you tomorrow," he said. He didn't leave immediately.

She couldn't speak. She just sat there, fighting to keep herself together until she heard the front door close behind him. Only then did she allow herself to cry—for herself, and for Hannah. For everything. And when Naomi wrapped her arms around her, she leaned into her sister's embrace, because Naomi was the only one who never blamed her—never once. Naomi was the only one who believed in her. In her little sister's eyes she wasn't a fuckup. Rachel clung to that.

And she refused to think that Trick might be right. She wasn't obsessed with Carnegie. She was certain of him. And she was not going to think about what would happen if she was wrong.

Eighteen years ago

Hannah's favorite part of the Met was the Costume Institute—and the gift store. She loved looking at fashion and it didn't matter when or where it was from or who designed it. A lot of people told her and Rachel that they should be models. Rachel loved it, but the part of the industry that appealed to Hannah was design. She'd rather be behind the scenes than up front, where people would grade her on looks rather than on talent.

"That's ugly," her friend Cara said from behind her.

Hannah met the other girl's disdaining gaze, reflected in the glass case. "It's Versace."

Cara shrugged. "It's still ugly." She was a short, curvy blonde who never had to worry about finding jeans that were long enough or bras that were small enough, or guys who were interested. And she never got freckles, no matter how much time she spent outside. Bitch.

"It's one of the biggest design labels in the world. They're innovators. Rule breakers."

"Maybe they should start following the rules, or innovate some taste."

Hannah's right eye twitched.

"It's the responsibility of a designer to try to break rules and barriers," came a new voice from beside them.

Hannah turned her head. Standing there was a woman a little shorter than herself, with bright red hair done up in a casual twist at her nape and grayish-blue eyes. She wore black pants, heels, and a boxy men's-style shirt, but it was obvious none of it came off a rack. She looked like she'd just stepped out of *Vogue*.

"Didn't Versace say that?" Hannah asked.

The woman smiled. She didn't look much older than Hannah, but she seemed so much more worldly. "He did." She extended her hand. "I'm Grace."

Handshakes were kind of old-fashioned, but the gesture made Hannah feel oddly grown up. She put her hand in the woman's and returned the gentle pressure. "Hannah. This is my friend Cara."

Grace didn't offer Cara her hand, and the other girl didn't seem to notice or care.

"Isn't your name supposed to be Rachel today?" Cara asked with a faint sneer.

Face warm, Hannah shot Grace a sheepish glance. "Rachel is my sister."

Grace smiled. "Let me guess, she's your twin?"

"She is. She didn't want to come on the trip today and she knows I love this place."

"I have a twin too," Grace confided with a small smile. "She and I used to switch places all the time. Everyone thinks you're so much alike, but you know how different the two of you are. Sometimes it's fun to pretend to be somebody else. People are fairly easy to fool."

"Exactly," Hannah enthusiastically agreed. "They see what they want to see."

Cara nudged her with her elbow. "We need to meet up with the group for lunch," she said.

Hannah nodded. "You go ahead. I'll be right there." She turned back to Grace. "Do you work here?"

The girl-woman smiled regretfully. "I wish. No, I'm an assistant. We're shooting an editorial for *Harper's* in the park." Her smile turned conspiratorial. "I came here to use the bathroom."

Hannah chuckled, but she was a little bit in awe. *Harper's Bazaar*—was that what she meant? Of course she was familiar with it. "That must be so cool—working with magazines like *Harper's*, I mean."

Grace lifted her shoulders in a gentle shrug. "It can also be incredibly tedious. But I suppose I should get back to it. It was nice meeting you, Hannah."

"You too," she replied a little wistfully. She winced and silently damned herself for sounding like a little kid.

Grace hesitated. "Look, I'm not really supposed to invite people along, but I would have loved to meet someone like me when I was where you're at. It's a tough industry, and it helps to know people. If you want to see what it's really all about—and promise to be discreet—I'll introduce you to some people. We'll be set up somewhere between the obelisk and the statue of Hamilton this afternoon if you have time to break free."

Hannah knew what the obelisk was—her father had pointed it out one time the family had come into the city and gone for a walk in the park. "Okay. Thanks." If it was the last thing she did, she was going to get to that photo shoot—even if she had to take the MTA train home after because she missed the bus.

She joined "her" class for lunch, and was cautioned by the chaperones not to be late again, even though they approved of her "enthusiasm." Whatever.

It was a gorgeous spring day, there were tourists every-where, and it was relatively easy for a teenage girl to sneak away—even one who was almost six feet tall and had flaming-red hair. Once outside, Hannah slipped on her sunglasses and took off in search of the nearest entrance to Central Park. She left without even telling Cara where she was going, because her friend was flirting with some guy as she pretended to know all about a particular painting. God, couldn't the girl tell he was gay?

The obelisk, otherwise known as Cleopatra's Needle, wasn't far at all. Hannah found it without any trouble—it was hard to miss. There was a photo shoot going on, and there was Grace, on the edge of it.

The older girl turned her head as Hannah approached. For a second, her expression looked almost...sad. Then she smiled. "Hannah. I didn't think you'd make it."

"Are you kidding? This is awesome."

Grace continued to smile. "When they take a break, I'll introduce you."

And she did. Grace introduced her to the wardrobe techs and showed her what the models would be wearing next. That was when Hannah realized one of the models was Kate Moss. Oh, God. Rachel was going to *die* when she heard about this! Kate and the others looked so thin and cool, sitting there smoking cigarettes and drinking bottled water while the makeup artist touched up their faces.

All the while, she kept watching him out of the corner of her eye. One of the most influential fashion photographers of the late twentieth century. He looked like he could be a model himself. How did every woman there not have a crush on him? Or on his assistant, for that matter? Both of them were beautiful.

"Boys, meet Hannah." Grace introduced her to the two men, but Hannah hardly heard it. Everything—even the breeze—seemed to stop and sigh at the sound of his voice. He was tall and tan, with blond hair and bright blue eyes. He had a camera in his long hands, and a smile on his face. He shook her hand and treated her like a professional. Hannah felt frumpy next to all of these beautiful people. Wearing her sister's clothes made it all the worse. There was no way she could be comfortable—she just hoped she didn't make a fool of herself.

"I bet you're incredibly photogenic," he said to her. Not that she could be a model, but that she'd photograph well.

"I don't think I am," Hannah replied. "My sister's the one who likes to be in front of the camera."

"Which one of us is the expert?" There was a teasing note to his voice.

Hannah flushed. It was bad enough she admired his work, but to have him be so terribly attractive made it even worse. She could barely speak.

"Kate wants to talk to you," his assistant said.

Hannah watched him walk away.

"You can breathe now," the younger man said with a grin. "He's a little overwhelming, isn't he?"

"Too much," Hannah replied, smiling back. "What's it like to work with him?"

He shrugged. "Awesome. Shitty. Inspiring. Demoralizing. Everything." He gave her a wink.

"Don't you have anything else to do but flirt?" Grace asked with a smile as she approached.

"Can you blame me?" he asked. Then he gave Hannah another grin before jogging away.

"Boys," Grace said with a sigh, and shook her head. "Always getting distracted by a pretty girl."

"Kate Moss is more than pretty."

"I was talking about you, sweetie. You're every bit as lovely as Kate. She just has help bringing it out."

Hannah smiled happily. She'd have to remember that.

She stayed with them all afternoon—willfully ignoring the time to catch the bus to travel home. She'd call her mother before she was supposed to arrive home and let her know she was taking the train. Rachel would have to pretend to be her a little while longer.

She was so glad Rachel had decided to skip that day. Losing her virginity would be such an abysmal disappointment compared to this. She hoped Cal would at least be gentle. Hannah's own first time hadn't been much to brag about, but of course, Rachel couldn't let Hannah know something she didn't. Ray Ray was so competitive.

She couldn't wait to share this with her twin. Rach was the only person who would understand.

And maybe she was a little competitive too, because Rachel would be so very, very jealous that she'd gone to a real photo shoot with such famous people. There were at least three supermodels there. Not that she got to meet them. Finally, she was doing something exciting. It was always Rachel who took risks, who broke the rules. But Grace had been right, it was a designer's job to challenge and break rules. If Hannah never broke a rule, how could she expect to be a famous designer someday?

At the end of the day, she was sweaty and hungry. Grace offered her a bottle of water, which she took gratefully and drained almost entirely in one go. Not long after, she began to feel funny. Woozy.

"I feel drunk," she said. "But I'm not."

"Heatstroke," Grace supposed, taking her by the arm. "Come sit in the shade." She led Hannah to a town car and put her inside. "Rest here. We'll give you a drive to Grand Central once we pack up." The hand she placed on Hannah's forehead was cool and almost maternal.

"Thanks," she murmured. She'd call her mother from the station and let her know what train she was taking.

But Hannah never made it to Grand Central. She never called her mother and told her she'd be late. Her best friend had no idea what had happened to her and, high on flirting with city boys, didn't think the meeting with the woman in the Costume Institute had been important enough to mention. When she did think to mention it, she couldn't remember the woman's name. It started with a "G," she thought. And Cara thought she had red hair. It didn't matter, because no one who worked at the museum remembered anything. Hannah and the mysterious woman had been but two in a sea of hundreds, possibly thousands.

The police checked with modeling agencies, designer shops,

even magazines. Two photographers had been shooting in the area, but neither of them knew an assistant with bright red hair. No one had a record of Hannah.

The girl had simply disappeared. It wasn't until the first photograph arrived that anyone realized the truth of who had taken her, and the police realized they were never going to bring Hannah Ward home.

CHAPTER SIX

They were six years old, playing hide and seek at their grandmother's house. It was Rachel's turn to be It. She closed her eyes and slowly counted to ten as her sister's excited footsteps faded away. She didn't have to count fast—Hannah always picked one of three hiding places. Always.

"Ready or not, here I come!" she called after reaching ten. She checked the upstairs bathroom shower—nothing. She checked the guest room closet—nothing. That only left one place. Rachel tiptoed into her grandmother's bedroom and looked under the bed.

Nothing.

She sat back on her heels, frowning. Where was her sister? This wasn't like her. For a second, panic filled her chest.

Then she felt it. It was weird—like a tingle. She peered over the top of the bed at the closet. The tingle intensified. She smiled. Carefully, she stood and crept toward the door.

"Gotcha!" she cried as she yanked it open.

Hannah was on the floor, among their grandmother's shoes. She let out a loud shriek and then started laughing.

"I knew you'd find me!" she cried.

Thursday

Rachel woke up to an empty house that morning. She slipped out of bed and opened the closet door. It was empty, except for her clothes of course. Had she actually expected to find Hannah sitting on the floor, shrieking in delight? Christ, she was losing it. She closed the door and headed for the kitchen.

Naomi had left a note saying she had to go to the university early and that she loved her. Rachel smiled and set the note aside as she opened the fridge and dug out the leftover pizza. Breakfast of champions. She really had to stop eating so much of it, though. *But not today.*

Trick had texted to say he was going to check in on Sydney Cole at the hospital, and that Rachel could meet him there if she wanted. She didn't. Well, she did, but she didn't want to see him and she didn't want to risk running into Carnegie again.

She ate the pizza standing over the sink before slamming down a cup of coffee and getting into the shower. When she got out, there was a voice mail on her phone from Morgan Cole.

"I was wondering if maybe you might...like, be free this morning? Mom kept me home from school, but they're at the hospital, and I would kinda like to talk to you."

Interesting. Rachel called the girl back and told her she'd be there as soon as she could. Then she brushed her teeth, pulled on some clothes, and applied some mascara and lip gloss before twisting her hair up into a bun.

She stepped outside into another bright, warm morning. She stood on the step for a moment and looked around. What was she expecting? To find her twin standing in the middle of the street? Or maybe to find a man outside her house holding a sign that said I AM GEMINI? The street looked as it always did. A young man with a backpack walked past, bobbing his head to the music on his headphones. A few cars drove by, but other than that, there was nothing out of the ordinary.

So why did she feel like someone was watching her? Was it part of the irrationality Trick accused her of having? Maybe he hadn't come right out and said it in so many words, but he thought it. Maybe she really was losing her grip on reality, but she didn't think so. It wasn't that absurd to think Gemini might be watching. After all, he'd been watching her for years. What no one knew—no one but her—was that Gemini watched her a lot. She had the photographs to prove it. They showed up randomly over the years, but she had quite the stack in a box in the back of her closet. Photos of her going to school, the academy, her first day at the FBI. The photo with Hannah didn't count, because that had been taken before she disappeared.

If only she'd gone on that fucking class trip. She never would have gone off with anyone. She wouldn't have been so naive. So trusting.

Rachel hit the button on the fob to unlock her car and climbed inside, coffee in hand. She punched the address into her GPS and started the engine. It was almost an hour's drive to West Hartford—and that was without traffic. It would have been more convenient if the Coles had taken their daughter to the hospital with them, but she supposed they wanted to keep her away from the drama—and the press—as much as possible.

The Coles lived in a large, gray stone house—the kind of thing you saw on TV or in magazines. It was ostentatious without being gaudy, and somehow still managed to seem warm and inviting.

Morgan answered the door when Rachel rang. "Are they gone?" she asked, peeking around her.

Rachel glanced over her shoulder. "News vans?" When the girl nodded, she said, "I didn't see any when I pulled up."

"They mobbed us when Dad and I came home last night, and were back when he left this morning."

"Your mom stayed at the hospital?"

The girl nodded again. "They got her a cot or something. Dad took her some clean clothes. Do you want something to drink?" They walked into the large, modern kitchen.

"You must be feeling a little forgotten right now," Rachel remarked when the girl got her a glass of water. "I remember that feeling."

Morgan held out the glass. "I'm just glad we got her back alive." Then she paled. "I'm sorry."

Rachel shrugged one shoulder. "It's okay." She took a sip of water. "What did you want to talk about?"

"You asked me why my sister would be in Alex's car yesterday."

Rachel straightened. "Yeah, I did." When the girl didn't immediately elaborate, she asked, "Was there something going on between your sister and Carnegie?"

Morgan's fair cheeks flushed in that bright red fashion Rachel had always despised in herself. "What do you mean?"

"I think you know. Were they having a romantic relationship? Anything that might have put her in harm's way?"

The girl laughed, but she looked away. "God, he's old enough to be our father."

Rachel raised a brow. "That's not really an answer. And it doesn't explain why the two of them were together when we believe Sydney to have been kidnapped."

"He didn't do it. He wouldn't hurt Sydney."

She said it with so much conviction, Rachel almost believed her. "Has he ever hurt you?"

Morgan jerked back, as if burned. "Fuck, no! Alex would never hurt me."

Something in her tone made Rachel's eyes narrow. "Morgan, is there something going on between *you* and Alex?"

The girl blushed so dark Rachel knew she'd just asked the right question. "Promise you won't tell my mother?"

"Yes." But that didn't mean she wouldn't tell Trick, and she couldn't speak for him. Morgan Cole was underage, and it was something she could definitely use against Carnegie. Excitement trilled in her chest. "Tell me."

"Alex and I have been seeing each other for about a month now. It just kind of happened when we all were together for Easter. He treats me like an adult."

"I'm sure he does." It took all her willpower to keep that

from sounding how she truly meant it. "I was once involved with an older man myself. It's nice being treated like you're as old as you feel."

Morgan's eyes brightened. "I thought you might understand."

Oh, she understood all too well, which made her despise Carnegie all the more. He should know better. "I do. Were you with him the night before last?"

"The night his car was stolen?" At Rachel's nod, she added, "No. But I was with him when Sydney was taken."

The confession was like a punch to the solar plexus. "I thought you were at a concert."

"I was. For a bit." The girl visibly squirmed under her gaze. "Alex picked me up there. Sydney was going to cover for me. When we came back to pick her up, she was gone."

"Fuck," Rachel swore softly, turning her head so Morgan couldn't see the confusion and rage in her eyes. If Carnegie hadn't been the one to take Sydney, then who the fuck had? Blake Kelly?

She couldn't be wrong about him. She just couldn't. Kelly could be his accomplice.

Calm down, said a voice in her head. *You've got him for statutory rape.* If she could get Morgan to turn on him, that was.

"Are you okay?" Morgan asked, her expression full of concern.

"Yeah, I'm fine," she lied. "Just thinking out loud. So, does Alex have a woman who works closely with him? Someone with light hair?"

"I don't know. I haven't been around his work that much. Maybe? Mom would probably know better than me. I've never even seen him with a girlfriend before." She blushed. "That's why I was surprised when things happened between us. I always wondered if maybe he was gay. Oh, wait."

Rachel waited—impatiently—for what felt like forever.

"There is a woman. I think she's his assistant? I've only seen her once. We came to visit and she was just leaving the room. She's tall—like maybe your height or taller—and blond. I think her name was Anne."

Anne. "Is she thin?"

"Yeah. I think so."

Tall and thin and blond. Could be the woman who dropped off the photo. The same woman who could have attacked Sydney. This meant there could still be a connection between Carnegie and Gemini. But she was going to have to do better than that to convince Trick. Hell, she was going to have to do better than that to convince herself.

"Thank you, Morgan. I appreciate your honesty."

"So…" The girl twisted against the counter. "You believe me?"

"Is your mother going to be pissed if she finds out about the two of you?"

Morgan's eyes widened. "So pissed, but Alex said you suspected him, and I had to tell you the truth."

Lowering her chin, Rachel looked the younger woman in the eye. "It *is* the truth, yeah?" She'd never wanted something to be a lie so much in her life. No, that wasn't true, but close.

"Here." The girl picked up her cell phone and swiped her finger across the screen a few times. "Look." She shoved the phone toward Rachel.

It was a selfie of Morgan and Carnegie. They were in bed, and Carnegie appeared to be sleeping. He also appeared to be naked.

"He'd kill me if he knew I took it, but I couldn't help it."

The look of adoration on her face, the hope in her voice…At that moment Rachel really hoped, for Morgan's sake, that the kid was tougher than she looked. Because no fifty-year-old man got involved with a sixteen-year-old girl because he fell in love with her. He either wanted to fuck her, own her, or destroy her. Question was, which one was Carnegie's reason? She knew Gemini's.

It was all three.

Amanda Forbes returned Jordan's call just as she was pulling out of the Dunkin' Donuts drive-thru.

"I'm sorry it took me so long to get back to you," the woman said. "I've had a crazy last couple of days."

Jordan popped the tab on her coffee to let it cool before drinking it. "No problem. I just wanted to talk to you about the incident you reported to the MTA yesterday. It might pertain to a case I'm investigating."

"Yeah, so I fell asleep on the train on my way into New Haven yesterday and when I woke up, my jacket was gone and so was the chick who had been sitting across from me."

"When did you wake up?"

"The stop right before New Haven. What is that? Westhaven. Yeah, that's it."

"Do you work in New Haven?"

"Mm. At the hospital. I'm a cardiac nurse."

"Did anyone around you see anything?"

"No. Those 'If You See Something, Say Something' signs have really been helpful, huh?"

Jordan didn't tell her that they had been helpful in a few cases.

"What did the woman sitting with you look like?"

A heavy sigh rang in Jordan's ear. "Tall. Skinny. Blond. Really pale. She was wearing a jacket that was way too big for her, but her jeans fit and her shoes were expensive. She kept her hands in her pockets and didn't talk, and she smelled kind of strange."

"Like what?"

"Like a handful of old pennies. I don't know how else to describe it. Metallic-y."

Blood, Jordan supposed. "If I send you a photo right now, could you identify her, do you think?"

"I'm not sure."

Jordan sent the photo Trick had e-mailed to her that morning. "I just forwarded it to you."

There was a pause. "I think that's her. That's definitely my jacket. See where it's missing a button? It's in the left pocket. I never got around to sewing it back on."

The thrill Jordan always felt when pieces started coming together blossomed in her chest. "You're certain that's your jacket?"

"As certain as I can be in black and white."

"The woman, do you remember anything else about her?"

"She was pretty, but there was something weird about her. You know when you want to pet a dog but you're not sure if it will bite you?"

"Yeah, sure."

"Well, that's why I didn't talk to her. So I just closed my eyes and listened to my headphones instead. Then I passed out. Like I said, it's been a crazy last few days. Long shifts and not much sleep. Speaking of which, I'm being called by a patient."

"One more question. Do you remember where the woman got on the train?"

"I get on in Southport and she was already there."

A creepy woman who smelled like blood, wearing a large jacket, and who got on the train prior to Southport, which was two stops after Westport headed toward New Haven. Sounded right. "Okay, thank you so much, Miss Forbes. I'll let you get to your patients. If you think of anything else, please give me a call."

The woman promised she would, said good-bye, and hung up.

She pulled into a parking lot and quickly texted Trick what she'd learned. Was it possible Gemini was a woman? That would be statistically rare, but not unheard of. But it was more likely this woman was his lackey or even a brainwashed lover. Christ, maybe she was even one of his victims. It wasn't that far-fetched—several of them had never been found. Rachel's sister was among them. Maybe that's why he could go years in between kills—he kept his victims alive for a while. Groomed them to do his dirty work.

Had he made Hannah Ward do his dirty work before he

killed and disposed of her? If he had, she hoped Rachel never found out. He'd already taunted and tortured the family enough.

She wondered how her old partner was dealing. Part of her wanted to reach out, while another part was glad she was Trick's problem now. Rachel had always been a good cop, but she wore her sister's abduction like a fucking coat. It influenced everything she did, and how people treated her. So many of the guys had thought she was so tragic and hot—and that somehow made her a better cop? Fuck that noise. Jordan worked her ass off to get where she was, and the FBI hadn't wanted her. But they wanted messed-up Rachel with her PTSD and first-hand serial-killer knowledge.

But she wasn't bitter. Not much.

Jordan was almost to Westport when her phone rang. It was Carl. "What's up?" she asked.

"Heya. Two things—we found the knife."

"You're fucking kidding me. Seriously?"

"Yup. Found it not far from the edge of the platform. Blood matches the Cole girl. We're running prints now."

"You beautiful man. What's the second thing?"

"I got something weird from the hospital."

"What is it?"

"The stab wounds on the Cole girl were made by both left- and right-handed people."

Jordan let that sink in. "So, two attackers?"

"Or one attacker who is ambidextrous. The wounds made by the right hand were much more vicious than those by the left. However, it was a left-handed cut that did the most damage."

"There was only one person on that train platform. One person who stole a coat."

"So maybe your guy was involved after all. We determined she was attacked elsewhere, right? One attacker dumped her and the other... fled, or some shit."

"You're so eloquent, Carl."

"Hey, I was hired for my looks, not my elocution." He chuckled. "Anyway, that's it for now. You talk to the Gallagher kid yet?"

"On my way to Carnegie's estate now. Gallagher's working today. I'd better get going. Call me if you get anything else."

"Will do."

Jordan hung up and pulled back onto the street. Once she got on the highway, it was a fairly clear drive to Westport. She was still nursing her coffee when she pulled into Carnegie's drive. Seconds after turning off the ignition, she was approached by a young man who didn't look to be much more than twenty-five, dressed in jeans, sneakers, and a Motörhead T-shirt. He was tanned and his brown hair brushed his shoulders. She would have been all over him in high school.

"Peter Gallagher?" she asked, getting out of the car.

He nodded. He looked nervous. "Detective Mancusi, I guess?"

"Yes. Thanks for taking time out of your day to meet with me. I just have a few questions."

"About Mr. C's stolen car? I didn't notice it gone until I arrived that morning. I mean, it was here when I left at four the day before, and gone when I got here at seven."

"Any security footage?"

He shook his head. "Cameras were down. They seem to glitch a lot. I've mentioned it to Mr. C, but he hasn't gotten anyone in to look at them."

She didn't tell him that "Mr. C" had made it seem like the faulty camera was a onetime thing. "Maybe this unfortunate incident will make him rethink that."

"Maybe." And then, "Hey, is Sydney okay?"

"She's in stable condition." And that was all she was going to tell him. Jordan nodded at his hand. "What did you do to your thumb?"

He held up his hand. There was a ragged, dirty bandage around the thumb on his left hand. "Sliced it open doing some yard work. Yolanda took me to the hospital."

"Can I see?"

If he thought the request strange, he didn't show it. He peeled back the dirty bandage to reveal puckered white skin beneath, and several stitches.

"Did you take the Audi to the hospital?"

"It was out, so yeah. Yolanda drove."

Which explained his bloody print on the door handle. "When did this accident happen?"

"Day before yesterday."

"You never thought to wipe down the car after?"

A blush crept into his cheeks. "I would have if I'd noticed.

I was a little light-headed, y'know? I almost passed out on Yolanda. I'm not much for the sight of blood."

Jordan nodded. She'd verify this with the housekeeper at another time. She had no doubt that he'd cut himself, but the whole "fainting at the sight of blood" thing she didn't quite buy. Still, maybe it was true. Or maybe it was simply to throw her off. If Rachel were there, she'd probably slice herself open just to see how Gallagher would react.

"Is your boss home?" she asked. She'd gotten a text from Rachel informing her that Carnegie had been sleeping with Morgan Cole. She wanted to ask the asshole about it. Liked 'em young, huh?

"Uh…no." Gallagher's lean cheeks reddened. "I think he went into the city this morning, or something. He took one of the cars."

"Which one?"

Pink gave way to stark white. "Um, the Porsche."

She nodded and glanced toward the house. Curtains fluttered in one of the upstairs windows, but she couldn't see anyone.

"Has Mr. Carnegie ever brought women home with him?"

Gallagher shrugged. "Since I've been here, there's only been one. Anne, I think her name is. She doesn't say much, but she's nice to me. And sometimes the Cole girls come by. Morgan, mostly."

"Don't you think it's weird, teenage girls hanging around with a man Mr. Carnegie's age?"

Another shrug. "He's known them forever, so no. I mean,

he's a rich, good-looking guy in the celebrity business. Who wouldn't want to hang out with him?"

Jordan arched a brow. "Is that why you work with him? Because he's famous?"

"Dude, he pays extremely well, and all I have to do is take care of his lawn and his cars. I didn't bother going to college, so it's a pretty sweet deal, you know? I make more than some of my friends with master's degrees and I don't have one cent of student-loan debt."

"Yay you. This Anne, is she the jealous type?"

"No idea. Anytime I've seen her, she's been pretty mellow. I think she likes her pills, you know? She's hot, though. Like I said, she's always been nice to me."

"What does she look like?"

"Tall, thin, blond. Like a model, you know?" He frowned slightly. "Except, I don't think she is one. I don't know."

"And the Cole twins, are they hot too?"

"Well, yeah." He looked surprised that she asked. "But they're, like, young. I like older women." He grinned.

He wasn't actually checking her out, was he? Jesus H. Christ. "So, if I asked either one of them, they'd tell me that you've never hit on them?"

Gallagher's face dropped. "No! They're underage, man. Gross. I look like a perv to you?"

Perfect segue. "You did have assault charges filed against you a few years ago, didn't you?"

The kid actually rolled his eyes. "That was a misunderstanding."

Jordan fought the urge to roll her eyes as well. "If only

I had a dollar for every man who said those exact same words."

"No, seriously. It was totally on me. I thought she was into me. I was drunk and I came on strong, but I stopped. She had to tell me a couple of times for it to sink in, but I fucking stopped, okay?" His face was pale. "I went to her house the next day and apologized to her and her parents. I hadn't hurt her, so she dropped the charges. You can ask her yourself—we're friends."

Jordan studied him for a moment. She couldn't detect any lie in his expression or tone. He seemed to have genuine remorse for what had happened. "Thanks for your time, Mr. Gallagher." She started to climb back into the car.

"Wait!" he cried, hurrying toward her. "Can I have your number? In case I think of anything?"

She wasn't sure if she ought to be flattered or insulted, but she gave him her card regardless. "In case you think of anything," she reiterated. Then she got into the car and started the engine. Gallagher remained where he was as she drove toward the main road, watching.

When she glanced in the rearview, he was looking up at the house, as if he was looking for someone.

Who was he looking for?

Eighteen years ago

This wasn't real. It had to be some kind of nightmare—a delusion. It was the kind of thing that happened on overly dramatic TV shows.

But it was real. Hannah realized that the next day, when she woke up in a room with no windows, wearing a nightgown she never would have chosen for herself, lying in a canopy bed. It was the lack of windows that confirmed it. Were it not for that, she might have believed the whole "sunstroke" lie a little longer.

At least she had a bathroom. She slipped out of bed and made her way to the toilet on legs that trembled and threatened to give out. Her bones had no more strength than pool noodles. At least her underwear was still her own.

She flushed the toilet, washed her hands, and returned to the bedroom. There was no dresser, no closet. She didn't even have a television. The bedside table had a few books and magazines on it—mostly fashion related.

The lock on the door clicked. Hannah turned around so fast her legs gave out and dumped her sideways into the wall. The door opened as she slid helplessly to the carpet, hands and feet scrambling desperately for support.

The woman named Grace entered the room, carrying a tray. The smell of bacon and eggs and coffee made Hannah's stomach growl roughly.

"Oh, you poor thing," Grace said, closing the door and locking it again. "Here, let me put this down and I'll help you." She walked past Hannah to set the tray on the bed, then came back and bent down, grabbing her beneath the arms. "Lift if you can, sweetie."

It didn't occur to Hannah to be deadweight. Once she managed to get one of her feet under her, she pushed herself up until the other fell into step as well. She leaned on Grace as she was helped back to the bed.

"It's just the drugs," Grace informed her, sitting down on the corner of the bed. "It will wear off soon. Do you take cream and sugar in your coffee?"

Hannah blinked at her. "Uh, yeah."

"Good. Now, this isn't normally what we have for breakfast—he likes to eat a healthy diet—but I convinced him you needed to eat a bit extra. I hope you like your eggs over easy."

She did. In fact, it was all she could do not to bury her face in the plate. "Are you going to watch me eat?"

Grace nodded, spooning sugar into the cup of coffee on the tray. "I learned my lesson not to leave any of you alone with the cutlery after a girl tried to cut her wrists with a butter knife."

"There have been other girls?" Suddenly the idea of food made her want to puke.

A serene smile curved Grace's lips as she poured in cream. "Of course. How do you think I got here? You think I chose to be his helper? No, he chose me." She offered her the cup. "Here."

There was a bitter taste in the back of Hannah's throat. She took the coffee and drank just to wash it away. For a second, it threatened to come back up.

"You should eat something," Grace suggested. "Coffee on an empty stomach can be so harsh. At least have some toast."

Hannah did as she was told. She couldn't have explained why if anyone asked. It was just that Grace seemed so nice, and she had such a soft, reasonable voice.

Hannah bit into a piece of bacon and then had some toast. Within a few minutes she'd cleaned her plate. She smiled when Grace clapped her hands.

"Oh, I'm so glad!" She smiled at Hannah. The younger girl watched as the smile slowly melted away. "You're going to be my replacement, you know."

Hannah shook her head. "No."

Grace nodded, her expression resolute. "Yes, you are. I saw how he looks at you. He's been getting tired of me. I can't be what he needs anymore."

"What does he need?" Her voice was a croak.

Long, beautifully manicured fingers stroked the coverlet. "Someone to support him. Someone who understands his needs, who can help feed his darkest appetites. I could do it—I have done it, for years now, but, I'm…broken. I can't do it anymore. You are the last girl I will ever find for him." Tears beaded on her lashes. "You'll take care of him, I know it. You'll do it and you won't break."

"No," Hannah insisted, breakfast churning sourly in her stomach. "I won't. I won't help him." She didn't even know what it was he did, but she had a pretty good idea.

Those pretty hands grabbed hold of hers—even though she still held her coffee cup. "Yes, you will. If you ever want the slightest hope of seeing your sister again, you will."

Those words cut right to her bones. Rachel must be so worried. So scared. Of course her parents would be too, but not like her sister—her other half. She was not going to die in a room with no windows. She was going to die the same day

Rachel did, within a few minutes of her. They were going out together—they'd promised.

"Okay," Hannah agreed.

Grace looked so relieved. She wiped at her lashes with her fingers, careful not to smudge her mascara. "Good. Okay, finish your coffee so I can take your tray. He'll be down to visit shortly."

He did come down. Hannah had no idea how long after. She was flipping through an issue of *Vogue*, trying to figure out her escape, when he came in wearing nothing but a pair of pajama bottoms. He had a beautiful face and a beautiful body, but the thrill she'd felt at the attention he paid to her in the park had twisted into fear.

"Hello, Hannah," he said in a silky tone. "I have to say, you've been a welcome surprise."

She didn't know what he meant, so she didn't respond.

"Take off your nightgown," he said.

She didn't move. If he was going to rape her, she wasn't going to help him.

"You can take it off, or I can rip it off," he said. "Would you rather spend all your time naked?"

Asshole. As defiantly as she could manage with a quivering lip, she rose from the bed and pulled the gown over her head, leaving her standing before him naked except for her underwear.

There was no hiding that he liked what he saw. "Lie down on the bed."

She did, keeping her gaze trained on the ceiling. Her heart

jerked against her ribs when she felt something clasp around her ankles. He was tying her down! She lunged upward, struggling against him, but he was stronger and heavier. He pinned her to the mattress and secured her wrists as well. Hannah glared at him. It was then that she realized he'd removed her underwear. She could only watch as he stood beside the bed and dropped the pajama bottoms. He was big and hard and there was nothing she could do.

A tear leaked from her eye and trickled into her hair. What would Rachel do? Rachel wouldn't lie there and be a victim. Rachel would plot how to get herself out of the situation. Rachel would slit his damn throat if she got the chance. She tried to hold on to the thought of her sister, but it kept dodging out of her reach.

When he climbed onto the bed, she waited for him to rape her, but he didn't. What he did was worse. He touched her. He kissed her. He did things to her no one had ever done before, and he kept doing them until her body responded. He made her orgasm—not once but twice. The second time was when he was actually inside her. Nausea and pleasure mixed inside her until she couldn't tell one from the other. When he released her, she jumped off the bed and bolted to the bathroom, falling to her knees hard beside the toilet. She threw up her breakfast, and then he insisted on cleaning her up.

There wasn't any mirror in the bathroom, otherwise she might have considered breaking the glass and sawing through her wrists with it. Fuck what her sister would do. Fuck being strong.

He put her back to bed.

"You rest now," he said. "I'll see you again later. I'll have Grace bring you some clothes, okay? If you're good, I'll get you a TV." He stroked her hair and left the room, leaving her alone, her body tender and throbbing. She curled into herself and pulled the blankets up to her mouth, biting into them as she cried.

The next time Grace came back, she'd be ready. She'd take the older girl down and then make her escape. She'd hit her until she couldn't get back up.

That's what Rachel would do.

CHAPTER SEVEN

There were no prints or any organic material on the envelope, card, or photo Rachel had received the day before, other than the bloody signature. They were running it against Sydney Cole's. It seemed half of her job was the rush to collect evidence, with the other half a long-ass wait for other people to process said evidence.

"They found blond hairs in Carnegie's car," Trick said, setting a coffee in front of her.

Rachel glanced up at him. "Thanks." She took a sip. "Do they belong to our mysterious Anne?"

He shook his head. "Not sure. No root. Carnegie wasn't home this morning—apparently he's in New York—but we've got an appointment with him tomorrow morning."

"We?"

He met her gaze. "Me and Mancusi."

"Ah." Her current partner and her former, working together. How sweet.

Trick sighed. He looked tired. That was her fault, she supposed. "Come on. You know this isn't personal."

"It is personal. Carnegie is trying to fuck me over and you guys are letting him do it."

"Look, Rachel—"

She held up her hand. "I'm being irrational. Got it. You don't need to say it again." She went back to her computer, Google searching Carnegie along with the name Anne. So far all she'd found was one photo and that was only from behind as the woman and Carnegie arrived at the Met Ball a couple of years ago. An article in *Vanity Fair* mentioned Carnegie's long-time assistant as "quiet and demure" and "doting."

"Do we need to talk?" Trick asked a couple of minutes later—just when she was starting to feel normal again.

She flashed a bright smile up at him. "Of course not. While you guys talk to Carnegie, I'm going to follow up with Cassandra Lennox and the Coles about our blonde in the security footage. And Blake Kelly's due back from LA tonight."

"I'm not sure you should do that alone."

Rachel stiffened. Right, because she was so certain of Carnegie she might bend responses to what she wanted them to be? Because she couldn't be trusted to do her job despite her feelings? "I'll take Maika with me."

"Good idea. Are you going to tell the Coles about Morgan's affair with Carnegie?"

"Not unless I have to. The kid's given me her trust. I'd like to keep it for a while. She might know more than she thinks, and we might need to use her against Carnegie at some point."

"Use her?"

Rachel closed her eyes. "She's the one concrete thing we have against him right now. I don't want her to turn against us prematurely."

"Why do you think she'll turn on us? Carnegie?"

"Because we're going to be asking her questions she thinks are personal. Because we're going to be prying into her life and the lives of her loved ones. I hated the feds and cops for years before I realized they were only trying to find the guy who took my sister."

"And then you became one of them."

"It was either that or become a killer, and I didn't have the stomach for it."

He didn't laugh at her joke. "Are you okay?"

She massaged her forehead. "I'm fine. Just tired of people questioning my mental state and my judgment. I'm not the only person who thinks Carnegie stinks."

"No, but you're the only one who's threatened him."

"I'm the only one whose sister he's kidnapped, raped, and killed."

"You can't prove it, Rachel. That's the problem. That's why people question your judgment."

She looked up at him. "You used to trust my instincts."

"I still do, just not where this case is concerned." He shrugged. "I'm sorry, but I can't lie to you just because I care about you."

"That's rich coming from a guy who had a girlfriend the first time we fucked."

Trick's jaw tightened. He looked around the bull pen to see if anyone had heard her. She didn't care if they had. It wasn't as though she had anything to hide.

"I broke up with her," he said, as if she needed a reminder.

"After we slept together. Look, Trick, if you don't trust me, then maybe we shouldn't be partners. Or anything."

"I was wondering when you'd give me an ultimatum." He shook his head. "It's gotta be your way or no way at all. Fuck that."

Rachel's heart skipped a beat as he turned away. She refused to apologize, not when she knew she was right. He'd hurt her first. Apologizing never got her anywhere. She'd apologized to her mother for more than a decade before she realized it was never going to make a difference. She wasn't about to do it again, no matter how much she thought she should.

Trick was wrong about her instincts. He was wrong about Carnegie, and she was going to prove it to him.

Cassandra Lennox and her mother and sister would be back from their trip to London Saturday afternoon. Cassandra was more than willing to meet with Rachel and Maika and show them the photographs she took of the woman who tried to abduct her six years ago. Mrs. Cole wasn't certain she wanted to meet with Rachel at all, until Rachel tempted her with the chance to prove Carnegie's innocence.

They met her in the hospital cafeteria, since it wouldn't be fair to expect her to leave her daughter's side. Though, Rachel had to wonder, who was paying attention to the woman's other daughter? Carnegie, probably. The idea made her skin crawl.

Victoria Cole looked tired and wan. She wore no makeup

and her hair was up in a messy ponytail. She wore yoga pants and a light tunic with sandals.

"Thank you for meeting with us, Mrs. Cole," Rachel said as she sat down at a table. "Can we get you anything? Coffee or tea?"

"No. I'm fine, thank you." She pushed a stray piece of hair behind her ear. "What did you want to talk about?"

"In the course of your association with Mr. Carnegie, did you ever meet a woman named Anne? Or a man named Blake Kelly?"

Victoria's eyes narrowed. "I thought this wasn't going to be about Alex." She tore jagged strips off her napkin. "I don't want to talk about him."

"It's not," Rachel placated, resting her forearms on the table. Was the woman being protective of Carnegie, or was she angry at him? It was hard to tell. "Not really. We're looking for a woman who might have information as to what happened to Sydney. We believe that woman might have been someone known to Mr. Carnegie, a woman named Anne. We also want to talk to Blake Kelly."

"Blake was out of town when Sydney disappeared. I know this because he was with one of my best friends when I called her to talk. Besides, his interest in girls isn't sexual. He has a longtime partner named Ben." She took a sip of coffee. "Alex has an assistant named Anne, but I haven't seen her in forever. I only ever met her once, and that was several years ago. She was never much for the limelight. Why would she know what happened to Sydney?"

"We're not sure," Rachel hedged. "Like I said, we just want to talk to her."

The woman shook her head. "I assume she's in New York. You should be asking Alex this, not me."

Rachel sighed. "If she works for Alex, he might not be so keen to say anything if he thinks it could get her in trouble."

"Mm," Victoria replied. "And I suppose you really can't talk to him, can you?" Her gaze locked with Rachel's.

Forcing a smile, Rachel continued. "No, I can't. But my partner can, and he will be chatting with Mr. Carnegie soon." She tried another tactic. "Mrs. Cole, I'm not your enemy. I want to find out who took your daughter."

The other woman looked away. "Forgive me, Agent Ward. I forgot that your sister was also abducted."

"That just makes me all the happier that you got Sydney back." She waited a heartbeat. "How is she recovering?"

"They say she's doing well. The surgery was a success and she's been awake a bit. She doesn't seem to remember much..." She raised her gaze to Rachel's. "My baby was stabbed... *everywhere*, and they say she's doing *well*. How is that even possible?"

"Because they mean physically she's doing well. The emotional healing will come later. You'll need to help her with that. Morgan too."

"Morgan?" The woman looked surprised. "Morgan's fine."

"Morgan feels an incredible amount of guilt for not being able to stop Sydney from disappearing."

Victoria put her hand over her mouth and closed her eyes. "Of course she does," she agreed, taking her hand away.

"Sweet, foolish girl. She's the older of the two, you know. She thinks she's Sydney's keeper."

"You don't blame her." Rachel knew she hadn't succeeded in keeping wonder from her tone.

Eyes that had stared out from dozens of magazine covers narrowed slightly. "Did your mother blame you?"

"Yes." Rachel cleared her throat. "Hannah was pretending to be me the day she disappeared."

"And your mother thinks that if you had been where you were supposed to be, nothing would have happened?" She sounded incredulous. "Doesn't she realize you would have been taken instead?"

"Sometimes I think she wishes that was the case," Rachel admitted, feeling Maika's horrified gaze beside her.

"You poor thing." Victoria Cole reached across the table and put her hand on Rachel's arm.

The contact made her throat tight, but Rachel couldn't bring herself to pull away. "Thank you. Mrs. Cole, is there any chance Sydney might have gone off with a boyfriend or friends?"

"No. Syd is far too conscientious. She's never been comfortable sneaking around. She wouldn't have gone off with someone she didn't know. That's why..."

"Why what?" Rachel pressed when the woman didn't continue.

Victoria picked at her nail polish. "Agent Ward, was Alex sleeping with Sydney?"

Rachel's eyes widened. "Not that we know of."

The older woman closed her eyes and shook her head. Her jaw was tight. "Morgan, then?"

Rachel and Maika exchanged glances. "Mrs. Cole..."

She opened her eyes and fixed Rachel with a piercing gaze. "I've known that man for years. I've seen the girls come and go from his studio. He loves my girls, but recently something changed—I just felt it. When Morgan called him that night instead of me, I knew something was going on between him and one of the twins. He's been too attentive. Too involved." She sighed. "I thought Morgan was too smart to fall for his charm. Sydney's the romantic one. Oh, that bastard. I trusted him."

"That's why we're trying to find Anne," Rachel confided.

"Ah, you think Alex was sleeping with her too? It's possible. They seemed quite close. She was very quiet, but I suppose any woman has it in her to become the jealous lover, doesn't she?" She smiled slightly.

"I'd take my jealousy out on the lover, though," Rachel allowed. Mrs. Cole's smile widened a little.

"Me too," the other woman agreed. "But we're not quiet women, are we?" She checked her watch. "I'd like to return to Sydney's room. Is there anything else?"

There wasn't, not for now.

"Does your mother really blame you?" Maika asked as they left the hospital.

"Yep," Rachel replied. "That doesn't stop her from calling me six times a day trying to get information on the investigation." The last time she'd checked her phone her mother had already called five times. She had enough conflict in her life at the moment with Trick; she didn't have the fortitude to deal with her mother too.

"That's whack."

Despite the deep ache in her chest, Rachel smiled at her friend's choice of words. "It sure is," she agreed. "It's fucking whack."

Her father called late that afternoon. Rachel was going through Carnegie's financials in the hopes of finding Anne's information. After all, as her employer, he would have had to pay her.

Apparently, he hadn't. Or, he paid her in cash. Regardless, she found employment records for Peter Gallagher and Yolanda Diaz—and others—but no one named Anne. No one, even, with that as their middle name. Surely even Trick would find that suspicious.

Rachel hesitated before answering the phone. Even though it showed her father's number on the screen, there was no guarantee it wasn't her mother using someone else's phone again to get her attention.

She accepted the call and lifted the phone to her ear. When nothing happened, she said, "Hello?"

"Ray Ray?"

She breathed a sigh of relief at the familiar deep voice. He was the only person who still called her by the ridiculous nickname Hannah had given her when they were toddlers. Ray Ray and Haha, that's what they called each other.

"Hi, Dad. How are you doing?"

"Keeping it afloat, sweetheart. How about you?"

"I'm okay."

"I know you are." His simple confidence in her made Rachel smile. He never asked if she was sure that she was okay. He never questioned anything she told him. He took her at her word, or at least believed that if she wanted to discuss it, she'd tell him. Her father would never tell her she shouldn't be on a case. He'd ask her what she thought and trust that she knew her own limitations.

She could work this investigation. She needed to. But she was in full agreement that she shouldn't be anywhere near Carnegie. Of course, no one had asked her opinion on that before they started telling her what she needed to do. She was the last person who wanted to mess up this investigation. The last.

"Are you at work?" he asked. His voice had a slight rasp to it that sounded like the beginning of a sore throat, but never was.

"Yeah. Almost done, I think. There's not much else I can do today."

"I won't keep you, regardless. I wanted to talk to you about your mother."

"Okay." Where was this going?

"I know she called you yesterday."

Rachel glanced up, but her gaze refused to focus on anything. "Yup."

"She probably said some things that weren't very motherly, or even very nice."

"You're right again. Dad, you don't need to apologize or make excuses for her."

"I'm not." Yeah, right he wasn't. He did it every damn time. "It's just this time of year, you know."

Wry amusement twisted her lips. "That's an excuse."

"You're right, and I'm sorry. I don't know why she treats you like that, and I hate that she does it."

"She blames me, Dad. She always has. We've talked about this a million times."

"I know. Make this a million and one. Blaming you means she doesn't have to blame herself. I don't understand why she has to blame anyone, but that's just how her mind works, I guess."

"I guess," Rachel agreed. "I'm tired of defending myself, Dad."

"I know you are, sweetheart. That's why I told your mother this morning that she needs to deal with this issue she has with you. I've let her hurt you for too many years and I'm ashamed of myself. I have no excuse except that I thought it would one day get better, but it's only gotten worse. I'm so sorry for not standing up for you sooner."

Hot tears gathered in the corners of Rachel's eyes. "You've stood up for me every time."

"Not like I ought to have. I made an appointment with a therapist for next week. I told her it was for all of us. She put up a fight, of course, but I told her we've lost one daughter, I'm not losing you too. She has to fix this—if you think it's fixable."

She swiped at her eyes with the back of her hand. "I don't know, but if she's willing to try, so am I."

"That's my girl." She could hear the smile in his voice. "I'm so proud of you, you know that?"

"Stop it," she said with a sniff. A quick glance around the bull pen proved that not one of the four agents present were paying her the least bit of attention.

"It's true. I don't say it often enough. One day you're going to find Hannah. You won't stop until you do. I admire that so much. You're the strongest of all of us."

Rachel fought against the prickling sensation behind her face. "Please, stop."

"Okay. I'm sorry. I don't want to embarrass you at work. I just want you to know I love you, okay? I need you to remember that, in case sometimes I don't show it enough."

"Thanks." Her voice sounded almost as rough as his. "I have to go. I'll call if I find out anything, okay?"

"Sure thing. Love you."

"Me too." She hung up and drew a deep breath. She sat there for a few seconds, processing how she felt about the conversation before finally packing up her stuff to go home. She left a note for Trick about the absence of any records for someone named Anne in Carnegie's employ, and emailed him her notes from the conversation with Victoria Cole. Then she went home for the day.

Blake Kelly's alibi looked good. He'd flown to LA a couple of days before Sydney went missing and wasn't due to return for another three. His social media was full of photos from the trip—including the dinner he had with Cindy Crawford the night Sydney disappeared. Unless he'd figured out some way to teleport himself back to New York, or had another identity, there was no way he could have been the one to take her. Still, it wouldn't hurt to talk to him.

Naomi wasn't home, and the house was still and quiet when Rachel entered through the back door. She punched in the code for the alarm, kicked off her shoes, and walked through to the front of the house to put her gun and badge in the safe. Once that was done, she padded to the kitchen and poured a glass of wine before running a bath.

She looked at herself in the mirror. Trick wasn't the only one who looked tired. The skin under her eyes seemed almost bruised. She found a facial mask in a drawer and slathered it on, just like when she and Hannah used to have spa days in their teens. They'd do facials and paint each other's nails.

When they were really bored, they'd sit facing each other and try to mimic each other perfectly. Hannah used to say they could join a traveling circus as the "living mirror." There'd been something calming about anticipating each other's movements. They'd gotten so good at it they could sometimes move completely in unison.

Rachel turned away from the mirror. She didn't want to see Hannah's face anymore.

Naomi came home for dinner, her girlfriend, Lynn, with her. Lynn was just barely over five feet tall, with a curvy figure and long dark hair. Naomi adored her, and so did Rachel. Anyone that made her baby sister that happy deserved to be liked.

The three of them ordered takeout from a local Thai place as Rachel silently swore she was going to start cooking more, and ate in the living room while watching a movie. There was more wine too.

It was just after eleven when Rachel crawled into bed, exhausted. She set the alarm on her phone, curled into her pillow, and fell asleep talking to Hannah in her head, as she sometimes did after a rough day. The conversations were basically entries in a mental journal. She thought about time they'd spent together, things they'd done.

Like the time Rachel tried to run away when they were twelve and Hannah found her. Or the time her twin explained algebra to her in a way she could understand. The time they dressed up like evil dolls on Halloween and scared the neighborhood kids. The memories weren't as vivid as they used to be.

It would be too much if eventually she began to forget Hannah. They were two halves of the same whole. How could time be so cruel as to take her away? She'd already lost her once.

Her phone rang shortly after three the next morning. Rachel jerked awake, fumbling for the cell on her bedside table. She knocked it onto the floor before putting it to her ear. "Hello?"

"Where are you?" Trick demanded.

"I'm at home," she replied, confused and indignant.

"Have you been there all night?"

"Yeah." She frowned. "I've got witnesses and everything."

"Good." There was audible relief in his tone.

What the hell? "Where are you?" she asked. "And why are you calling me in the middle of the night?"

"Open your damn door."

Phone still at her ear, Rachel slipped out of bed and walked through the darkness of the house. The streetlights shining through the windows made it relatively easy for her to see, though she really didn't need to. She turned on the outside light and peeked through the peephole. Sure enough, there was Trick on her doorstep.

She unlocked and opened the door. He stepped inside before she could ask him to come in. He grabbed her in a fierce hug.

"What the hell happened?" she demanded, struggling for breath.

"Carnegie was attacked earlier this evening," he replied against her hair. "Someone tried to kill him."

Jesus Christ. And then the puzzle pieces fell together. Rachel shoved against his chest, pushing him away. "Son of a bitch! You thought I did it?"

"Yes."

She stared at him. "And you came here to what? Arrest me?"

"I came here to help you." That was when she noticed that his shirt was buttoned up wrong and his hair was a mess. He'd been woken up as well, and had come straight over. "I thought you might need an alibi."

The anger festering inside her gave way to something softer, and harder to name. "I thought you wouldn't risk the investigation for me."

"I didn't think I would, then I got the call about Carnegie and all I could think of was that if you'd done it, I needed to help you get away with it." He laughed humorlessly. "Jesus, I can't believe I just said that."

"I can't either." She really couldn't. The tears she'd been fighting since her conversation with her father came spilling over her cheeks as she wrapped her arms around his waist.

"It's been a shitty couple of days," she said.

He stroked her back. "I know. I'm sorry I doubted you."

She lifted her head. "Stay?"

Trick nodded. So Rachel locked the door, turned off the outside light, and reset the security alarm. Then she took his hand in hers and led him through the darkened house.

"Rach?" came Naomi's voice from upstairs. "Everything okay?"

"It's Trick," she called back. "Everything's fine."

In the darkness of her room, Trick shrugged out of his jacket and pulled off his shirt. She heard the jangling of his belt as his jeans hit the floor. When he joined her in bed, he wore only his underwear, the skin of his chest warm as she pressed her back against it. He wrapped his arm around her waist and fit his body as tight to hers as possible. They didn't speak. Rachel simply twined her fingers through his as they rested on her stomach.

"I wouldn't let you lie for me," she whispered.

"I know," he replied. "But I would try."

She squeezed his hand, but didn't speak again. She was too afraid of what she might say.

CHAPTER EIGHT

Eighteen years ago

"Are you hungry?"

Hannah pulled down the blankets that covered her face and looked up at Grace, who stood over her with a tray. She didn't know how long she'd been in that room, but Grace had brought her four breakfasts so far. Judging from the smell, she'd guess this was breakfast number five.

Five days she'd been their prisoner—she no longer counted Grace as an ally. *He* visited her every day, bringing gifts or doing something for her that might be seen as kind if he hadn't been a psychopath. He had sex with her every day too. Was it still rape if she enjoyed it? Because he made sure she enjoyed it. Her body didn't know to be repulsed by him. Sometimes her mind didn't know it either. He had to be drugging her somehow. The food, maybe? The air? She didn't know how. All she knew was that when he touched her, she made noises she'd never made before. Felt things she'd never felt before. And if she asked him to stop, he did, but then he did things that made her beg him to continue.

It had only been five days and she already looked forward to his touch rather than feared it.

Hannah sat up and let Grace put the tray on top of her lap.

"I made you an omelet," the older woman announced proudly. "It's egg whites, because that's healthier, but I threw in a little extra cheese when he wasn't looking." She smiled— as though she'd done something terribly rebellious.

"Thanks," Hannah murmured. She took a forkful, chewed, and swallowed. It was good, but she'd eat it even if it wasn't. She needed to be strong. To be able to fight. She had to be ready when the opportunity to escape came.

She knew better than to ask Grace for help. Grace had been there a long time and her loyalty was to him, even though she knew it was wrong. He knew how to make people loyal to him, to make them love him.

"I don't know how much longer I'll be here."

Hannah's head snapped up. "What do you mean?" she demanded around a mouthful of omelet.

Grace seated herself on the edge of the bed. Hannah noticed how much the bones in her wrist stood out. She was so thin. So delicate. She could probably snap her entire arm like a twig. She considered trying it.

"He likes you." This was said like it was something wonderful. "That means he's going to keep you. It also means that he no longer has any use for me."

Hannah shivered. "You mean he's going to kill you?"

"I think so. He doesn't look at me the same anymore. He's had me three years now—the longest he's kept anyone." That also was said with pride. "I've made him happy, but I always knew this day would come. Will you do something for me?"

Unable to eat anymore, Hannah nodded. "What?"

"Take care of him—and yourself."

Hannah met her gaze unflinchingly. "I'm going to fucking kill him."

Grace smiled. "Okay. I also need you to do something else."

"I will not love him, if that's what you're going to ask."

"No." She shook her head. "That's not it." She scooted closer on the bed, until her hip touched Hannah's knee. "I want you to stay strong, okay? You become whatever or whoever you need to be to survive, because I think you will survive, Hannah Ward. And when they find you, you tell them about me, okay? Please? So they'll let my family know. You tell them that I never forgot them."

The tears trickling down Grace's face made Hannah's throat tight. She couldn't eat even if she wanted to. "I will. I promise."

"Good." Grace wiped her eyes. "Now, who's the strongest person you know?"

"My sister, Rachel."

"You think of her when he comes for you. You use her to stay strong, and he won't be able to break you like he did me."

Hannah didn't tell her that she was afraid she was already broken. "Okay."

"You haven't finished breakfast. He'll be upset with me if you don't eat."

"I can't."

Grace ate it for her, then gathered up the dishes on the tray and rose to take it away. "I'm sorry," she said. "For talking to you at the Met, for luring you in. I want you to know that I didn't want to, but he threatened to hurt my sister. You understand, don't you?"

Hannah nodded, her stomach churning.

"Okay." Grace bobbed her head once, then took a step back. "See you later."

But she didn't see Grace later. She never saw Grace again.

Friday

"How much do you figure this place is worth?" Trick asked as they pulled into Carnegie's drive the next day. They'd stopped by his place on the way so he could shower and change for work, and Rachel was still enjoying the smell of his soap.

She shook her head at the almost obnoxiously manicured grounds. "Four or five million?" She'd seen photos of it once, in a magazine, but they hadn't done it justice. And of course, she hadn't given its worth much thought when she'd originally shown up there, questioning him about her sister.

"Jesus. I guess there's good money in taking pictures of people."

"You'd think he'd have twenty-four-hour staff." She glanced up at the camera placed inconspicuously on the side of the house. "I wonder if he ever got his security system fixed."

"Funny you should mention that," Trick began as he put the car in park. "Last night CSU told Mancusi the system had been tampered with."

"Interesting. The elusive Anne, I wonder?"

"No idea. I don't believe anymore that his hands are clean of this, though. Too much of this has centered around him."

His confession ought to make her happy, but it didn't. It felt too little, too late. He only believed in her because there was now too much stacked against Carnegie. "Anne might be his assistant in more ways than one," Rachel offered up, saying what they both had suspected. "She could be the partner we've wondered about."

"But why attack him if they're in it together?"

Rachel gave him a grim smile. "Ever heard about a woman scorned?" she asked.

"Good point." He opened the car door.

They were greeted at the door by a Spanish woman, who took one look at Rachel and scowled. "*You*," she said.

Trick shoved his badge at her. Rachel opened hers as well, but let him do the talking. "Agents Patrick and Ward, ma'am. We'd like to talk to you about the attack on Mr. Carnegie."

The woman gave Rachel another dark look before focusing her attention on Trick. "I'm Yolanda, Mr. Carnegie's house-keeper. What do you want to know?"

"May we come in?" Trick asked.

Yolanda stood back and let them enter.

"Is Mr. Gallagher around?" Rachel asked. "We'd like to talk to both of you since you're the only staff."

"He's in the kitchen," the other woman said. "Follow me."

The house was over-the-top opulent for Rachel's tastes, but she had to admire it all the same. The kitchen was large, with lots of gleaming marble and stainless steel. A young man with long hair sat at the table drinking coffee with another man. When asked, he confirmed that he was Pete Gallagher, and the other was Blake Kelly

Rachel studied Gallagher as she and Trick joined him at the table. He didn't look like he'd been in any kind of physical altercation—no visible marks or bruises. Given that every piece of evidence they had led to a woman being the missing piece of the puzzle, it was unlikely that Gallagher was responsible for the attack on Carnegie.

Blake Kelly was immaculate in his jeans and pale yellow button-down. He was certainly tall and thin enough to have been the person in the video, but he had far too much facial hair.

Yolanda set two cups of coffee in front of them, along with cream and sugar. Normally they would refuse refreshment, but Rachel went ahead and fixed hers the way she would normally take it, if only for show.

"Were any of you notified of the incident?" Trick asked.

Gallagher shook his head. "I came in this morning and the police were here."

Yolanda pursed her lips. "I did not like finding them in the house. It felt like a violation."

Kelly cleared his throat. "Alex called me afterward. I called the police and came straight over."

"Mr. Carnegie was found in his bedroom?"

"Yes," Kelly replied, his dark eyes wide. He looked haunted by what he'd seen.

The housekeeper made a face. "They won't let me clean it."

"May we take a look?" Rachel asked.

"Why?" The woman shot her a narrow glance. "The police have already ripped it apart."

"Because while we work with the police, we're also independent of them. We might see something they missed."

Yolanda's expression said she found that unlikely, but she nodded. "Now?"

"In a moment," Trick said. "Have any of you seen Anne, Mr. Carnegie's assistant?"

"Like I told the police, I don't really know her," Gallagher said. "I haven't seen her around."

"Anne?" Kelly asked. He glanced at Yolanda. "I thought she quit."

"She was with him the last time he visited," Yolanda revealed.

"Were things alright between them?" Rachel asked.

The housekeeper shrugged. "I didn't notice anything amiss."

"So, does Anne have her own room when she's here?"

Now the woman looked offended. "Of course she does."

"I get the impression you don't like her very much," Trick joined in, hands wrapped loosely around his coffee mug.

Yolanda looked down at her own clasped hands. "I don't. I know that is unfair of me to say, but she wasn't very friendly. She never spoke." That dark gaze locked with Rachel's. "You remind me of her."

Rachel arched a brow. "How so?"

"I don't know. Her hair is blond, her eyes blue, but your mouth is similar. She didn't smile much either."

Nice. "Does she have a temper?" Rachel asked.

"I never heard her raise her voice, but there were times I could feel her rage. Does that make sense?"

"She kept to herself," Kelly joined in. "But Yolanda's right, you do look like her. Of course, Alex has always liked women with full lips and high cheekbones, so there's that."

"How does Mr. Carnegie feel about twins?" Rachel asked.

He frowned. "I have no idea. Alex and I tend to stick to work when we're together. We don't exactly talk about our love lives."

"You're not close?"

"Professionally, yes. Personally, not really. Alex doesn't 'get' homosexuality." He laughed. "You'd think being in the fashion industry would have cured him of that, right?"

It was obvious that Kelly didn't harbor resentment. He was genuinely amused by his employer's intolerance.

"What were you doing in LA?" Rachel asked.

"Shooting. I'm working with a makeup artist friend on his book. He's my partner, actually. He's brilliant." He blushed a little as he spoke.

"So, you're branching out on your own?"

"I have been for a few years now. Working with Alex has opened a lot of doors for me, and I appreciate it, but it's time to do my own thing, you know?"

"Is that why you thought Anne had quit? Because she wants to do her own thing?"

"No. Because Alex chases tail like it's an Olympic sport."

"So she and Alex are involved in a relationship?" Trick asked.

Kelly shrugged. "They were." He glanced at the others.

Yolanda and Gallagher both nodded.

Trick's gaze touched on all three of them. "Do you think Anne might have wished to harm Mr. Carnegie?"

Yolanda and Gallagher exchanged a look. Kelly's gaze was fixed on Trick—like he was studying the angles of his face. Rachel couldn't blame him—it was a beautiful face.

"Her or Mr. Cole," the younger man said.

Rachel glanced at Trick. "Morgan and Sydney's father?"

Gallagher nodded. "He was here yesterday. Really angry. He went after Mr. Carnegie. Accused him of raping Morgan."

"Whatever went on between them wasn't coerced," Kelly said.

Yolanda made a dismissive noise. "As if that man would have to rape a woman."

There was so much wrong with that statement Rachel didn't know where to begin. "Morgan is underage. That's statutory rape."

The other woman shrugged. Rachel didn't know what to do with that, so she left it alone, though it was on the tip of her tongue to suggest that maybe the housekeeper's sparkling personality was why Anne hadn't been friendly.

"Did they have an altercation?" Trick asked.

Gallagher shrugged. "No one threw a punch, if that's what you're asking. But Mr. Cole did say that he'd kill Mr. Carnegie if he ever came near his daughters again. Mr. Carnegie told him he would never hurt Morgan, and that he cared for her. I thought Mr. Cole was going to hit him, but then he saw me and he left instead."

"That girl knew what she was doing," Yolanda insisted. "It's not like Mr. Carnegie forced himself on her."

Yeah, right. Rachel forced herself to smile. "We'd like to see the crime scene now, please."

They were led to a large master bedroom with plush carpet, cream-colored walls, and dark wooden furniture. There were bloodstains on the carpet and quilt, even a bit on the wall closest to the bed.

"Doesn't look like there was much of a struggle," Trick commented when they were alone.

Rachel slipped on a pair of nitrile gloves. "He was probably asleep."

"You think Cole could sneak in here?"

"The family seems to know his security codes. Stupid to threaten him and then come back later and make good on the threat."

"Mm," Trick agreed, pulling on gloves of his own.

There was a case of watches on top of the hand-carved dresser. She wasn't an expert when it came to men's accessories, but even she had heard of some of the designers. The drawers of the dresser were mostly filled with socks, underwear, and casual clothes. Carnegie's idea of casual was Ralph Lauren and Calvin Klein, though Rachel doubted he shopped at Macy's. She found nothing in any of the drawers to cause suspicion.

"Anything?" she asked Trick, who was looking in the bedside tables.

"Condoms, some ticket stubs, a paperback, and a pair of glasses. The other one had a handful of sex toys—mostly fairly vanilla—and a book on the history of photography."

"I'll check the other bedroom," Rachel offered. Yolanda had

shown them the door to Anne's room. While it wasn't officially part of the police investigation, she kept her gloves on as she turned the knob.

This room wasn't as large as Carnegie's, but it had more personality. The walls were painted a pale sage, and the bedding had hints of rust and teal. It was serene and comfortable, with lots of cushions on the bed and airy curtains in the windows. She opened the closet and felt a pang of envy as she turned over a pair of Prada shoes. She and Anne wore the same size. The clothing appeared to be designer—and there was a little too much of it for Anne to be just a business acquaintance.

There were so many perfumes and lipsticks on the vanity table it was like a department-store counter. High-end makeup filled the drawers, the palettes well cared for. The foundations were pale and warm—the shades Rachel herself would wear. The perfumes were soft but woodsy with a hint of spice.

She opened the armoire and blinked. Among the shelves of accessories was one that held three wig stands, one of which was bare. The other two held light-blond wigs that were obviously human hair, lace front, and very expensive.

Anne wore a wig. Or, at least, she did on occasion. Which meant that they might not be looking for a blonde after all.

There were also three cases of colored contact lenses—green, blue, and brown. Did Anne like to play with her appearance because she liked to try different looks or because she didn't want law enforcement to have an accurate description?

"Anything?" Trick asked from the door.

She stood back and gestured to the wigs and lenses. "We

should take them. See if there's any DNA on them. The wigs explain why there wasn't a root on the hair found in the car."

"We don't have a warrant," he reminded her.

"We were allowed in," she argued. "And she is a suspect."

He nodded. "Alright, bag them."

It just so happened that she had evidence bags in the tote slung over her shoulder. "You find anything?" she asked.

Trick held up his own evidence collection. "Two volumes of child porn disguised as art and one that there's no disguising."

Rachel arched a brow. "He just had it out in the open? How did the cops miss that?"

"They weren't in the open. I found them in his closet inside a suitcase."

"Is it bad?" she asked.

Trick tilted his head, and she knew she shouldn't have asked. "Let's just say that between it and his relationship with Morgan Cole, it might send him away regardless if he's our guy or not."

That observation made Rachel far happier than it ought to have.

When they left the house—the door shuting behind them with just enough force to be passive aggressive—Rachel's attention was snagged by a small garden out back that she didn't notice until they were almost to the car. Frowning, she moved closer for a better look. The magazine article she'd seen on this place didn't have many photos of the grounds.

There were rows of rosebushes around a rectangle of grass. Marble statues stood behind the roses on three sides. The one in the center appeared to be older than the other two, judging from its slightly more weathered appearance. The one to Rachel's right was definitely the newest of the three. There was something oddly familiar about the statue's face.

There was something strange about the rectangle of grass. The way it was slightly raised...

"Trick!" she yelled.

He came running, stopping beside her. "What is it?"

She gestured to the plot with a shaking hand. "What does this look like to you?"

It took him a second. "Jesus Christ," he said, pulling out his phone to take a photo. "It looks like a fucking grave."

Trick sent the photo to Mancusi and then called her to see if she thought she could get a warrant.

"Because he's got a creepy garden?" she asked. "You better have something more concrete than that."

"The third statue looks like Rachel," Trick said, voice low.

"Excuse me?"

He glanced over his shoulder to make sure Rachel wasn't within hearing distance. She was talking to someone on her own cell, so he was probably safe. "Jordan, it looks *just* like her. And take a look at the center one. Who does that look like?" He waited for her to do as he instructed.

"Holy shit," came her inevitable reply. "Is that—?"

"It's Suki Carlton," he confirmed. "I'm sure of it. Rachel agrees, and you know no one knows as much about Gemini victims as she does." Except, of course, for the man himself.

"Christ. If she's been right about Carnegie all this time, you and I are going to have some apologizing to do."

"If we catch the bastard, I don't care how many times I have to say I'm sorry."

"Right. Shit. This is definitely something I can take to a judge. Give me a couple of hours."

Trick hung up and walked over to where Rachel stood on the edge of the garden. As he approached, he heard her say, "Mom, I can't talk about this right now...I'm not lying!...How can you say that?...Yeah, well, maybe I wish it had been me too." She hit Disconnect with her thumb. For a second, he thought she might throw the cell phone.

If there was one thing he knew about Rachel, it was that her mother had a way of getting to her that no one else did. The woman seemed to take some kind of satisfaction from hurting her, and Rachel didn't like to talk about it, of course. It was a vulnerability, and she was mortified anytime anyone witnessed it.

"Hey," he said in a loud voice. "I spoke to Mancusi. She's going to get a warrant."

As Rachel turned, she blinked several times. Trick could see wetness in her eyes. "Great. What do we do until then?"

"Let's go to the hospital and check on the condition of our Mr. Carnegie. See if anyone's been in or called to check on him."

"I'm not supposed to go near him."

Trick shrugged. "Fuck him." That got a smile out of her.

They walked to the SUV side by side. Trick got in the driver's side, as was their usual custom.

"Do you think my mother will finally forgive me if we arrest him?" she asked when they were on the road.

"I think your mother should hope you'll forgive her."

"That's not how we work, but thanks." And then, "We should check on Carnegie's other properties. He's got a place in New York, right?"

"And probably a few other places." Trick stopped at a light. "Let's see what the warrant uncovers first." He didn't say "no pun intended," because it could very well be her sister under all that dirt and it felt in poor taste.

"I'll send the wigs and lenses to the lab," Rachel said. "Have we gotten anything back from the blood on the card yet?"

"No. I'll check." He resumed driving. "Suki Carlton—wasn't she one of his earliest victims?"

"The first that we know of," Rachel replied, removing her coffee from the cup holder between them. "Then Grace O'Brien. I'm pretty sure she's the second statue, but I need to compare it to a photo. The Grecian style makes them look different, of course."

"Right."

"It's okay, you know," she said, glancing at him.

He met her gaze for a fraction of a second before looking back to the road. "What?"

"That the third statue looks like Hannah. You can talk about it."

Oh, hell. He ought to have known. Heat crept up his neck. "I wasn't sure you'd noticed."

"It's a reflection of my own face, Trick. Of course I noticed."

She played with the plastic tab on her coffee. "Part of me hopes that's her grave."

"And the other parts?"

Rachel looked out the window. "You asked me if I thought she was alive and I told you I hoped she was dead. That's true, but there's a part of me that wants her to be alive. I want my sister back, even though I know it wouldn't be the same."

He couldn't imagine her loss, and it broke his heart. "We'll find her." It was all he could think of to say. Everything else seemed disingenuous.

"What if Anne's one of his victims?" she asked after a few moments' silence. "What if that's what he does with the ones he keeps? He makes them help him."

"We have no record of a victim named Anne."

"Maybe no one reported her missing. Or we didn't make the connection. Or maybe Anne's not her real name. Maybe she's Grace. Maybe she's…"

Trick reached over and squeezed her hand. "Don't go there."

Rachel was silent.

When they arrived at the hospital, they found Morgan outside Carnegie's room. She looked as though she'd been crying.

"You okay, sweetie?" Rachel asked.

Morgan nodded. "The police think my dad did this."

"They're going to look at everyone who might have had a motive," Rachel told her.

"Even you?" the girl asked.

Rachel nodded. "It wasn't me, and I don't think it was your dad either."

Morgan sighed. "Mom knew—about me and Alex. Somehow she figured it out, and she told Dad. Now, he's in there and I can't see him." Trick heard the anger in her voice, but what had the kid expected? She was underage, and that made Carnegie a predator in his book.

"I know it seems unfair," Rachel said. "And I know you feel you're old enough for the relationship you and Alex have, but it's against the law, Morgan. He could be charged with statutory rape. That's not your dad's fault, or your mother's. It's not your fault either. It's Alex's. No matter what he feels for you, he's an adult who knows better."

The girl gave a glum nod.

Trick's phone buzzed, so he walked away to answer, giving the two of them a little privacy. Morgan might say something to Rachel that she wouldn't with him present.

"Hello?"

"Is Rachel with you?" It was Mancusi.

"She's talking to the other Cole girl. Why?"

"They got a hit on the blood on the card she got. It's a match for Rachel."

"Meaning it's a match for Hannah."

"The paper was still damp, Trick."

His heart skipped a beat. "Jesus Christ. You think Hannah's still alive?"

"Maybe he saved some of her blood. Maybe it's Rachel's."

He laughed. "What, you think she sent the card to herself?"

"Maybe. Maybe she wants to make sure we're on the case, or maybe she freaked out when there wasn't a delivery that morning. Maybe she can't let go."

"Yeah, don't give up your day job to pursue psychology, Mancusi. You used to be her partner. You think she'd do that?"

"I think her sister getting taken fucked her up, Trick. It would fuck me up too. Just do me a favor and follow up with her sister—make sure Rachel really was at home all night last night."

"You follow up with Naomi," he said. "I believe Rachel."

"Christ, you're in love with her."

"Call me when you've got the warrant," he said, and hung up.

He walked back to Rachel. Morgan was gone. "They got a hit on the blood on the card."

"It's Hannah's," she said, not looking at him. "And Jordan's wondering if it could be mine."

"You heard?"

"Enough to guess, yeah. I mean, it would be the best way to mess with me. He likes to do that, remember?"

She didn't have to remind him. "I told her I believe you."

This time she looked up at him, and her smile was more real. "Thank you."

"Agent Ward?" the nurse asked when she stepped out of Carnegie's room.

Both Rachel and Trick turned their attention to her. "Yes?" Rachel asked.

"Mr. Carnegie has asked to see you."

CHAPTER NINE

Twenty years ago

Rachel hid under the doorstep. There was no way Hannah would find her there. Now, she could have some privacy to read the note Aaron Grant gave to her in math class that day. She didn't like math, but she liked Aaron. He'd written *READ WHEN YOUR ALONE* on the folded paper. She didn't even mind that he'd spelled "you're" wrong.

Hannah made fun of her for liking Aaron. She said he was a dork, but Hannah was a dork, so what did she know? She was just mad because Aaron was the one person who did better in algebra than she did.

Hannah would tease her for the note. She'd want to read it, and at fourteen, Rachel didn't think she and her sister had to share everything anymore. It wasn't like Hannah had told her when Finn Walker tried to kiss her. Now, Finn was a *dork*.

Rachel unfolded the note, her heart racing.

I LIKE YOUR SISTER. CAN YOU FIND OUT IF SHE LIKES ME?

Her heart plummeted. Tears gripped at her throat and burned the back of her eyes.

"Found you!" came a triumphant singsong as Hannah's head appeared in the opening in the lattice. "Rach?"

Rachel pushed her aside as she crawled out from underneath the step. She shoved the crumpled note into her sister's chest. "Sometimes I hate you," she whispered as tears trickled down her cheek. She stumbled to her feet and ran up the steps into the house, slamming the door behind her.

The hospital room smelled of cleaning solution, blood, and flowers. Rachel wasn't sure what she'd expected to find inside, but the man in the bed wasn't it. She stopped just inside the door, and stared.

Whoever had attacked Carnegie hadn't wanted to kill him, or he'd be dead. Whoever had done this had wanted to hurt him. Ruin him.

His once-handsome face had been slashed in several places, and there was a thick bandage over one eye that made her wonder if there was anything left in the socket beneath. They'd cut his lips too. Because he was a liar? His arms and chest were heavily bandaged as well.

"Hello, Agent Ward," he said in a rough voice not much louder than a whisper. "Like what you see?"

"Not particularly," she replied. "Someone really wanted to mess you up."

"Yes," he agreed. "She did."

"She?" Rachel jumped on the word. "Did Anne do this to you?"

"Anne?" He laughed harshly. "*My* Anne? No. She didn't do this to me."

"Then who did?"

"Come closer."

Rachel hesitated.

"You're not afraid of me, are you?" He smiled, then winced.

"No," she said. And she wasn't. Yet…it took all of her strength to move closer to him. She stopped at the foot of the bed. That was close enough.

Carnegie watched her with his one free eye, his gaze sharp as a new razor. "That's a good girl." He lifted a straw in a plastic cup to his lips and drank before setting the cup on the table positioned over his lap. "Tell me why you think I took your sister."

That wasn't what she expected. Rachel tilted her head as she studied him. "Because every time I look at you, I hear her voice in my head screaming that it was you." She'd never confessed that to anyone—not Trick, not Naomi. Not even to her shrink.

"You *hear* her, even though she's dead?"

Rachel's hands gripped the footboard. "Is she dead, Alex?"

His myopic gaze brightened at the use of his first name. "I would think so, but then, you know monsters better than I do." He shifted against the pillows. "Which would hurt more, knowing she was dead or knowing she was alive?"

"That's an odd question. I'd answer it if I didn't think you'd masturbate to the answer."

Another laugh—followed by a groan of pain, which pleased her more than it should have.

"Where's my sister, Alex? Is she in your garden?"

That wiped the smirk off his face. "My garden?"

She leaned into the footboard. "Did you think I wouldn't notice Suki, Grace, and Hannah keeping watch over your backyard?"

"There are so many things you haven't noticed, Rachel darling."

"Where's Hannah?"

"How should I know?" He shifted again, face tightening in pain. "Why'd you do this to me?"

"Excuse me?"

"Why did you attack me last night?"

Now Rachel was the one to laugh. "I didn't. You and I both know that."

"I know it was dark and that I was attacked by a woman with a knife. A woman who claimed to be you."

There was a challenge in his gaze, but Rachel let her anger take over. "If I wanted you dead, you'd be dead," she informed him. "And I wouldn't use a knife."

Carnegie shrugged. "I'm just telling you what I told the police."

Blood turning to ice in her veins, Rachel went still. "You told the police I attacked you?"

"I told them the woman who attacked me identified herself as you, yes. I imagine they'll want to talk to you about that."

"You son of a bitch." She'd have killed him at that moment if she thought she could do it and get away with it. Shove her gun in his mouth and pull the trigger.

"Ah," he whispered. "There she is. You want to finish the job, don't you?"

This was dangerous and she knew it. Trick was just outside the door. All she had to do was walk out, and sanity would return. She wouldn't be thinking about what Carnegie's blood would feel like on her face.

Hannah wouldn't be screaming in her head for her to do it. *Kill him. Kill. Him.*

Her breath caught. She could do it. She knew she could.

Letting go of the bed, Rachel pivoted on her heel and lurched toward the door.

"I hope you find your sister, Rachel," Carnegie called after her.

"We will," she promised as she reached for the door handle.

"No."

Something in his tone stopped her. Gripping the handle, she turned her head and met his singular gaze. For a second, she was sure she saw the killer he was, in the bright blue depths.

"I mean it," he said. "I hope *you* find her."

Ice slithered down her spine. She yanked open the door and stepped out into the corridor. Only Trick stood there now. Morgan was gone.

"Are you okay?" her partner asked, straightening away from the wall as she approached.

"She's there," Rachel told him, her fingers closing around his forearm. Her teeth were chattering. "Hannah's in that fucking garden."

Seventeen years ago

"When you look in the mirror, do you see your face or your sister's?" he asked her.

Hannah took another drink of wine. "Mine." He liked to ask questions like this. He seemed obsessed with the fact that she and Rachel were reflections of each other.

"If I fucked you in front of a mirror, it would be like fucking her," he mused, running his fingers up her arm.

She shivered and licked her lips. He'd put something in the wine. Some kind of drug that enhanced sex—she could feel it buzzing between her thighs, tingling along her skin.

He took her by the hand and led her into his bedroom. He'd started letting her out of her room a few months ago. She'd run if she thought she'd get far. Where would she go? Home? How would she get there with no money and no clothes? She'd be raped or murdered, and not by anyone who treated her as well as he did.

He placed her in front of the mirror in his room. The light was soft, making her hair glow like it was on fire. Her body was hardly concealed by the thin gown and robe he'd chosen for her to wear. He liked touching her through thin fabrics. Hannah watched as he took her wine and set it on the dresser. Then, standing behind her, he untied her robe and slipped it from her shoulders.

Her nipples were tight. She blamed the drugs, but she knew that wasn't all of it. She closed her eyes when his hand came up and cupped her breast. His other hand bunched the fabric of the gown in the back, hauling it up until she could feel the rough fabric of his pants against her bare ass. He nudged her legs apart with one of his, working those same fingers between her thighs.

"You're already wet," he murmured.

Hannah tried to stay silent as his fingers slid inside her, but he knew just how to do it. He knew what she liked. When he pinched her nipple, she gasped.

"Sweet Rachel," came his rough voice.

Her eyes sprang open, her gaze locking on his in the mirror. He shoved his fingers so hard and deep inside her that she had to grab the dresser to keep from crashing into it. "Oh, God," she said.

"That's it, Rachel," he said. "Fuck my hand with your tight, wet cunt."

She hated that word, but when he said it...she whimpered. Rachel wouldn't have whimpered.

He took her to the edge of orgasm, then stopped. He liked to do that. His fingers slid out, leaving her cold and stretched. In the mirror she watched as he started taking off his clothes.

She hated him.

Hannah spun around and pounced at him with all her weight. It wasn't much, but she knocked him back onto the bed.

"What the fuck?" he snarled, lifting his head from the mattress.

She straddled him, her hands closing around his throat as her knees grasped his hips. She squeezed as hard as she could as she lowered herself on top of him, slipping down on his erection. She smiled at the surprise on his face.

"You want to fuck Rachel?" she asked. "This is what Rachel would do to you." She squeezed harder, thrusting her lower body down onto his.

He smiled then, his fingers digging into her hips.

Hannah's fingers were already tiring, and she knew she wouldn't be able to take it all the way. He knew it too, but that was okay. Glancing up, she caught her reflection in the mirror on the other side of the room. It wasn't her face she saw. It was Rachel's. Strong, capable Rachel.

Beneath her, he gasped for breath. Her back arched and her fingers went slack as orgasm ripped through her, making her roar like some kind of animal. He gave one last thrust and came as well, sucking in air like he'd been drowning.

Hannah collapsed on top of him, feeling the pounding of his heart beneath her hand.

"Of all my girls," he said, his voice hoarse, "you're my favorite."

She smiled at the compliment, and when she looked at the mirror again, it wasn't her sister's face she saw. It wasn't her own either. It was one she didn't recognize.

Jordan didn't believe Rachel was stupid enough to use her own blood to write a threatening card to herself. However, she did think Rachel was smart enough to use her own blood and say it was her twin's if it kept her in the investigation.

She liked Rachel—for the most part. They'd worked well

together back in the day, but Jordan never really felt close to her. Rachel didn't let people get close. She'd never seen her go out with friends or heard of her dating. She kept to herself and didn't share. To Jordan, that was weird. Normally people who acted like they had something to hide, well…had something to hide.

And then there was her obsession with Alex Carnegie. She'd threatened bodily harm against the man because of circumstantial evidence and a "feeling." It was unprofessional and reckless. How the hell the woman had made it to the FBI, Jordan would never know. Not that she was jealous, because she wasn't.

But now Carnegie was saying it had been Rachel who attacked him. Actually, he'd said he was attacked by a tall, redhaired woman who in the dark looked a lot like Rachel. He claimed she took off when he said her name.

He might be lying—either to protect Anne or to make things difficult for Rachel. Or he could be telling the truth, which would be hard to wrap her head around, because if Rachel wanted someone dead, she had the knowledge and the means to make it happen. She wouldn't leave her intended victim bleeding out on his steps.

But it was her job to follow up on all leads, so she would talk to Rachel's sister Naomi, and if she had to, she'd get a warrant for information from their security company. She would have thought Trick would be on board with that, but he was thinking with his little brain rather than the big one. Some men just couldn't resist crazy.

As she stepped off the elevator onto the floor where Sydney Cole was being kept, Jordan's pulse kicked up a notch. She was there because Mrs. Cole had called and said her daughter had remembered some details about her abduction and attack. She half expected to see Trick and Rachel there, and was surprised when they weren't.

She lightly knocked on the doorframe. The whole family was there, Morgan sitting on the bed beside her sister while her parents sat in nearby chairs.

"Sorry to interrupt," Jordan said.

"Detective Mancusi." Victoria Cole rose to her feet and came to greet her. The woman still looked drawn and pale, but there was a lightness to her gaze that hadn't been there the last time Jordan saw her. It had to be the relief of knowing that her daughter was going to be okay. Physically, at least.

"Is this an okay time?" Jordan asked.

"Of course. Come in."

Mr. Cole rose to his feet as well, and nodded at her. He looked like a man with rage seething just below the surface of his skin. Probably because he'd found out a man a little older than himself had been sleeping with his teenage daughter.

"Sydney, honey. This is Detective Mancusi. Do you feel up to telling her what you told me?"

The girl in the bed looked frailer than her twin, though they were the same size and height. Dark circles hugged her tired eyes and her skin looked thin as paper. She had a few bandages on her forearms—defensive wounds, most likely. She was fortunate nothing vital had been punctured.

"Yeah," Sydney said, wrapping her hand around her twin's. "If Morgan can stay."

"I have no problem with that," Jordan told her. She moved to the bottom of the bed—close enough to hear, but not so close that the girl felt pressured. "You go ahead and tell me whatever you can. Go as slow as you need to, okay? If it gets to be too much, we'll stop. It's all however you want it to be."

She nodded. "Where do you want me to start?"

"What do you remember about the night you were abducted?"

"We went to the concert." She glanced at her sister. "Well, I did. Morgan went...somewhere else."

"Son of a bitch," Mr. Cole muttered.

Morgan flushed, but remained silent. Her twin leaned against her.

"Afterward, I was walking out to wait for Morgan to come back and get me when I heard someone call my name. It was a woman in a car parked on the street."

"Did you recognize her?"

"Not at first, but then I saw her face. It was Anne—Alex's assistant."

Jordan kept her excitement hidden. "Do you know Anne well?"

"No. I've met her a couple of times, and talked to her a few times on the phone to set up appointments with Alex to work on my portfolio."

"What happened next?"

Sydney frowned in concentration. "I walked over to her,

and she said that Alex and Morgan had gotten stuck somewhere and that she would take me to meet up with them." A tear trickled down her cheek. "I never should have gotten in that car."

"It's okay," Morgan whispered, hugging her. "You didn't do anything wrong."

Jordan smiled sympathetically. "Your sister's right. You did nothing wrong. Where did Anne take you?"

"I don't know. When I got in the car, she offered me a bottle of water. I was thirsty and hot, so I drank it." Her brow puckered again. "I must have fallen asleep, because when I woke up, I was in a strange bedroom."

Jordan glanced at the monitor tracking the girl's vitals—her heart rate was up slightly. "Take a deep breath, Sydney," she urged. "You're doing great. Just relax. None of it can hurt you now."

Her head bobbed in a jerky nod as Sydney sucked in a breath, then winced when it pulled at her wounds. "I wasn't tied up or anything. My head hurt, but I think I heard people arguing. I couldn't hear what they were saying, and I don't know who they were."

"That's okay. What happened next?"

"I don't know. It was all blurry, you know? Anne brought me food, but I think she must have drugged it, because I'd just start feeling a little better and then I'd fall asleep again. And then...I woke up and she was there. She told me she was going to take me home. That she was going to save me."

"From who?"

"I don't know. But she helped me out of the room."

"Do you remember anything about where you were kept?"

"That's what's weird. The room was strange—unfamiliar—and in a basement, but when she took me upstairs, I thought I was in Alex's house."

Thank God the warrant she requested was for house and grounds. They were going to dig up the garden the next morning. They could have done it that afternoon if the judge hadn't been in a meeting that ran late.

Sydney looked at her sister. "I couldn't have been there, right? Alex would have known I was there. He would have saved me."

"Yeah," her sister assured her. "He would have."

Or else he was the one Anne was arguing with, Jordan thought but didn't say. "Do you remember anything else?"

"It was really early in the morning. She put me in a car, and then there was more arguing. And then…" Another tear ran down her cheek. "I remember it hurting. It hurt so much. And she was telling me that it was all going to be alright. That she was saving me. She just kept saying it over and over as I begged her to stop." She began to cry in earnest.

"I think we need to stop," Mrs. Cole said.

Jordan nodded. "Of course. Sydney, you're incredibly strong and brave. I want you to know that. That's how you survived, and that's how you're going to heal and get through this. Your family is going to help you. Meanwhile, I'm going to find Anne and make sure she never hurts anyone again."

Sydney wiped her eyes. "Thanks."

Jordan said good-bye and walked out of the room with Mrs. Cole. In the corridor, the other woman turned to her with a fearful expression. "Tell me the truth, was my baby sexually assaulted?"

Jordan put her hand on Mrs. Cole's arm. "The rape kit came back negative. There was no sign of sexual assault."

"Oh, thank God." She pressed a hand to her chest. Once she'd collected herself, she raised her gaze to Jordan's once more. "What are the chances of Alex not knowing she was in his basement?"

"We don't know if it was even his house," Jordan replied—mostly because she didn't want Mr. or Mrs. Cole heading over to Carnegie's room and finishing him off. "A lot of these criminals keep their victims drugged so they can't give credible accounts of what happened. The house might have only looked like Alex's, or she could have seen something that made her think of him. We'll know more once we conduct our search."

"He's always liked young women," Mrs. Cole confided. "I heard rumors from some of the models I worked with that he didn't care if you were underage, but he never tried anything with me. I trusted him with my girls. My precious girls." She began to sob.

Jordan hugged her. "He was your friend. You had no reason to think he'd take advantage of that. It's not your fault. As for the rest of it, try not to jump to conclusions. All you need to do right now is care for your daughters. They need your full attention. Everyone else can wait."

Mrs. Cole pulled out of the hug and began wiping under

her eyes with her fingers. She must use a good mascara, because there wasn't even the slightest smudge of black on her face or fingertips. "Thank you, Detective. I appreciate your advice, and you don't have to worry about either my husband or myself going off like a vigilante. I'm afraid that, for all our anger, neither one of us have it in us to get revenge."

"If only everyone was the same," Jordan said with a faint smile. "I'll come by and check on you tomorrow." Then she said good-bye and walked back to the elevators. As she stepped in, her phone rang. It was Trick.

"Hey, we got the warrant. The digging crew's coming tomorrow."

"You need to meet us at Rachel's."

Jordan froze. Christ, what had Rachel done now? "Why?"

"She just got a call from her security company about an alarm going off at her house. They think someone's broken in."

CHAPTER TEN

Twenty years ago

I t's not my fault Aaron likes me," Hannah said defensively.

"Go away."

"It's only because he's afraid of you. You like making people afraid of you, but boys don't like it."

"GO AWAY!" Rachel screamed. At least she wasn't crying anymore.

Hannah fixed her with a narrow gaze. "You know, Mom says boys will come and go, but we'll always have each other."

If her sister wouldn't leave, then Rachel would. She shoved past her to leave the bedroom.

"You and I are more important than any boy!" Hannah called after her. "Especially a dork like Aaron Grant!" Rachel heard the tears in her voice, but she kept walking. Hannah was right, it wasn't her fault Aaron liked her, but Rachel was going to blame her anyway.

"You think I did this too?" Rachel asked when she saw Jordan walking up her drive. They were in the backyard while police checked the house.

Her former partner stopped a few feet away, the late afternoon sun lighting her features as it filtered through the trees. She shoved her hands in her jacket pockets. "Of course not."

She shouldn't have asked, Rachel realized as she turned away. Now she just felt like a shit.

The crunch of gravel clued her in to Jordan's approach. "You okay?" the other woman asked.

"I will be, once I see the face of whoever did this." And once the locksmith changed the locks.

"How'd they get in?"

"Must've picked the lock," she allowed. "They ignored the alarm."

"They search the house?"

Rachel rolled her shoulders to ease the tension knotted there. "That's what they're doing now. Trick's with them. Once it's clear, I can go in and see if anything's missing."

"Well, we know it's not Carnegie."

She gave the cop a droll look. "Yay us."

Silence fell between them. Jordan scuffed the toe of her shoe against the drive. "Look, Rachel…"

"Don't." Rachel held up her hand. "Just do your job. You got to, right?"

Jordan nodded. "I spoke to Sydney Cole today."

"What?" She couldn't believe it. "Why weren't we notified?"

"I guess my number came up first in her phone." It was a shitty excuse and they both knew it. Jordan sighed heavily. "I didn't call you because I didn't know what the girl was going to say and I didn't want you to get upset."

Rachel shot her a dubious glance. "You're kidding."

"Look, I might not be your favorite person, but I'm not a complete ass, okay? If I had my way, you wouldn't be at Carnegie's tomorrow either, but I know better than to try and stop you."

"I'm not going to fall apart if she's there."

She shrugged. "I would if it was my sister."

Was that a judgment? Rachel opened her mouth to ask, but was stopped by Trick coming out of the house. He wore gloves and had what looked like a shoebox in his hands. It was smeared with fingerprint powder.

"What's that?" Rachel asked, moving to intercept him.

"It was on your bed," he told her before setting it on the hood of one of the police cars. "I think you should take a look. Both of you." He offered them gloves, then removed the lid from the box.

It was a box of photographs. On top was a note—written in the same hand as the card she'd received, only this time not in blood: *For the Family Album.* Rachel began going through them.

"Fuck," she whispered as invisible fingers tightened around her heart. "They're all Hannah." And a few of her and Hannah together. God, they were taken so long ago. As she went through them, horror unfurled in her stomach, rising up until it threatened to choke her. It wasn't even that the photos were terrible—Gemini had sent her ones that were far more upsetting in that regard. No. What was terrible was that Rachel could see her twin's age progression.

"She had to be at least twenty in this," she said, holding one so Trick and Jordan could both study it. Tears scorched the back of her eyes. It was one she hadn't seen before. Gemini had been holding out on her.

"Rachel," Jordan said, handing her a photo.

It took a second for her vision to clear so she could see it clearly. It was Hannah in what looked like a designer dress—very skimpy and not the sort of thing flattered by underwear lines. Her sister wore makeup and had her hair done—she looked like a frigging model, so thin and chic. She was sitting on a sofa with a glass of wine in her hand.

"Look at the playbill on the coffee table," Jordan said in a soft voice.

She did. "*The Book of Mormon.*" She shrugged. "So?"

Her former partner's expression was almost anguished. "It opened in 2011."

That's when it all became too horrible to contemplate. "She was alive in 2011." *Twelve years* after she'd been taken. "Oh, Jesus Christ." Before she could stop it, bile rushed up from her stomach. Still clutching the photograph in her fist, she doubled over and vomited on the weeds growing by the foundation of the house.

Twelve years.

Twelve years.

Twelve. Fucking. Years.

"*Ughnnnn,*" she moaned. "Oh, no, no, no."

"Rachel." It was Trick's voice. Trick's arms that caught her before she crumpled.

"I could have saved her," she croaked. "She was still out

there, and I left her with him." She couldn't stop the tears that poured from her eyes. Couldn't stop the sobs that followed, racking her body until it felt like she was having a seizure. She didn't care who was there, or who saw. All she could think about was the fact that her sister had been Gemini's prisoner for so long. So many years of abuse, while Rachel had lived her life and played at being a cop. It was too much. Too sickening. Too heartbreaking.

She didn't put up a fight when Trick picked her up and carried her into the house. She didn't speak when he told the CSUs to get the fuck out of her bedroom. She didn't stop crying when he set her on her bed and took off her shoes, or when he put a blanket around her. And when someone—Naomi, she thought. When had her little sister gotten home? She shouldn't see her like this—pressed pills against her lips, she opened her mouth, swallowing them and the water to wash them down without any fuss.

Trick stayed with her, holding her as the darkness came on. As it took her down, she imagined Hannah in that little garden, shovels full of rich soil raining down upon her cold skin, and she hoped—she prayed—that her sister had found some peace.

Because Rachel would never know peace again.

Saturday

Trick didn't try to stop Rachel from attending the search of Carnegie's home, though it was painful to watch. Her breakdown the night before had left her with swollen, red eyes with a haunted look in them. She was pale and quiet, as though she was in the world, but not of it.

He took the key out of the ignition and looked at her. She was staring through the windshield at Carnegie's house, probably wondering what they'd find within. The search the two of them had done the other day would be nothing compared to what was about to go down.

"If any of this gets to be too much..." he began.

She turned her head and smiled faintly at him. "Yeah. Thanks."

He squeezed her hand. She surprised him by leaning over and kissing him. Usually she was so careful about people finding out about them. Then she opened her door and stepped out of the SUV. He followed suit.

Mancusi had pulled in behind them and had just gotten out of her car as well. She walked up to Rachel. "Good?" she asked, her expression neutral.

Rachel nodded. "Good."

They let Mancusi take the lead. Yolanda was not happy to find two federal agents and a small police squad on the front step, but there was nothing she could do when faced with a search warrant.

"Where's the basement?" Mancusi asked her. They were led to a door at the back of the house. It was carefully concealed within a panel of the wall.

"That's not suspicious," Trick remarked.

They were geared up so as not to contaminate any evidence. CSU followed them through the door, down the narrow steps. Cool, slightly stale air rose up to greet them, but no death. Though, had he really expected the place to smell like a slaughterhouse?

Rachel followed behind him as Mancusi led the way down. Once they reached the bottom, Trick looked around. It looked like a normal basement—except for the custom wine cellar and corner full of photographic equipment.

"Is that a darkroom?" he asked.

Mancusi nodded, and gestured for the crime-scene team to start there. "I'd say that one over there is what we're looking for."

Trick followed her line of sight. The door to this room had several heavy locks on the outside. Just the sight of them made his stomach turn.

Rachel stepped forward, but Trick stopped her from opening the door. Mancusi did it instead. Inside, the room was dark. She flicked the switch to fill it with light. It was a small bedroom with an attached bath. Nothing nearly as fancy as the rest of the house, but nothing to scoff at either. Except there weren't any windows.

It was empty.

"Not a guest room," Mancusi commented. "I'm guessing it's pretty soundproof too."

Rachel pulled free of Trick's grasp and stepped inside, her gaze traveling everywhere, as though searching for some sign of her sister. He watched her flex and fist her left hand, like she did when she had those weird pins and needles. She seemed to get them only when she was thinking of Hannah.

CSU began doing their job, checking out the bath, going through the dresser, stripping sheets off the bed.

"Wait," Rachel said. "What's that?"

There was something etched into the wall by the bed. It was so small, Trick had no idea how she'd seen it, except that she was looking for it—for anything.

One of the CSUs bent down to look at it. "It says *Hannah*."

It was as though someone punched Rachel in the stomach, so visible was her physical reaction. "Photograph it," Mancusi ordered. Then, to Rachel, "Why don't you wait outside? If we find anything else, we'll let you know."

It said a lot about her emotional state that Rachel agreed. Trick gave her arm a squeeze as she walked past him. He and Mancusi exchanged concerned glances.

"Got some hairs from the pillow," another investigator announced. "Red."

Mancusi glanced at him. "Willing to bet on whether or not those belong to Sydney Cole?"

Trick shook his head. "I think that might be an easy bet."

"Trick?"

He turned. Standing in the doorway was Agent Richard Carter, from their office. Beside him sat a black retriever in an FBI harness.

"Rick," he said in greeting, offering his hand. "Thanks for coming."

"Sure." The shorter man glanced around. "Is it true this guy's a Gemini suspect?"

Trick nodded. "Yeah, so we're looking for the usual—drives, servers, recording equipment."

"Gotcha. If there's anything here, Pepper will find it." They turned away to begin working the rest of the house. There were already too many people in that small bedroom.

One of the best things the FBI had ever done, in Trick's estimation, was employ electronics-sniffing dogs. They were amazing. In his previous position he'd watched the dogs find servers and concealed drives that they never would have found otherwise. It was especially helpful in cases where pornography was involved.

The thought of which made him leave the room and approach the officers working the dark room. "Find anything?" he asked.

"Some prints," a female officer informed him. "A few rolls of undeveloped film that we'll take back to the lab. Nothing interesting yet." And by "interesting," she meant incriminating.

He glanced toward Rachel, who was looking at a photo on the wall with wide eyes.

Oh, shit. He joined her, his heart pounding hard. It was a large black-and-white photograph of a partially nude woman sitting with her back to the viewer, glancing coyly over her shoulder among a cascade of thick hair. One look at the profile and his breath caught. She looked so much like Rachel he knew it had to be Hannah. Rachel wasn't so thin that her ribs were visible when she moved.

Rachel's fingers shook as she reached out and touched the photo. "Why did he keep her so long?" Her voice was a thin whisper.

Twelve years was a long time to keep a victim, but Carnegie wasn't the first predator to do so. Jaycee Dugard, for one, and

Rosalynn McGinnis had both been held for well over a decade by their captors.

He didn't know how to answer her question, so he didn't try. Dugard and McGinnis had been victimized for eighteen and nineteen years respectively, but they'd survived. There was no evidence here that Hannah had done the same.

"She photographed better than me," Rachel remarked, her fingers trailing over the image of her sister's hair and shoulder. "And I was the one who wanted to be in front of the camera."

The dog barked, making both of them jump.

"Over here," came Rick's voice. Trick and Rachel exchanged glances before rushing over to the back wall where Pepper sat expectantly.

"There's something behind this wall," Rick told them.

It took only a moment to find the seam. A bookcase of photography manuals and books also served as camouflage for a door. All Trick had to do was give it a hard tug and it swung open.

"Jesus Christ," he breathed.

It was a small room—smaller than even the bedroom, but there was a table with a computer monitor on it and boxes stacked against the wall. Trick turned on the monitor. It flickered, then showed an eerily clear picture of the crew in the bedroom.

"He liked to watch," Rachel commented from behind him.

Trick thought about kicking her out of the room, but she was already moving toward the neatly stacked storage bins. She selected one off the top row and brought it down to the floor. Crouching over it, she removed the lid.

"There's a server in here," Rick said, grabbing Trick's

attention. The dog had sniffed out another spot inside the room—another panel—behind which was a stack of equipment Trick recognized. He'd seen many such servers in his days of taking down pornographers.

"Fuck," he whispered. Then he stuck his head outside. "Mancusi!"

"Oh." It was a small word, but it echoed in his head like a thunderclap. He turned and saw Rachel with her hand pressed against her mouth as she stared at a photograph. Quickly he went to her, crouching down so he could better see what she was looking at. It was an image of Tricia Douvall, who'd disappeared in 2010, having sex with another woman.

Having sex with Hannah.

Trick took the photo from her and put it back in the box. There were CDs in there as well—probably filmed versions of the photographs. Jesus. He snapped the lid back into place.

"You shouldn't be here," he said, taking her by the arm and helping her to her feet. "Come on."

"No," she said, pulling against his grip. "I don't want to go."

"You're going." Usually he gave in, but not today. How much did she think she could take? How much abuse did she want to heap upon herself? How much guilt? Wanting to know what happened to her sister was one thing, but she didn't need to know every horrible thing Hannah had been made to do.

He hauled her upstairs into the main part of the house. Yolanda and Gallagher were in the kitchen, drinking coffee, waiting. Neither of them was talking.

"Did you know?" Rachel demanded when she saw them.

Yanking free of Trick's grasp, she rushed at them, making Yolanda draw back. "Did you know he kept girls down there? That he filmed them? Did you know my sister?"

Their expressions were ones of matching horror—too real to be faked.

"Your sister?" Yolanda whispered. "No. I...I never."

Pete Gallagher had gone totally white. "He brought a girl home once. She looked at me and said, 'Help me.'" He swallowed. "I thought she was drunk, so I just helped her out of the car. Mr. C laughed and said she couldn't hold her liquor. Oh, God." He looked like he might throw up.

Rachel shoved her phone at him. "Was this her?" Heather Montgomery, Trick saw, the most recent victim.

The young man leaped out of his chair and rushed to the sink. He just made it before he retched. He turned on the tap as he continued to heave.

Rachel moved toward the exit. "I need to get some air," she said.

Trick went with her. They sat on the steps in the sunshine. There was a lovely breeze, and seagulls cried in the distance. There seemed like there could be nothing terrible in such a beautiful place.

Rachel wrapped her arms around her bent legs and pressed her forehead to her knees. "I think you were right. I shouldn't be here."

"I can take you home."

She shook her head. "No. You *have* to be here, and I *need* to be, regardless of whether or not I *should*."

"Has seeing any of this made it easier?" he asked. "Because it seems like it's making it worse."

"I don't know. I just know I can't leave. If she's here...she needs to know I found her. *I* need to know."

Trick rubbed his hand over her back. Helplessness wasn't something he'd felt a lot in his life, but he was feeling it at that moment. There was no way he could make this any easier for her.

A rumble caught his attention and he looked up as a couple of larger vehicles pulled into the drive. One of the vehicles had a dog in it, and his heart sank at the sight. It was a cadaver dog.

The digging crew had arrived.

Nineteen years ago

"I can't wait until we move to New York," Hannah said as she flopped down on Rachel's bed.

"I know," her twin agreed excitedly. "It's going to be fucking awesome."

"Promise to remember me when you're a famous model?"

Rachel shrugged. "I don't know if that's ever going to happen."

"Why wouldn't it?"

"Because I'm not skinny enough. I'm not pretty enough. Alex Carnegie turned me down."

"Only because he's like one of the top photographers in New York. You have to start smaller than that, Ray Ray."

"I don't want to start small."

"You're going to be on the cover of *Vogue* someday, I know it." She took her twin's hand and squeezed. "And I'm going to buy copies for all my friends."

"I'll be wearing something you designed," Rachel said, joining the fantasy. "Every shoot I do will have something of yours in it—it will be in my contract."

They rolled on the bed to face each other, hands still clasped.

"We're going to live together, right?" Hannah asked.

"In an industrial loft we totally decorate ourselves."

"And we'll have awesome parties with Leo DiCaprio and Johnny Depp."

Rachel grinned. "And John Cusack."

"He's old."

"So's Johnny Depp. Besides, you like old guys."

"Not that many. I like Leo more. Hey, do you think you'll marry a male model?"

"Nah. I want to marry a normal guy—like a cop or something. Someone who will keep me grounded but doesn't care that I make more money than him."

"I want to marry a guy who loves me more than anything. I don't care about the rest."

Rachel smiled at her. "Of course he'll love you, dweeb. Everyone loves you."

Hannah returned the smile, unsure of herself. "You think so?"

"I know so. Everyone who meets you loves you. It's a fact. And if he doesn't love you more than anything, I'll beat his ass."

Laughing, Hannah hugged her sister. "I love you more than anything, Sissy."

"Dweeb," Rachel replied. But she hugged her back. "I love you too."

"According to Gallagher, the newest statue just went up just this spring," Trick informed Mancusi when she joined them outside. Rachel had collected herself and was sipping at a cup of coffee Yolanda had made for her.

Mancusi shrugged out of her jacket. "Yeah, he calls them his 'muses,' apparently."

Rachel took another sip to ease the tightening in her chest. Her former partner glanced back at her from where they were gathered on the edge of the garden. Mancusi nodded. Rachel nodded back. She could do this. She was going to do this. She owed it to Hannah, but most of all, she owed it to herself to see this through.

But that didn't stop her head from spinning a little when the cadaver dog sat down on the rectangle of earth guarded by those damn statues.

Trick—beautiful, too-good-for-her Trick—was immediately at her side. When he laced his fingers with hers, she held him as tight as she dared.

"Do you think he used Hannah to lure other girls?" she whispered.

Trick turned to her. "Maybe. He's a good-looking guy, and charming. I don't think he needs a lot of help."

"You think so?" Or was he just saying it to make her feel better?

He smiled slightly. "He's very chiseled and white."

Rachel chuckled. God, how could she laugh at a time like this? Still, it felt good. "He's a little too chiseled and white for my taste, I guess."

"What is your taste?"

It was just the two of them, but this was still dangerous—not to mention inappropriate. Still, the levity was just the distraction she needed at the moment. "I think you know." She raised her coffee cup to her lips.

Trick seemed to study her face. He smiled wryly. "Careful, Ward. I might start to think you like me."

"I do like you," she admitted. "A lot. I just think you could do better."

He squeezed her fingers. "I don't. You'd be a hard act to follow."

She didn't say anything, but she moved closer to him. They stood together, watching as the small backhoe took shallow scoops of earth from the section of the garden. Then a small group of men with shovels and tools began carefully removing dirt. Other CSUs sifted through the discarded soil for evidence.

Rachel's anxiety rose with every fall of the scoop. Gripping Trick's hand, she watched and waited for a scrap of fabric, a hint of hair or bone. Anything. An hour went by of painstakingly slow work, then another, and nothing.

Her parents had wanted to have a service for Hannah several years ago. They called it closure. They wanted to bury some of her favorite things, just so there'd be something with an emotional connection in the grave. Rachel hadn't agreed with the idea, but they'd done it anyway. She refused to visit the spot, even though they'd buried her grandmother beside it.

If she couldn't know where her sister was, she wouldn't mourn her where she wasn't. Maybe that made no sense, but it only made her angry to talk about it. Of course, her mother took it as a personal insult. Just one more thing Rachel did to fail her and Hannah.

"Jesus Christ!" a voice yelled. "Stop digging! Stop digging!"

Rachel and Trick shared a startled glance before racing over to the hole. Everyone stopped talking and moving, and an eerie silence fell over the garden. Forensics were already in the hole, uncovering the rest of what had been spotted.

"Holy shit," Trick whispered.

Rachel could only nod. There, partially covered by rich dark soil, dotted with bits of grass and flower petals, was the skeleton of a woman laid out with her arms over her chest, as though she'd been placed that way. She wore the tattered remains of a long dress, and her hair—what was left of it—though clotted with dirt, was still a vibrant red.

"Hannah," she whispered.

CHAPTER ELEVEN

Rachel watched as the state death investigator and her team carefully removed the skeleton from the grave and placed it in a body bag for transport back to the coroner's office.

"We'll run dental," Trick said. "It will be faster."

She knew that. "It's Hannah."

"We'll know for sure soon."

She was too tired to fight with him. She knew he didn't want her getting her hopes up. She almost laughed out loud. Who got their hopes up that their sister had been tossed into a hole like garbage?

She drew a deep breath. It felt like something was about to pop in her brain. She turned away from the scene as her phone rang. "Ward," she said.

"It's Maika. How you holding up?"

Of course she knew they'd found a body. "I'm fine," Rachel told her. If she faked it enough, maybe it would come true.

"I got a call about those wigs you found at Carnegie's. I've got friends in the business."

"Of course you do." Rachel allowed herself a smile. "You have friends everywhere."

"What can I say, I'm popular. Anyway, one was high-quality synthetic and one was human—like, high end. My friend says the synthetic one retails for about three hundred and the human one closer to two grand. Now, that's a good wig. My aunt Cece loved herself some wigs, but I doubt her entire collection cost two grand."

"Is that odd? To have both synthetic and real hair?"

"No. Synthetics retain their style longer don't get all frizzy in Connecticut humidity. We also found traces of skin and hair inside the caps, so the lab is running that now. You want to share this with the staties, or do you want me to?"

"Mancusi is here. I'll fill her in. Thanks." After hanging up, she filled Trick in, and the two of them went to join Jordan, who was talking to the death investigator.

"I'll make sure the office knows this is priority," Charlene assured her. "As soon as we have dental, you'll have it too." She nodded to them, then got back to her crew.

Rachel told Mancusi about the wigs.

"If she was wearing wigs that expensive, then she really wants them to look natural," Mancusi mused. "It's not just for fun."

"Maybe Carnegie made her wear them in public to conceal her identity," Rachel suggested just as her phone rang again. This time it was Naomi.

"Everything okay?" she asked.

"Yeah," her sister replied. "Mom's only called twice today. Don't worry, I didn't tell her about the break-in."

"Don't. She'll only find some way to blame me for it."

"A guy from the police and I went through the footage from the camera. It was a tall, light-haired woman in a large hat and sunglasses that walked up the driveway and opened the back door."

"I'm not surprised. She's been getting around."

"Yeah, but Rach—she used the spare key."

Rachel froze. "What?"

"She knew where we kept the key. And the security guys gave me the codes she tried to enter on the alarm. Your birthday, my birthday, and the day Hannah disappeared."

"Someone's done their homework, but not good enough."

"She's been watching us? Fucking hell."

"Stay with Lynn this weekend. The locksmith is coming on Monday."

"What about you?"

"I'm a federal agent with a weapon."

"Have Trick stay over. Or stay with him."

Rachel glanced at Trick out of the corner of her eye. She wasn't sure how much more she could ask of him, but if he offered, she'd take it. She thought of herself as strong for the most part, but she wasn't stupid.

"Did she put the key back?" Rachel asked.

"Yeah. I've got it now, though."

"Good." She squinted up at the sun. "Okay, if I don't see you before I get home, I love you."

"What's happened?"

"Nothing," she lied. "It's just been a rough day." There was no point in both of them waiting on the lab results.

"Rach—"

"Listen, sweetie, I gotta go. I'll talk to you later." She hung up before her sister could dig any further. She just didn't have the energy to lie convincingly.

She joined Trick and Mancusi. "I'm going to see what I can do about getting a rush on these dentals," Mancusi said.

Rachel nodded. "All three of the women represented by those statues were redheads. I don't think that's a coincidence. You'll speed things up by comparing records for just Suki Carlton, Grace O'Brien, and Hannah. Also, given that Carnegie seems to have a thing for gingers, we need to dig into his past. See if we can figure out the obsession with red-haired twins."

"I'm surprised you don't know that already," Mancusi remarked. "Given your...research into the guy."

Research. Now that it was looking like Rachel had been right the whole time, it was funny how obsession became something more positive. "I dug into his family life and his career, not things that might have been going on around him. We need to talk to his sister, Everly."

Mancusi nodded. "On it. Meanwhile, you should go home and rest. You're freaking everybody out."

"Nice," Rachel replied. "Thanks. I'd rather keep busy."

The detective slapped Trick on the shoulder and smirked. "Oh, I'm sure Agent Patrick here can think of something to keep you occupied." She pivoted on her heel and walked away before either of them could respond.

"Let's go," Trick said. "We're done here for now." It was the tricky part of their job. How much could they do before step-ping on police toes? Serial killers were federal cases, but it was important to keep up a good relationship with local law en-forcement, as it was also a state concern.

They drove back to Rachel's place. Rachel punched in the code on the alarm—426624—"H-A-N-N-A-H" in numerical form. It felt strangely quiet without Naomi there. The break-in had been an invasion of their privacy—a violation. She didn't want to leave, but she wasn't going to feel completely safe or comfortable until the locks had been changed and Anne was in custody.

Anne, who she was beginning to think was just as deranged as Carnegie.

"Can you stay?" Rachel asked Trick as she kicked off her shoes. "*Will* you stay?"

"Yeah," he said with a nod. "Sure."

She smiled at him. She could feel the stretching of her skin over her face—how much effort it took. "Thank you. You're so good to me. I don't think I deserve it."

He took her hand and kissed the inside of her wrist. "Shut up."

She laughed and twined her fingers in his, tugging him through the house into her bedroom. Once there, she began to strip off her clothes.

Trick arched an eyebrow. "Rach?"

"I don't like to feel vulnerable," she told him, tossing her shirt on the floor. "I don't like to feel weak or needy."

"I know."

She unfastened her pants. "But I *need* to feel *something*. You make me feel like I can handle this. You make me feel safe. What I need, Trick"—she slid her pants down and kicked them off—"is to feel you. Inside me." It was the most emotional and dramatic declaration she'd probably ever made, and if he rejected her now, she didn't think she'd ever get over it. Standing there, in her mismatched underwear, waiting for him to tell her that she mattered as much as her sister. That she didn't have to deny herself things she wanted just because Hannah would never have them.

Trick stared at her for a moment, then pulled his shirt over his head. For a second, Rachel thought she might cry, but the urge went away. She'd cried enough lately. A beautiful man was getting naked in front of her—it was not the time for tears.

Carnegie might have destroyed her sister, but he wasn't going to destroy her too.

Sixteen years ago

"Why are we here?" Hannah asked. They were parked across the street from the pizza place where she and Rachel always liked to eat. Her stomach growled at the thought of all that cheese and pepperoni and crust...

Alex offered her a cigarette. He'd made her smoke to stay at a size four. At first he'd tried to get her down to a size two, but he didn't like how bony and weak it made her.

Hannah took the cigarette and stuck the tip in the flame of the lighter he offered. She sucked the smoke deep into her lungs and the hunger subsided. It always did.

"We're here," he said finally, "because today would have been your graduation day. This is where Rachel and her friends are celebrating the end of high school."

The mention of her sister was like a punch to the chest. She felt it so acutely that she actually placed her hand against her breastbone. She could feel the ridges and dips of it beneath her shirt. She hated the way he made her dress. He bought her clothes that belonged on someone else—someone who lived in the pages of *Vogue*, not her. She missed the comfort of long skirts and peasant blouses.

But she liked the way her cheekbones stood out, though that seemed a small reward for having been separated from her family for two years. She did what Alex wanted her to do and he was good to her until he wasn't. It didn't seem to matter how well behaved she was; sometimes he just had to do something to cause her pain.

That was why they were parked in front of the pizza shop. It wasn't so she could see Rachel, it was so he could see her see Rachel, and so she could see Rachel *not* see her. He wanted her to see her twin having a life without her. He'd probably take a photo of her with the shop in the background and send it to Rachel on the next anniversary of that fateful trip to the Met.

God, if only she hadn't left the group. If only she hadn't been so stupid.

"There she is," Alex piped up in his infuriatingly cheerful drawl. "Look at all that baby fat."

Hannah didn't say anything. She couldn't have spoken if she

wanted to. She could only sit there and watch her sister across the street, walking with friends from school. There was Ashley and Brittany and Gina. Oh, and Cara. The sight of her—the last familiar face she'd seen before her life changed forever—hurt more than Rachel's. But this wasn't the first time she'd seen Rachel. Last year Alex had driven by the house so she could see her family on the anniversary of her disappearance. It had turned him on so much he'd fucked her in the car.

If it weren't for the fact that he had her feet tied together, she might try to escape. But she wouldn't get far before he jabbed her with one of those needles he always seemed to have nearby. From almost the beginning he'd made sure she knew that Rachel's life—and her own survival—hinged solely on her being exactly what he wanted her to be. Lately she'd stopped caring so much about her own life, but Rachel's still meant something.

"Do you wish you were with them?" he asked.

She knew what he wanted to hear. It didn't matter if she meant it or not. "Yes." In reality she would rather die than have her sister see her like this.

"Do you think Rachel is thinking about you?"

"I know she is. We had a lot of plans for this summer and the fall."

"How do you feel knowing you'll never get to do any of those things?"

She took another drag off the cigarette before tossing it out the window. "I feel sad." Then she gave him a bright grin. "But I feel so much better knowing I'll be with you instead."

His blue eyes narrowed. "Maybe I should go in there and tell Rachel I know where you are. Think she'd come with me?"

She would. Hannah was sure of it. Rachel would put a knife in her purse and follow him willingly.

"Think of the fun the three of us could have together," Alex continued.

"But who would you send pictures to?"

"I suppose I'd have to kill both of you and start over with someone new. It wouldn't be the first time."

"No," she agreed, and turned her attention back to the window. Rachel had gone inside and Hannah could no longer see her. "It wouldn't be the first time."

She felt him look at her. "I don't think you appreciate that I've brought you to see your sister."

"You didn't do it so I'd be thankful. You did it so I'd be sad."

"I do it because someday it won't make you sad. It will make you angry."

"At you?" she asked, turning her head to meet his gaze. Her defiance was going to get her into trouble, but she couldn't seem to stop it. She'd lost everything because of him. Everything except the love she felt for Rachel.

He grinned. "No, at her. Someday you'll hate her more than you could ever hate me."

"That will never happen."

"It will, I promise you."

She glared at him. "There's no promise you could make me that I will ever accept."

All the good humor drained from his face, stripping away

the handsome mask, revealing the monster beneath. She'd seen it before, but it was still terrifying.

"I think someone needs to spend a little time in the cellar when we get home," he said. "Maybe then you'll learn some gratitude."

The cellar. The thought of it made her want to scream. She hated the cellar, its darkness, its smell. Most of all she hated what he did to her in the cellar, and the things he made her do. She wanted to beg his forgiveness, promise him she'd be good, but Rachel would have told him to go fuck himself.

So Hannah compromised and remained silent. She'd survived the cellar before, she could do it again. She'd do whatever she had to do.

To survive *him*.

Cassandra Lennox said the woman in the photos could be the same woman who approached her in the mall six years ago, but she couldn't say for certain without seeing her face. The woman had been tall and thin with long blond hair and eyes that were light blue—she thought.

Thought. That was the problem with memory; it sometimes wasn't reliable.

Jordan had one thing left to do before she could go home and pop open a bottle of wine and have dinner with her girlfriends, and that was to stop by the hospital.

There was an officer outside Carnegie's room now, and there would be until she had the son of a bitch in custody, behind bars. It wasn't just to make sure he didn't run but to make sure no one decided to go vigilante on him before charges could be laid.

"Any visitors today?" she asked the cop.

He nodded toward the door. "Just the girl."

Jordan sighed. Of course. Opening the door, she stepped into the room just in time to see Morgan jump back from Carnegie's side. The stupid girl looked embarrassed, but he...he looked smug.

"Miss Cole, I need to speak to Mr. Carnegie alone, please."

The girl didn't even speak, she just hurried toward the door. "Oh, Morgan."

The girl turned.

"Stay away from him."

Morgan's face blanched. She turned on her heel and ran from the room.

"Was that necessary?" Carnegie drawled. "I was just telling her the same thing."

Jordan arched a disbelieving brow. "*You* told a teenage girl to stay away? I somehow doubt it."

His one visible eye glittered with amusement. "Detective Mancusi, you insult me."

"I doubt that too." She moved closer—but not too close. He was still dangerous. "Who is she, Mr. Carnegie?"

"Her? Why, that's Morgan Cole, as you know."

Jordan gritted her teeth. He was having fun now. The ones like him always liked to have their fun. It made them feel superior or some shit. "The girl we found buried in your garden. Who is she?"

He didn't even try to feign surprise. "A girl in my garden? How shocking."

"Listen, you son of a bitch—"

"*No*," he said in a tone that actually made her mouth snap shut. "You listen to me, *Detective*. I will not be answering any of your questions, nor will I see you at all without my attorney present. You will not dictate who can visit me and who can't, and you will not sashay in here like you're on a fucking catwalk."

"Or what?" she challenged. "You won't tell me who she is? We're getting DNA, Carnegie. Even if we don't identify her, we still have you with a dead body on your property."

"That you cannot prove I had anything to do with," he shot back.

"You want a lawyer? Fine. Call your lawyer. It's not going to save you this time. We've got you."

"But you don't have Anne, do you?" he taunted. "Tell me, has she gone to visit our dear Rachel yet?"

The cruel curiosity in his expression made Jordan want to take a step back, but she held her ground. "What do you mean?"

"Only that the poor thing is quite unstable. Without me around I don't know what she'll do. Look what she did to sweet Sydney."

"Why did she do that?"

"To hurt me, of course. She probably thought Sydney was Morgan. They look so much alike, you know."

Jordan studied him. Fucking psychopaths were so hard to

read at times. "So, you're saying she stabbed a girl and left her to die out of jealousy?"

"That's exactly what I'm saying." His face brightened. "I wonder if she killed that poor girl you found on my property."

"Did she set up the cameras in your basement room too?" she asked. "What about the photographs we found in your little hideaway? And your server. What are we going to find on that, I wonder?"

Brightness gave away to glittering darkness. That was the real him—the monster that lurked beneath his once-pretty exterior. "You mongrel bitch."

Jordan couldn't help but smile. "I've been called worse by better. I'm going to enjoy locking you up, Alex. I really am."

"I still have something to bargain with," he told her.

"Oh, what's that?"

He smiled. "I know where Hannah Ward is."

CHAPTER TWELVE

Sunday

R *eady or not, here I come...*"
    "It's not her."

Rachel looked away from the kitchen closet—another of Hannah's favorite hiding spots. She had to shake her head, the memory of playing hide and seek was so vivid. "What?"

Trick's gaze was soft and sympathetic. "It's not Hannah. The dental records of the woman we found match Grace O'Brien."

"Grace," she whispered. "If it couldn't be Hannah, then I'm glad it was Grace. Her parents have suffered for too long. Have they been notified yet?"

"Mancusi's got someone going to see them later."

"I'd like to do it."

His brows rose. "What? Are you sure?"

"I spent a lot of time with them years ago when I was on the force. Mrs. O'Brien was really nice." What she didn't say—what she didn't have to say—was that Mrs. O'Brien never made her feel like it was her fault, what happened to Hannah. "Their other daughter, Marley, helped me get through Gem—Carnegie's cruelty. So, yeah. I'd like to be the one to tell them they don't have to wonder anymore."

He leaned across the table and kissed her. "I'll tell Mancusi we'll deliver the news."

"You don't have to come with me."

"Until we catch this Anne person, consider me your shadow."

"So, you'll tell Jordan we want to be there when she makes the arrest?"

Their gazes locked. He understood how important this was to her. "I will."

After breakfast they made the drive up to Farmington to see the O'Briens. Rachel had called Marley and asked her to meet them at her parents'. When Mrs. O'Brien opened the door, she took one look at Rachel and burst into tears. Rachel cried too.

"We found her," she said as the older woman fell into her arms. Mr. O'Brien hugged his daughter before shaking Trick's hand.

Once the initial tears had stopped, the five of them sat in the living room. Rachel and Trick told them as much as they could, as gently as they could.

"Did she suffer?" Mr. O'Brien asked.

"I don't think so," Rachel told him. "That's not how the person that took her operates."

"Gemini," Marley sneered. Her gaze latched on to Rachel, and Rachel could see the lines around her eyes, the gray starting in her hair. She wasn't that much older than Rachel herself, but she'd aged. "Tell me you've caught that bastard."

The three of them pinned her with their stares.

"We have a suspect in custody," Trick said, taking over. "We expect to make an arrest soon."

Mrs. O'Brien reached over from her seat at the end of the sofa and took Rachel's hand. "What about your sister, dear?"

Her eyes stung, but no more tears fell, thank God. "Not yet." The sympathy in their faces was almost too much to bear. "Once the autopsy has been done, you'll be able to give Grace a proper burial."

"Can we see her?" Mr. O'Brien asked.

Rachel gave him what she hoped was a gentle smile. "Mr. O'Brien, she doesn't look like you remember, and she's not how I would like you to remember her. Of course, I can't stop you if that's what you need to do, but I suggest you just take a good look at Marley and then work out the differences to get an idea of what she'd look like now."

The man nodded. She couldn't tell if she'd helped him or not.

"Will you come to her funeral?" Marley asked. "It would mean a lot."

Oh, Christ. She was going to cry again. She smiled to push the tears back. "I will."

"And when you find your sister, you let us know," Mrs. O'Brien instructed. "We'll come say good-bye to her with you as well."

A tear she could no longer fight trickled down Rachel's cheek. "Thank you."

They left a few minutes later, after Mrs. O'Brien showed Trick photos of Grace and after Rachel got a chance to find out if Marley was okay.

"I knew she was dead," the older woman told her. "I felt

something break inside me years ago—not long after your sister was taken. I don't know if it was just that I knew he wouldn't keep more than one girl at a time, or if I felt her leave, but I knew."

"I've never felt that," Rachel confided. "I envy that you had that kind of connection."

"If only it had helped me find her." Marley smiled grimly. "I envy you getting to bring that bastard down. You'll sit with me at his trial?"

"You know I will." They all hugged then, and Rachel decided it was time to go. She needed to be there to see Carnegie's face when they charged him with murder.

"You okay?" Trick asked her as they drove south again.

She glanced at him from the passenger seat. "Yeah, why?"

"You keep rubbing your left hand."

She curled her fingers into a fist. "I think I've been spending too much time at the computer. I just need a massage."

He smiled at her. "I'll give you one later."

"Now you're just talking dirty."

Trick chuckled, and flicked on the signal to get into the on-ramp for the highway. "That was good, what you did with them."

She shrugged. "They've been good to me. They deserved to hear it from someone they know. Someone who understands." And then she decided to ask him, "Have you been telling Crouse about what I've been like these last few days?"

He shot her a startled glance. "Are you serious? Of course not."

"I didn't think so, but I just wanted to be prepared if you had."

"Look, you've been understandably shaken up, but I haven't seen you do anything that might fuck this investigation. Until you do that, I'm not telling Crouse dick."

"Listen to you, using all the naughty words."

Shaking his head, he merged into traffic. "I'm glad you're feeling better."

"I feel like shit. I've felt like shit for eighteen years. But some moments are less shitty than others."

He reached over and took her hand, and she let him. He didn't let go until he needed both hands on the wheel, and then she put her hand on his thigh. The contact kept her centered.

It was hard to explain to anyone who didn't understand, but she was almost looking forward to finding her sister's body. It really would be closure, though she was sure she would still need to grieve. The only thing that made it marginally better was knowing that Carnegie hadn't beaten or brutalized his victims when he killed them. He put them to sleep. God knew what he did to them when they were alive, but he let them die with a little dignity. He was a sadistic bastard in many ways, but he liked to fuck with heads, not with bodies. Still, she'd make sure he paid for the damage he'd done to her sister, and to her family.

An hour later they arrived in Westport. They parked in the hospital lot and rode the elevator up to Carnegie's floor. Mancusi was already there waiting for them. "Took you long enough."

Rachel frowned at her. "We went to see the O'Briens."

"Oh," the cop said, looking at least a little contrite. "How did that go?"

"Pretty much like I expected. Thanks for letting me tell them."

"Thanks for offering. It's not usually a job people ask to take on." She smiled slightly. "Ready to arrest Carnegie?"

Rachel grinned. "So ready."

She and Trick followed Mancusi into Carnegie's room. He had a man with him—one wearing a shirt and pants that were obviously tailored for him. His lawyer, no doubt.

"Hey," the man said, standing up. "What's going on?"

"It's alright, Elliott," Carnegie said. "Let them have their moment."

Let them have their moment? What Rachel wouldn't give for five minutes alone with Carnegie, his smirk, and a baseball bat.

"Alexander Carnegie," Mancusi began. "You are under arrest for the kidnapping and murder of Grace O'Brien. You have the right…" Rachel didn't listen to the rest. She couldn't hear much over the pounding of her heart. Eighteen years she'd waited for this day. No, they hadn't found Hannah, but this was almost as good.

They left Carnegie handcuffed to his bed, because there was no way they were taking a chance on him escaping. A man with his resources could get to a country with no extradition laws in short order, and manage to live a long and comfortable life.

Victoria Cole met them in the corridor. "You arrested him?" she asked.

Mancusi nodded. "What Sydney told me matched up. Mrs. Cole, we found one of the missing girls on his property."

Trick caught the woman before she collapsed. A nurse rushed over with some water, and together they got her to a wheelchair parked against a wall.

"I'm fine," she protested. "It was just…Oh my God, I've known the man for years. I trusted him with my kids." She looked horrified. "I should have guessed after what he did to Morgan…"

"He's very good at pretending," Rachel told her. "A skilled liar."

The woman shook her head. "And your sister?"

"Not yet."

"I'm so sorry." She meant it too, Rachel could tell. "Would you…would you come see Sydney? She's asked to meet you."

"Sure," Rachel agreed. After the morning she'd already had, what was one more emotional upheaval? "Are you okay to walk?"

Victoria waved a dismissive hand. "I'm fine." But when she stood, Rachel thought she was a little shaky. She stayed close to her as they walked, just in case. Trick was on her other side.

Sydney's room wasn't far from Carnegie's. Rachel wondered if they were going to ask to have her moved to another floor. Rachel would have. When they walked in, Morgan and Sydney were on the bed, watching a video on Morgan's phone.

"Sydney," Victoria said. "Honey? I brought Agent Ward to see you."

Rachel smiled as Morgan lowered the phone. Sydney Cole looked up, right into Rachel's eyes.

And began to scream.

Rachel thought she might be sick. They were back in the corridor—out of Sydney Cole's line of sight. She could still hear the girl's distress, though Dr. Pillai was in there with her, giving her something to calm her down. Gradually, her cries turned to whimpers. Her whimpers to silence.

Trick paced a small section of floor, running a hand over the top of his head. "She must have remembered the photo of Hannah at Carnegie's house and seeing you triggered memories."

Rachel shrugged, chewing on the side of her thumb. "Maybe." Truth be told she was a little freaked out by the girl's reaction. That wasn't just a triggered memory, that was outright terror. What had the girl seen?

He turned to her. "What else could it be?"

"Well, that went well," Mancusi said as she joined them. "Anyone else you want to pop in on while we're here?"

Rachel shot her a narrow look. So did Trick.

"I wasn't blaming anyone," the cop said a little defensively, though Rachel had felt the weight of that nonexistent blame. Of all of them, Rachel herself ought to have been the one to realize what seeing her might do to Sydney Cole, but she'd spent close to half her life being one rather than half of two, and in her eagerness to solve the investigation, she'd forgotten her face didn't belong to her alone. She just never expected such a strong reaction. There had to be a reason for it.

She winced as her stomach rolled. She needed a minute. "I'm going to the restroom."

In the restroom, the smell of cleaner and feces mingled unpleasantly, but other than the odor, she was alone. Rachel braced her hands on either side of one of the sinks and leaned closer to the mirror, studying her own reflection. She used to stare into mirrors a lot and pretend she was looking at Hannah. Did Hannah ever do the same? They were mirror twins—identical but not.

She stared at herself a few seconds longer, and when she was certain her stomach wasn't going to come up, she left the room and found Mancusi. Trick was talking to Mr. Cole, who cast a wary—angry—glance in Rachel's direction.

"Can I talk to you for a second?" She kept her voice low as her heart pounded in her ears.

Mancusi shifted on her feet. "Look, it's not your fault she freaked out."

Rachel shook her head. "That's not what I wanted to talk to you about."

"Okay. What do you want to talk about?"

She shifted self-consciously. "Your witness on the train. I want to send her some mug shots, see if she can identify the woman she thinks stole her coat."

Mancusi frowned. "You have someone in mind?"

"Yeah, I do. But first, I need your word that you won't mention anything to Trick. Let me do it."

Mancusi's frown slackened. As it drained away, it seemed to take some of the color from her face with it. "Fuck."

Rachel hugged herself. She was actually trembling a little. She didn't want to say it out loud, but she had to. "I think the woman on the train—the woman who stabbed Sydney—is my sister."

Jordan hoped to hell that Rachel was wrong, because if she wasn't, that meant Hannah Ward wasn't just Carnegie's victim; she'd become his apprentice.

Holy hell, what had Carnegie done to her? He'd had eighteen years to do it.

Quickly, while Trick was still trying to smooth things over with the Coles, Jordan took a photo of Rachel with her phone and used an app to change it to black and white. Then she sent it, along with random photos of five other light-haired women, to Amanda Forbes.

"Now we wait," she said.

Rachel nodded. She was shaky and pale. Jordan had never seen her former partner so unsettled. She couldn't imagine what was going through her head at that moment, the fears she must have. It was one thing to think your sister had been killed by a serial killer, another to think she might have willingly helped one.

"What are you going to do?"

With a shrug, Rachel sat down in one of the chairs in the waiting room. "Crouse will kick me off the investigation."

"Well, yeah. She'll have to. It could jeopardize everything if she didn't, you know that."

"I know." Rachel sighed and closed her eyes, leaning the back of her head against the wall. "God, I hope I'm wrong."

"Me too." Silence fell for a few seconds. "How long has it been since you ate?"

One gray-blue eye opened and looked at her suspiciously. "A few hours, why?"

Jordan took a cereal bar from her blazer pocket and tossed it to her. "Eat that."

Rachel caught it. "I'm afraid I'll puke it back up."

"Hang on to it for when you feel better."

"Thanks." She slipped it into her pocket. "Promise me you'll let me tell Trick."

Jordan nodded. "I promise." She didn't know what else to say. The situation was like something out of a soap opera.

After a few minutes of awkward stillness, Trick walked into the room. "We're done here for the day," he announced. "The Coles have shut us down until a therapist can talk to Sydney."

Rachel stood. "I feel like I should apologize."

"They don't blame you," he told her.

"Mr. Cole looked like he does."

"He's blaming the world right now. Come on, I'll buy you sushi on the way home."

Rachel looked like she might puke at the thought.

At that same moment, Jordan's phone pinged. She pulled it out of the clip on her belt and looked at it. Her heart actually skipped a beat.

"It's Amanda Forbes," she said. Rachel looked at her, pale and wide-eyed. "She picked number three."

Number three was Rachel.

CHAPTER THIRTEEN

There was nothing as disgusting as the taste of coffee and bile. Rachel shuddered as she retched into one of the toilets in the restroom.

Hannah was Anne. Her sister was alive. Her sister was wanted by the police.

She could barely process the thoughts running through her head. There were so many, and so many emotions came with them. Why had she hurt Sydney? Where was she? *What* was she? The damage that Carnegie must have done to her...

She wiped her mouth with the back of her hand, flushed, and left the stall. Then she washed her hands and rinsed her mouth at the sink. When she left the bathroom, she walked purposefully past the room where Jordan and Trick waited for her. They stood close together in conversation and never even noticed her walk by. She went straight for the room at the end of the hall and walked in.

His lawyer was gone, and he was handcuffed to the bed. When Carnegie saw it was she who'd entered his room, he lost some of the tan in his cheeks.

This man had been with her sister longer than she had.

Birthdays and Christmases. He'd photographed her, degraded and hurt her—turned her into his accomplice and God only knew what else. Now Hannah was out there, alone. She could have come home, but she didn't. Was she afraid? Ashamed? Or had Carnegie brainwashed her into thinking her family had forgotten her? He'd turned Hannah into someone who sent anniversary cards signed in her own blood, and broke into her family home to leave a killer's photographs.

Slowly she walked toward him.

"I heard screaming," he said. "What was all that?"

She'd tell him, but he'd get off on it, probably. "Where's my sister?"

"I don't know," he replied, and for once she believed him.

"Where would she go?"

"I'm not saying anything without a written guarantee it will get me a lighter sentence."

Rachel pressed her thumb against one of the many bandages on his chest where she could see the shadow of blood. She pressed as hard as she could, until warm wetness blossomed through the gauze and he moaned in pain.

"Good," she whispered. "Where's my fucking sister?"

Carnegie's lashes fluttered, but he still managed to look up at her with barely concealed hatred. "I'm not giving her up to you. You'll put her in a cage."

"She needs help."

He laughed. "Hannah doesn't need anything from you. She's become something you'll never understand. Something beautiful."

"What did you do to her?"

"I allowed her to become what she was supposed to be."

"Bullshit. You did this to her."

He actually laughed. She shoved her thumb against the wound again, pressing until he grabbed her wrist with his free hand.

Rachel pulled her weapon.

Carnegie smiled then. "The two of you aren't so different after all. Only, your sister would have used something sharp in the wound." He released her arm, and Rachel slowly lowered her gun.

"Did you get her to abduct Sydney for you?"

He rubbed his hand over the bloody bandage. "She did that on her own."

"I don't believe you."

"She thought I was going to replace her with Morgan—as if I could—so she wanted to hurt me. Hurt Morgan."

"You're lying."

"Oh, I'm afraid this is the terrible truth, Rachel dear. Your sister abducted that girl and then tried to kill her when it didn't work out. The only reason she didn't finish the job—and I can only guess at this—is that she wanted to send a message to me. And to you."

Rachel blinked. "To me?"

"All she wanted in those early days was for someone to find her. Then that someone became you. That's what she wants. If you want to ask someone where she is, ask yourself."

"What are you doing?" came a voice from the door.

Rachel lifted her head and met the gaze of Carnegie's lawyer. "Talking," she said. Then she realized she still had her gun in her hand. "He grabbed me."

"You need to leave. Now."

She reholstered her weapon and walked toward the door. The lawyer stepped back to let her pass.

"Oh, Rachel," Carnegie singsonged.

She should have just kept on walking. Ignored him. Instead, she turned to look at him. "What?"

"Don't worry if you can't find my darling Anne. Eventually she'll get bored and come for you."

"My sister's the woman we've been hunting," Rachel mused as they drove back to New Haven that afternoon. "How fucked up is that?"

Trick barely glanced at her. He was still pissed at her for going into Carnegie's room and talking to him alone. When he'd found her, she was being ushered out of the room by Carnegie's lawyer, who accused her of threatening and assaulting his client. Rachel didn't deny it. He could see the blood on her hand, and on Carnegie's bandages. And then she told him about it, and he couldn't fucking believe it. He didn't know whether to hug her or scream at her.

So he drove her home instead, and decided he'd figure it out when he had both hands free.

"He said she'd come for me. What does that mean?"

Jesus, was she in shock? He thought it was pretty damn clear what that meant. It was a threat. Hannah had carved up her lover for betraying her and took out his eye. What would she do to the sister she thought had abandoned her?

"If you were held prisoner for years, where would you go if you were finally free?" he asked, directing her train of thought away from what her sister might have planned for her. They had to find Hannah before she came for Rachel, because the next time she wouldn't just leave a gift.

"Home. I'd go home." He felt the weight of her stare. "But Hannah didn't run home."

He shrugged. "Maybe after all these years, there's another place she thinks of as home."

She perked up. "Have we searched any of Carnegie's other properties?"

"Not yet, but now that we found Grace O'Brien and those boxes of photographs, we will."

"You'll call me, won't you? If you find her?"

Trick nodded. He didn't like it, but he knew her removing herself from the case before Crouse could do it was the only next move she could make. Hopefully, her interaction with Carnegie wouldn't harm their case. The man was, after all, a serial killer. He deserved worse than being poked in a healing wound. "I will."

They made the rest of the drive in silence. Leaving her alone with her thoughts might not be the best thing, but he didn't know what else to do. He too was reeling from the revelation that Hannah was Anne. And if he was honest, he was kicking himself for not seeing it sooner. Once he'd kept Hannah alive for twelve years, what was six more? He'd turned her into his idea of the perfect woman.

Back at Rachel's house, while Rachel ran a bath, Trick did a sweep of her house to make sure "Anne" hadn't stopped by again. He poured her a glass of wine and took it in to her a little while later. When he opened the bathroom door, his heart broke.

She was in the tub, her hair pinned on top of her head, crying. On the floor was an open photo album filled with photos of her and Hannah as children.

"She was such a wimp," Rachel told him with a sniff as she wiped her eyes. "She'd never hurt anyone—not even to fight back. I was always the one getting into scrapes."

"That doesn't surprise me," Trick replied, setting the wine on the side of the soaker tub. "You're still the first one in."

She smiled slightly. "I didn't really fuck things up today, did I?"

"Would poking Bundy make him less of an asshole?"

"I guess not."

"Then there's your answer."

She turned the page of the album. "God, look at those outfits. What was Mom thinking?" She buried her face in her hands. "Oh, God. What am I going to tell my fucking mother?"

"You don't have to tell her anything right now," he said. "We'll figure it out."

"We?" She glanced up at him with those smoky eyes. "You're going to stick this out, are you?"

"I am."

She smiled. "You are the strangest man. I can't figure out if you're punishing yourself for something or if you've just had such rotten luck at relationships that I look good."

"Neither. I think it's sexy that you poked a serial killer." It was a joke. A horrible, horrible joke. But it made her laugh, just a little.

"You like the crazy," she said. "Okay, well, if you're serious, get in this tub with me and look through this album while I wallow a little."

Trick hesitated, but only for a moment. Then he stripped off his clothes and stepped into the tub behind her, sliding his legs around her hips so that she could lean back against his chest. The water was just hot enough, and a little slippery with the oil she liked to use. He rubbed her shoulders as she flipped through the pages, trying to loosen up whatever knot was causing the tingles in her left arm.

"Mm." She took a drink of wine, then offered him the glass. He took it.

She held the album so they could both look at the photos. He'd never seen pictures of her as a child before. "You were cute," he said, pointing at the photo in the top right. "I like that one of you."

Rachel glanced over her shoulder at him. "You don't know which one I am."

"You're the one in the purple shorts."

Her mouth fell open. "How did you know?"

He shrugged. "I know you, I guess." He took a drink of wine and handed the glass back to her. "That's you in the sparkly dress right below it too."

"Huh." She slid her right foot along the inside of his calf. "Most people could never tell us apart. Even teachers and friends."

"I could be dramatic and say something about how I've always seen the real you, but that's horseshit. I just know you when I see you."

She tilted her head back and kissed his jaw. "That's why you scared me so much before. I figured you'd eventually take off running once you figured out just how much of a mess I am."

"You're not a mess," he told her. "You're handling this better than I would." He couldn't even imagine what it would be like to find out a person he thought dead was alive, let alone that they had become something twisted.

"I feel like I'm keeping myself together with luck and spit." She took a drink of wine and sighed. "For years I've been waiting for this to be over, and I've put my life on hold because of it. Now that it's becoming reality, I'm not sure what to do with myself. I felt that way before I realized the truth about Hannah. Maybe I realized it before all of this and just never admitted it."

"You did say you've never felt like she was gone."

"No. I just hoped in here that she was." She took his hand and placed it over her heart. It was always a surprise to remember that hers was on the opposite side of most people's. Her Medic Alert bracelet had soapsuds on it.

"Show me some more pictures," he urged. Maybe these happy ones would take away some of the terrible photos she'd seen over the last few days.

Rachel flipped to the next page. "Oh, God. Here's our tenth birthday. Look at that cake. Hannah wanted chocolate and I wanted vanilla. We ended up with marble and were both miserable."

As she pointed out various people in the pictures, Trick found his gaze going more and more often to Hannah. In every new picture she seemed to look a little more villainous to him—like something out of a bad movie. It was just his imagination, he knew, but it was unsettling all the same. He glanced to where he'd set his holster on the floor. It was within arm's reach, just in case.

In case Hannah Ward decided to come home.

Monday

"Take a few days off," Crouse told her. "In fact, take all of next week. You've earned it."

Earned it. Right. In addition to being off the Gemini investigation she was off any and all investigations until her superior thought otherwise. It wasn't vacation, it was paid suspension without the write-up.

And she didn't have to turn in her gun and badge.

It really didn't matter what explanation she was given, Rachel was honestly—secretly—glad to be cut loose. Glad that for a few days, at least, she could just be a woman worried about her sister, because she had so many emotions boxed up inside her it would take ten years of Christmas to open them all. She needed to deal with at least some of it before she came apart. So she scheduled an appointment with her therapist and then went for a massage.

She still hadn't talked to her mother about Hannah. She hadn't told Naomi either. What they didn't know couldn't upset them, and what didn't upset them, Rachel didn't have to deal with.

She had the locksmith come by in the morning and change the locks on the front and back doors. There wasn't much else she could do, other than find a new place to hide the spare key. Of course Hannah had known where to find it—it was in the same place it had always been.

It was nice to feel safe in her own house again. Nice to be alone for a little while. Oh, having Trick around had been fabulous—and a little scary. She couldn't change all at once, and after letting herself be so vulnerable to him, thoughts of running had kicked in. Was it self-preservation, or cowardice? She wasn't sure, but she wasn't going to give in to it, not yet. He was the best man she'd ever met. He'd seen some of the worst of her, and still chose to see the best. That was a gift, she realized. A gift her sister would never have, because a maniac had gotten his hands on her.

Hannah might very well be suffering from Stockholm syndrome, or from some kind of mental break. Whatever it was, they'd deal with it. Even if Hannah had stabbed Sydney with the intent to kill her, they'd handle it. Whatever therapy or care her sister needed, Rachel would make sure she had it. There was no question about whether or not she would be there for her sister.

No, the question was—what sort of danger was Hannah to herself and to others while she was out there alone? In a perfect world, Trick would find her at Carnegie's New York apartment and bring her in. Hannah would give evidence against Carnegie, and they'd put the son of a bitch away for life. Rachel's family could begin to heal. Maybe her mother wouldn't hate her so much. And maybe, eventually, she'd have her sister back.

She'd settle for Hannah not killing anyone before she was brought in. And for her testifying against Carnegie. The rest she could work around.

Her mother had texted while Rachel was in the tub. She hadn't read it yet. Was dreading having to. It was one of two things—a further lament on what a disappointment Rachel was as a daughter or an apology for the way she'd spoken to her the last time they talked. Sometimes her mother found it in herself to apologize, especially if her father and Naomi gave her hell for it. Either way, it didn't matter. Her mother's love had been a poisonous thing ever since Hannah's abduction. One minute she was sweet and loving—clingy, even—and the next she was vicious, going straight for the jugular. It all depended on whether or not she was taking her meds like she should.

Rachel heard the mailbox open and close. It was too late for mail, so it had to be Naomi checking. It was about the normal time her little sister arrived home from her job at the university.

A few moments later there was a knock. Right, Naomi hadn't been there when the locksmith came. Rachel got off the couch and went to open the door. The energy of the house lifted when Naomi breezed in. It was as if even the furniture was glad to see her.

"Oh, I'm so glad you're home," her sister said, setting down her messenger bag. "I forgot about the locks until I tried to use my key."

"I'm taking a few days off now that Carnegie's in custody." It wasn't really a lie.

Naomi smiled at her. "Oh, that's good. I have to be honest, I really don't want you to be there when they find her."

Rachel bit her tongue. She didn't want anyone else to find Hannah. "I'm going to the gym later. Want to come?"

"Thanks, but I have too much work to do. Hey, did you have company?"

Rachel hesitated. "What makes you ask that?"

"Because I saw a woman leaving as I pulled up. At first I thought she was you and you were going back to work, but then I realized she was way too dressed up."

Rachel raced for the door. She yanked it open and ran down the steps in her bare feet—just in time to see a silver Audi peel away.

"Hannah," she whispered, her heart pounding, eyes burning. She raised her hand.

Brake lights. Her breath seized in her chest. For a second the world stood still.

And then the car sped away, leaving her standing there, the sidewalk warm beneath her feet, with her damp hair wrapped up in a towel and dressed in yoga pants and an oversized FBI

T-shirt. The neighbors would think she'd lost it, but she remained there until the Audi was out of sight, and even a little while after, hoping to see it reappear.

"Rach?" Naomi called from the door.

She turned and met the concerned gaze of her sister. It was what made her move—come back up the steps. "I'm okay," she said. But then she looked at the mailbox, its lid slightly open. She'd gotten the mail when she came home, but she slipped her hand inside once again. She wasn't surprised when her fingers touched paper. It was an envelope—the size of a greeting card.

"What's that?" Naomi asked.

"Let's go inside," Rachel suggested calmly, despite the pounding in her chest. Only when the door was firmly closed behind them—and locked—did she tear open the side of the envelope. The steadiness of her fingers was a surprise, and she was careful when she handled it, knowing it was probably evidence. She pulled her sleeve down over her fingers before gripping the card and pulling it out.

Thinking of You, it read, in gold script on the front.

"That's nice. Who's it from?" Naomi asked.

Rachel shoved the card back into the envelope. She didn't even look inside. "Mrs. O'Brien," she lied. When her sister went up to her room, she grabbed a Ziploc from the kitchen and put the card inside it. Then she took it to her room and texted Trick. It wasn't until he responded with *What does it say?* that she took it out of the plastic and actually opened it. This time her sister had written in cursive rather than block print, and her penmanship was immediately recognizable. The message, however, was both heartwarming and bone-chilling.

Ready or not, here I come. Love, Hannah.

She walked into the hospital just before the end of visiting hours that night. She nodded at the nurse at the station, who glanced up, and continued down the hall, the heels of her shoes clicking rhythmically against the tiles.

She smiled at the guard outside the door. "He awake?" she asked.

The guard shook his head. "Been in and out. Heard you had some trouble with him earlier."

She shook her head. "Nah. Just the usual. You know that sometimes you have to play bad cop with these assholes. He's a killer, you know."

With a tilt of his head, the man said, "That's what I hear. You need to see him?"

"Just checking in. Has the nurse been by?"

"Just a few minutes ago." He checked his watch.

"Something wrong?"

"My relief should have been here by now."

She offered him an encouraging smile. "Probably just caught in traffic."

He rolled his eyes. "It's always traffic. I was supposed to take my wife out to dinner tonight."

"Go," she said. "I'll watch him until your replacement shows up."

"You sure? What if he doesn't show up?"

"Then I'll make a call." She smiled. "Look, take off. It's fine."

He hesitated. "I don't think—"

"Hey, I know you've heard this guy took my sister, but no one wants to see him go to jail more than me. I'll guard him with my life, trust me. If he dies, I'll never know what happened to her." Tears filled her eyes as she spoke.

The cop's expression softened. "Oh, hey. Are you okay?"

She sniffed and dabbed at her eyes. "I'm fine. Please, go be with your wife. I'll watch our Mr. Carnegie. Promise."

He grinned. "Thank you."

She watched him walk through the door at the end of the corridor before walking into Carnegie's room. Slowly, she approached the bed, her heart pounding. She gazed down at him as she stood there. He looked so innocent and peaceful. So beautiful—like Lucifer after the fall. Even with his ruined eye, he was gorgeous.

She stroked his hair back from his forehead. It felt silky between her fingers—like a child's.

He stirred in his sleep, brow puckering. His eyelashes fluttered open, revealing the eyes of dark blue. She could see herself reflected in his gaze—see the moment he realized who she was.

She took her hand away. Carnegie had to pay for what he'd done. He could never be allowed to tell anyone what he'd done to her sister. Then, her expression grim, she drew the needle from her pocket and injected its contents into the IV line in his arm.

"Good-bye," she whispered, and kissed him on the forehead.

She was gone by the time staff reached his room.

CHAPTER FOURTEEN

When Rachel arrived home, Trick was in the living room with Naomi, waiting for her. Was she late? No, he was early. She'd hoped to be home and showered before he got there to collect the card.

"What's wrong?" she asked, setting her water bottle on the nearest table. "Has something happened with the case?" Was it Hannah? Jesus, she was going to have to tell Naomi.

He stood up, walked over, and caught her in a hug so tight she could hardly breathe.

"Tell me you have to badge in at your gym," he said against her hair.

"Yeah." She pulled back as much as his tight hold would allow. "There are security cameras too. Trick, what's going on?"

"What time did you get there?"

"Seven thirty." She pushed hard against his chest and he let her go. "Tell me what the fuck is going on."

The doorbell rang. Rachel pivoted on her heel and marched out to the foyer. When she opened the door, Mancusi stood on the step.

"Hey," she said. Then she noticed the two troopers behind the detective. "Not a social call, huh?"

Mancusi crossed the threshold, her gaze sweeping the area as she entered the house. "At approximately seven fifty-seven this evening, a lethal amount of heroin was injected into Alex Carnegie's IV line."

Blood fell from her head to her feet. Rachel had to brace her hand against the back of an armchair to keep herself upright. "No."

The detective's expression didn't change; it remained impassive. "The cop who was supposed to be on duty was found unconscious in his cruiser in the parking lot. He'd also been drugged, though to a lesser degree. The previous-duty guard said that you volunteered to watch Carnegie until his replacement showed up so he could keep plans with his wife."

Rachel stared at her. The words her old partner had said swirled and dipped in her brain, teasing and taunting her until finally coming together as something comprehensible.

"He said I was there?"

She nodded. "He talked to you."

Naomi came to stand slightly behind Trick. "Rach, what's going on?"

Rachel shook her head so hard she was dizzy. "No, he didn't. I was at the gym, not the hospital."

"Rachel, there are cameras at the hospital."

"There are cameras at my fucking gym, Jordan," she snapped back with a scowl. "Do you really think I'd murder a suspect?"

"No," her former partner admitted. "I think your sister did it."

"What?" Naomi exclaimed, the blood rushing from her face.

"Not you," Mancusi said. "Hannah."

"Fuck," Rachel whispered.

Naomi turned to her. The poor kid was trembling. "What's she talking about?"

Mancusi looked confused. "You haven't told her?"

Shaking her head, Rachel turned to her younger sister. "Hannah's alive. She's who attacked Sydney Cole."

Naomi's face went white. "No."

"I'm sorry, Squirt. I didn't want to tell you until I found her."

Her sister looked murderous. She didn't speak, she just turned on her heel and left the room. A few seconds later her bedroom door slammed shut.

"Sorry about that," Mancusi said.

Rachel didn't think she was really all that sorry.

"Okay, we still need to do this the right way. You need to come with me and give a statement and I'll follow up with your gym. Give me the name and address."

Rachel did. One of the troopers wrote it down. "Can I shower first?"

Mancusi nodded, then turned to the troopers. "You two go to the gym, get the logs and any security footage. She used to be one of us, so be professional and do this exactly by the book, got it?"

They both nodded, then left. Rachel entered her bedroom, grabbed a change of clothes, and went into the bathroom. She showered quickly and pulled on jeans and a shirt while her skin was still slightly damp. She left her hair piled up on the back of her head but spritzed it with a light spray of perfume. When she came back to the bedroom, she shoved her feet into a pair of flats. She grabbed the plastic baggie with the card in it on the way out.

"Let's go," she said when she returned to the living room. Trick and Mancusi were sitting across from each other, having an intense conversation that stopped when she walked in. She didn't have to be an agent to know they were discussing her.

The house phone rang as they left the room. No one ever called that line but telemarketers and the occasional family member.

"Rachel," Naomi said, entering the foyer where her sister was gathering up her things. "Call for you."

"Take a message." She dropped her keys into her purse.

"It's important."

Rachel whirled around. "Nothing's that impor—" She froze when she saw the pallor of her sister's face. "Shit." She reached out her hand.

"Seriously?" Mancusi asked. "Do I have to arrest you just to make you hurry the fuck up?"

"For Christ's sake, Jordan. It's her," Rachel said in a harsh whisper. "It's Hannah."

"Hi, Sissy."

Rachel's heart broke at the sound of those words in that familiar voice, so like her own.

"Hi," she replied, her emotions betrayed by the roughness in her throat. She felt naked and vulnerable standing there with Mancusi and Trick staring at her.

"Is that all you've got to say? It's been eighteen years."

Rachel blinked back tears. "I don't know where to start."

"No? You're not going to ask me where I was earlier this evening?"

Rachel pushed the speaker button on the phone so Trick and Mancusi—and Naomi—could hear. She opened those boxes in the back of her head and started throwing stuff in, but it was like the lids wouldn't close. She didn't know if she could keep it together any longer. "Where were you?"

Hannah's soft chuckle filled the room. "No fair putting me on speaker, Rach. Are Jordan and that delicious Dason listening in? What about Naomi? God, I can't believe how grown up she sounds."

Rachel swallowed. She didn't bother to look at Mancusi or Trick. "She's twenty-eight."

"Jesus. Does she even remember me?"

"She does."

"I saw her earlier. I stopped by Nan and Gramp's. Were you home?"

"I was." She drew a deep breath. "You should have rung the bell." Rachel glanced up to see Mancusi leave the room, her phone to her ear. Probably calling to get a trace.

"I didn't have time to chat. Things to do." Hannah's tone was light, like she hadn't just killed someone. Rachel would be more concerned about her sister's sanity if she didn't sound so damn sane.

"Like a visit to the hospital pretending to be me?"

"I'm good at pretending to be you, remember? How many times did I cover your ass?" There was a slight bite to her words—just enough to make the hair on Rachel's arms rise.

"About as many times as I covered yours."

Another laugh. "Touché." There was a pause. "It's really good to hear your voice, Rach."

A tear slid down Rachel's cheek, scalding hot. "Yours too."

"I'm actually crying right now. Are you crying?"

"No."

"Liar."

"Where are you, Han? Carnegie's dead. You don't have to keep running."

"Are you going to get in trouble for it?"

She didn't have to ask what "it" was. "It's more of a pain in the ass than trouble. It could have been worse. It was smart of you to pretend to be me."

"Don't condescend to me, Sissy."

"I'm not. You were always smarter than me. You were the one with the great grades and the popular friends. If either of us felt like less, it was me. I was always trying to catch up with you."

"If that was true, I wouldn't have spent the last eighteen years of my fucking life with a man who thought it was fun to cause pain. A man who thought he owned me because my hotshot FBI sister couldn't find me and I was right under her fucking nose."

Rachel went still. "What do you mean, right under my nose?"

"Forget it."

"No. You called to talk. Let's talk."

"Oh, Rach. Now you're just trying to play me. I hate that. You just want to keep me on the line so you can trace the call."

"Yeah, but I also don't want to let you go. I don't want to lose you again."

There was silence. For a moment, Rachel thought they'd been disconnected. "You mean that."

"I do."

"I'm sorry, but they've probably gotten a trace by now, and I'm not about to let the cops find me. That's your job, Rach. After eighteen years I'm not going to make it easy for you. Come find me, Sissy."

"Han—" But there was the unmistakable *click* of someone hanging up. Her sister was gone, and Rachel felt her loss as keenly as she had the first time.

Almost eighteen years ago

"Good work, Hannah," Mr. Avery said as he handed back the tests.

It was October. Her sister had been missing for just over five months. "I'm not Hannah," Rachel said, her voice rough.

Mr. Avery's face turned a dull red above his beard line. "Right. Sorry, Rachel. It's just…well, good work." He dropped the test and practically ran away.

He'd called her Hannah because she'd gotten a ninety-eight on a math test. Rachel hadn't scored that high in years.

Mrs. O'Keefe, the biology teacher, called her Hannah when she walked into her class the next day. It was an honest mistake; she was wearing one of Hannah's skirts. It still hurt.

By the end of the week, Rachel was back to her own clothes, but she kept her grades up in an effort to make her mother happy.

"You'll never be Hannah," her mother told her, taking the peasant blouse from Rachel's stiff hands. "Never."

No, she would never be her sister. Rachel knew that. She didn't want to be Hannah. She just wanted to feel close to her again, and wearing her clothes had made her feel closer to her twin.

But the change in her grades was for something else. Rachel wasn't planning to move to New York anymore. She was going to be a cop, and one day she was going to work with the FBI, and she was going to find her sister. Because she always found her.

Trick went with her to Bridgeport. Mancusi wanted everything by the book, so she insisted on bringing Rachel in to her troop office to question her.

"Did you find anything at Carnegie's New York apartment?" Jordan asked Trick.

He glanced at her, his attention focused on navigating 1-95 traffic. "Electronics dog found some more stuff. I'm not sure what all of it is."

But he had an idea, Rachel was certain. "I guess you're not really allowed to talk to me about the investigation."

"Not here," he agreed. And then, "How are you holding up?"

"I am surprisingly numb," she replied. "I don't think it will last much longer, but as long as it holds out until Mancusi's done with me, I'll be happy."

"She's just doing her job—I don't like it either."

Rachel shrugged. "Doesn't matter. I didn't do anything, and the evidence will prove it."

The Bridgeport office wasn't anything fancy—a plain brick-and-white building that looked more like a doctor's office or school than a cop shop. Mancusi took them to an interview room and closed the door.

Rachel sat down at the table and Trick sat beside her. "Are you going to read me my rights?" she asked.

"You're not being charged with anything," Mancusi said. "We're just having a chat."

"I've heard you say that to suspects before," Rachel replied.

Her old partner held her gaze. "Are you helping your sister, Rachel?"

She jerked back, the front legs of her chair lifting off the ground. "Excuse me?"

Trick grabbed her hand, pulled her back down into her chair. "What the hell, Mancusi?" he demanded.

Mancusi ignored him. "Have you actively worked to keep law enforcement from finding your sister?"

"You have to be fucking joking." She couldn't believe it.

Mancusi's expression didn't crack. "So, you're telling me it's a coincidence that your sister killed her abductor on the same day you had an altercation with him? The night before your having been removed from the investigation became known to all parties involved in the case?"

Rachel felt like she'd been slapped. "You've known me for years. Do you honestly think I'd let that monster keep my sister if I could have brought her home?"

The detective pinned her with a dark gaze. "Tell me about the apartment."

"What apartment?"

"The one almost directly across the street from your house. It was rented five years ago—by you."

Fingers digging into the table, Rachel tried to keep the world from spinning out beneath her. "I never rented an apartment."

"No? Because the woman who did used your name and your Social Security number."

"Jordan, I'm telling you I don't know anything about it. Did you search it?"

"We're waiting on the warrant," came the quick reply. "What are we going to find there, Rachel? Did Hannah and Carnegie rent the place so the two of you could see each other?"

Whatever friendship she'd felt toward Mancusi was being stripped away in great swaths. "How fucking dare you? I would never set my sister and her rapist up in an apartment. I would do anything for Hannah, but I'd see him dead before I lifted a finger to help him."

"Convenient that he's dead, then. And your sister has somehow managed to avoid being found." Mancusi folded her hands on the table. "Do you know how we found out about the apartment?"

"Enlighten me."

"It's where we tracked the phone call from Hannah to. Imagine my surprise when I ran the address."

Rachel ran a hand through her hair. "Well, there's your answer. If my sister and I were in league with one another, would she incriminate me?"

"She might, to save her own ass. She's been Carnegie's accomplice for a long time."

Her chair flew back so hard it bounced off the wall. Rachel planted her hands on the table, digging her fingers in as if she might rip right through the veneer. "Don't you call her that. She was a kid when he took her. He manipulated, brainwashed, and tortured her. Nothing she did for him was voluntary."

Jordan leaned back, putting distance between them. "Okay," she said.

Frowning, Rachel regarded her warily. "Okay?"

The detective nodded. "I believe you, and now everyone who watches this interview will too. We're done."

It had all been for show? To prove her innocence? Mancusi had grilled her and insinuated things just to see how she'd react? Of course she did—Mancusi didn't trust anyone. "You're a piece of fucking work," Rachel told her. She stood up and walked toward the door. Trick rose and followed after her. He'd been mostly silent through the whole thing, but she could see the tension in his jaw and neck.

"Rachel," Mancusi said as she opened the door. "This isn't personal."

"Fuck you," she replied, and walked out. Whatever friendship she'd had with the cop, it was over now. Rachel could forgive a lot of things, but she'd never forgive Mancusi for informing her that Hannah really had been just under her nose.

And Rachel still hadn't been able to save her.

CHAPTER FIFTEEN

Rachel was silent for most of the drive back to her place. It took her that long to calm down. When she finally did speak, it was to say, "You should probably stay away from me for a while."

Trick didn't even glance at her. "Martyrdom doesn't suit you."

"That's not what I mean. Mancusi already suspects there's something between us. If Crouse finds out, it could cast doubt on the investigation. On you. I don't want to drag you down."

Of all the reactions she might have expected, laughter wasn't one of them.

"What the hell?"

He shook his head, and she could tell then that the laughter hadn't been in humor. "I can't believe you're using the investigation as an excuse to end things between us."

"It's not an excuse. It's a valid and genuine concern."

He shot her a "bitch, please" look. "You're such a rotten liar."

"I'm not lying! Jesus, Trick. If I didn't care, I wouldn't even mention it. I'd just take you home and fuck your brains out and let Crouse do her worst."

"I'm not big on associating Crouse with sex." His smile was hesitant.

Rachel laughed. "Neither am I." She leaned back against the seat. Reaching over, she put her hand on his thigh. "Look, I won't lie—I could use all the support I can get right now. I feel like I'm standing on a glass bridge and I don't know where the ending or beginning is. One wrong step and I'll just drop."

He squeezed her hand in his. "You've got my support. You know that, right?"

"I do. I just won't forgive myself if it comes back to bite you on the ass."

"You let me worry about my ass."

"But it's such a nice ass." God, she was being ridiculous. Was this what a nervous breakdown felt like? "I just want to give you the chance to get out while you can."

"I appreciate that, but I'm not going anywhere. Do you need food?"

And that was the end of it, Rachel supposed. A little voice inside demanded that she push it—and push him away—but she couldn't. She didn't want to. Above all else, Trick was her friend. He knew her better than most people and still wanted to be with her. With him, she knew someone had her back, but most of all, she liked him. Adored him. There was no such thing as the perfect man, but Trick was pretty close to it.

"No," she said. Then, "Yes. I want French toast. Make me some?" It was the perfect way to tell him she was okay with him sticking around if he wanted.

He considered the invitation for a moment. "My place? Or do you need to be home for Naomi?"

"She texted me that her girlfriend's coming over, so she's got someone. She's also still pissed at me, so let's go to your place." She couldn't quite explain that his place would feel safer—a place where nothing could touch her—without sounding weak and needy, so she kept it to herself.

"That was a real bitch move Mancusi made."

Rachel exhaled sharply. "I can't believe Jordan actually went there. She's known me for years."

"I'd like to say she was just doing her job, but I think she handled it badly. Anyone who'd been there when Hannah called could see how shocked you were to hear from her. She didn't have to come down on you like that to sell your innocence."

"I suppose she didn't want to be accused of going easy on her old partner."

"Someone else could have questioned you."

"But they wouldn't know what buttons to push."

"Are you defending her?"

Rachel frowned. "I am. Fuck that. It's bad enough that I'm trying to find excuses for Hannah."

"You haven't talked about the phone call."

She was still trying to make sense of it. To believe it had actually happened. "Hearing her voice again . . . It was so weird."

"How did she sound?"

"Angry. Hurt. Loving." She shrugged. "She feels absolutely no guilt for Carnegie's death."

"I wouldn't either," Trick remarked.

A bark of surprised laughter tore from her throat. "No, me neither. She's not right, Trick. He broke her, I think. I don't know if she can be fixed." Her throat tightened, but no tears came. She was all cried out.

"What do you need from me?" he asked. "How can I help?"

He broke her heart sometimes, he really did. "Just be there—like you already are. I need someone who can handle my crazy."

Trick smiled. "I can do that."

They pulled up in front of his building a short time later. Trick had a condo in an old building that had retail space in the bottom, but had been converted on the second and third floors and then connected to the neighboring building by a bricked-in alleyway that now served as lobby and stairwell. Each unit was two floors and fairly spacious. The bedrooms were on the lower floor when you walked in, and the living area and kitchen were upstairs. It seemed backward to Rachel, but she had to admit it was interesting. One wall was rough brick, the floors wide hardwood boards that had been reclaimed. It had a slightly industrial feel mixed with a modern aesthetic. And she loved his renovated kitchen. The whole place was masculine, relaxed, and beautifully put together—much like Trick himself.

"Drink?" he asked, flipping on the light as they walked in.

"Yes, please. Wine if you have it." She toed off her shoes, hung her light jacket over the banister, and followed him upstairs to the kitchen. It was all stainless steel and navy cupboards with a natural wood counter.

He took a bottle of Riesling from the fridge and got a corkscrew from a drawer. Butterflies danced in her stomach— as if she would have any reason to be nervous with Trick. Maybe it was because she always insisted on him coming to her place that had her off center. Or maybe she was starting to crack under the strain of the last eighteen years.

He handed her a respectable glassful and got a beer for himself. "Still want French toast?" he asked. When she shook her head, he offered, "I can cook, or we can order."

"I don't want you to go to any bother," she replied. "We can order."

She loved that he didn't try to insist cooking wasn't a bother. "Thai?"

"Perfect."

They ordered food from a place nearby and settled on the sofa in the living room. It was also navy, and overstuffed. It was ridiculously comfortable and was adjustable like a recliner.

Trick found a movie for them to watch, and that's what they did when the food arrived. They sat on the sofa and watched TV as they ate. It was such an incredibly normal thing to do, and Rachel was thankful for it.

Trick's phone pinged when he paused the movie to get more wine and beer.

"You're not going to check it?" she asked.

"It can wait."

She set the wine on a coaster on the coffee table. "Right. You probably don't want me looking over your shoulder, especially if it's work related."

He shot her a scowl. "No, I don't want to check messages while enjoying dinner and a movie with a gorgeous woman. It can wait. If it's important, they'll call."

Feeling stupid, Rachel picked up her chopsticks and funneled more pad Thai into her mouth. It was such comfort food.

His phone didn't ring again and they were able to enjoy the rest of the movie. Only when the credits rolled did he pick up the cell and check it. He smiled.

"It was Naomi who texted," he told her. "She wants to know if you're staying here tonight."

Rachel met his gaze. "I don't know. Am I?"

"If you want."

She nodded, watching as he typed a response to her sister, who was sweet to worry about her even though she was mad, and had to be shocked by everything going on.

They sat up for a while after that, watching the Discovery Channel. Trick had his arm around her, she was curled up against his side. It was all very comfortable. Very domestic.

When they finally went to bed, it was well past midnight. Trick gave her a T-shirt to sleep in and a new toothbrush. She was in bed when he turned off the lights and crawled in beside her. Then he pulled her against him and draped his arm over her waist.

Rachel stared into the darkness, waiting. She wasn't sure for what. For the other shoe to drop. For the sky to fall. For the earth to open up and swallow her whole.

None of those things happened, of course, but the sense of doom didn't go away.

"I can't sleep," she whispered.

"Mm."

She turned to him, sliding one hand up the back of his lean, muscular thigh. "Want to make me sleepy?" she asked.

He chuckled, but he obviously didn't have to be asked twice. His hands and mouth were on her almost instantly, winding up Rachel's insides like a jack-in-the-box. When she finally climbed on top of him, her thighs trembled with anticipation. Their bodies came together easily, naturally, falling into sync as they moved.

It didn't take long. Rachel's head tilted back. Her fingers clutched at the hands holding her hips as tension built inside her and then finally bubbled over. She couldn't keep herself from crying out, and a few seconds later, Trick answered her.

Afterward, she curled against him, wrapping her legs around his. He kissed her forehead and stroked her hair. The last thing she remembered before drifting off to sleep was the feeling of his fingers against her scalp.

The ringing of his cell phone woke them the next morning. Groggy, with wine mouth, Rachel watched Trick put the phone to his ear. "Patrick," he said.

He sat up and pulled back the blankets. "What?" he demanded. Obviously he didn't like the answer, because his frown quickly became a scowl. "I'll call her." He hung up.

"What is it?" she asked.

He set the phone on the bedside table. "That was Crouse. Apparently, Sydney Cole wants to talk to you. And the entire police force of Connecticut is looking for your sister on murder charges. And Crouse is pissed because neither of us told her about Hannah's phone call."

Rachel fell back against the pillows. "Fuck."

Tuesday

"I'm surprised Crouse didn't just GPS my phone," Rachel said later, as they drove to her place so she could shower and change.

"I wouldn't be surprised if she did," Trick replied. "She'll be watching both of us now."

"I'm sorry to drag you into this. If I hadn't left my phone upstairs, this probably wouldn't have happened."

"It's fine," he said. She wanted to believe he meant it.

At her place she took only enough time to shower, brush her teeth, and change. While she was doing that, Trick called Crouse to let her know that he was with Rachel and that together they would come by the field office after Rachel talked to Sydney and bring Crouse up to speed.

"Mancusi apparently wants to record the conversation," Trick informed her when they were back in the SUV and headed to the hospital.

Rachel nodded. "In case either one of us says anything to incriminate me, I guess."

"Is she really gunning for you?"

"A little. She actually did me a favor with the interview—I'll look innocent. But I think she blames me for losing Carnegie."

"You didn't kill him."

"The person on the security footage looks just like me, and I don't think she's ever forgiven me for joining the Bureau."

"This feels like a lot more than jealousy." He frowned. "I mean, does she honestly think you'd protect your sister who's wanted by the police?"

Rachel glanced at him. "You don't have siblings, do you?"

"No."

She smiled. "Mancusi has a brother and a sister. She knows what she'd do for them."

"I still think it's harsh," Trick said. "How do you feel about Sydney wanting to talk to you?"

"I'm afraid of what she might tell me," Rachel confided. "Carnegie had eighteen years with my sister to mold her into whatever he wanted. She's done things I won't be able to understand, no matter how much I want to rationalize them."

"Might be a good idea to talk to someone. Professionally, I mean."

"Already made the appointment," she told him.

Trick turned on the radio and sang along with some of the pop songs that played. He had a nice voice, and Rachel enjoyed listening to him. It helped keep her from dwelling on Hannah, but of course she couldn't stop herself from thinking about her sister and what sort of help she would need. Their father had several friends who were defense attorneys, so they would at least have help on the legal side. Hannah would need therapy but trying to gauge how much or how little at this point was futile and a waste of energy.

She had to find Hannah before she could help her.

The cops at the hospital stared at her as they walked toward Sydney's room. Rachel wished she could talk to the security guard who saw Hannah the night before.

Had it only been a few hours since her sister had killed her monster? God, it felt like days had passed.

There was a guard stationed outside Sydney's room. He studied Rachel as they approached. Probably memorizing her in case Hannah showed up again. Rachel didn't bother to tell him her sister wouldn't come back. Hannah had never been one to press her luck. Besides, people who had known them their entire lives got them mixed up, so checking her out for a few seconds wouldn't make him an expert in telling the two of them apart.

Mancusi was there waiting for them.

"Thought maybe you'd taken off," she said with a slight smirk. She wasn't completely joking. That's why she was angry, Rachel realized. She thought Rachel had duped her.

Rachel looked her in the eye and didn't blink. "You thought wrong."

The detective motioned with a tilt of her head for them to move. Rachel and Trick followed her a few feet away.

"I want you to record the conversation," Mancusi said.

Rachel frowned. "Doesn't that kind of go against her wanting to talk only to me?"

"Yeah, but if we don't, it means I have to take your word on what's said, and I'm sorry, but your word isn't going to mean much in court, given your sister was the one who attacked her."

She bristled, but pride wouldn't let her cause a scene.

"Whatever, but we do it with police equipment so the parents will know who to blame for betraying their daughter's confidence."

Mancusi produced a small digital recorder from her pocket. "Here."

Rachel looked at it before shoving it in her jacket. She wanted to make sure she could find the Pause button if necessary.

When they finished, the rest of the Cole family came into the hallway. Rachel was glad to see that Morgan was with them instead of being left alone at home. The poor kid looked like shit. She probably felt all kinds of guilt for having fallen for Carnegie's charm. And she probably realized how lucky she was that he hadn't decided to keep her.

"How are you doing?" Rachel asked her.

The girl nodded. "Okay. You?"

Rachel shrugged. "I'm about how you'd expect." As far as conversations went, it was weak, but Rachel saw everything she needed to see in the girl's gaze. She stepped forward and wrapped her arms around Morgan. "It's going to be okay," she whispered.

The girl hugged her hard, then stepped back. "Thanks," she said.

"I'll leave the door open," Rachel told the parents. "You can watch from out here to make sure Sydney is okay. If either of you have any concerns, you can step in at any time."

"And we will," Mr. Cole assured her. It might have been meant as intimidation, but the man was so tired and pale that it lacked any real threat.

Sydney was sitting up in bed when Rachel entered her room.

Her long red hair was up in a messy bun and her pale face was bruised, but other than that she looked good. Her fingers trembled as they fidgeted with the blanket over her lap.

"Hi. I'm Rachel."

"Yeah. They told me." The girl's voice was a little hoarse, and slightly higher than her twin's. "You're Anne—I mean, Hannah's sister."

Rachel didn't get any closer than the foot of the bed. It was obvious that just looking at her kind of freaked the kid out. "I'm sorry that seeing me upset you so much."

"It's not your fault you have a face like hers. It scared me then, but I can now see that you're not her. You're not as skinny, or weird. Sorry."

She forced a smile. "I'm not offended."

"She said that hurting me was the best way to hurt my sister—that Alex had taught her that."

Swallowing, Rachel tried to ignore how much hearing that hurt. "I'm sure he did."

"She said he'd kidnapped her years ago."

Rachel nodded and finally pressed the Record button. "Alex Carnegie kidnapped my sister eighteen years ago when she was pretending to be me on a school trip."

"Wow. That's not a guilt trip or anything."

Rachel laughed. "Tell me about it."

Nervous fingers pleated the stark white sheet. "So, I guess that's why you became a cop?"

"You guess right. For all the good it did. I was never able to find her."

"She said Alex owned a lot of property. I only saw the Westport house. Hannah said he would probably take me somewhere else."

"I'm glad he never got the chance."

Sydney glanced down. "She also told me that Morgan was going to be her replacement. That he was going to kill her and take Morgan instead. She said part of the reason she had to kill me was so I wouldn't know what it was like to have my sister disappear. And that if she killed me, then it might save Morgan from what Alex planned to do."

A hard lump formed in Rachel's throat. She couldn't imagine what Hannah's life had been, but she wished Carnegie was alive so she could kill him herself. "I suppose that seemed logical to her."

"She looked me right in the eye and shoved that knife into my stomach."

The hairs on the back of Rachel's neck stood on end. If only she'd thought to press Pause on the recorder. And then she realized that was exactly why Mancusi didn't trust her. Shouldn't trust her.

"Did she say anything?"

Sydney tilted her head, her brow furrowing in concentration. "Yeah, but not to me. It was like she was talking to herself, and she kept switching the knife from her left hand to her right and back again. I can't remember what she said, though. Something about 'saving' her, but I don't know if she meant me or someone else."

Herself, maybe, Rachel thought. Maybe Hannah had been talking about how no one had saved her.

"Will you do something for me?" the girl asked.

"Of course."

"If you talk to Hannah, tell her it's okay. I understand why she tried to kill me and I forgive her for it."

"You do?"

Sydney nodded. "I'd rather die than have my sister turn out like yours."

Ten years ago

There was blood. So much blood. And cramps. Hannah curled into a ball and moaned.

Alex was there, fussing over her like a mother hen. She wanted to hit him with something. This was his fault. He'd gotten her pregnant despite her birth control, and now she was paying the price.

Thankfully, Nature wouldn't let his child take root, flourish, and grow. At least that was one monster she wouldn't have to look at every day. How could she love a child born from this insanity? How could she ever hope it would be normal with either of them for parents?

She had to pee. He helped her to the bathroom.

"Give me a minute," she said.

Alex hesitated. "I don't want to leave you alone."

"You left me in that room for days at a time," she reminded him sharply. "You can leave me in the bathroom for a few fucking seconds."

He blinked at her tone. Normally he'd react, reassert his

dominance, but this scared him, she could tell. He only nodded and backed out of the room. He even shut the door. She
didn't push her luck by locking it.

She passed the remainder of the tissue sitting there on the
toilet, sweating and panting through the cramping. Felt it slip
out of her, plop into the water. Relief washed over her. Hannah
pressed her forehead against the cool wall, her body empty now
and raw.

How much longer would he keep her? Why hadn't he killed
her by now? She'd begun to hope for it, but wasn't strong
enough to do it herself. He'd begun to trust her a few years ago,
and had made her into his accomplice. She'd helped him lure
two girls to their deaths, and knew of one other that he'd lured
on his own. There was no redemption for that, was there? That
blood was on her hands.

Rachel would be so disappointed in her. There were times
when she slipped away, let her thoughts of Rachel take over,
pretended to be her sister like she used to. It was one of the few
things that kept her from breaking completely.

She'd been with Alex for eight years. She should be in college
now, or just finishing a degree. She hadn't even finished high
school. Alex told her Rachel was becoming a cop. He thought
it was funny—thought it was because of him. Hannah didn't
correct him, didn't tell him he didn't have that kind of power
over her twin. Rachel wasn't becoming a cop because of him—
she was doing it for Hannah. Rachel was going to find her, and
if Hannah died before that happened, Rachel would be the one
to capture Alex and put an end to him.

There'd be no more girls killed with heroin, made up like models, posed in some semipublic place to be gawked at and inspire fear. No more press to feed his ego, no more photographs.

There were statues in the garden in Westport of Grace and the girl before her. Sometimes he went outside and talked to them at night. He thought she didn't know, but she watched from the bedroom window. *What did he say to them?* she wondered.

And why did none of his friends who came to visit ever notice that his art looked like dead girls? Why didn't any of them ever ask about her? His waif in the background, who disappeared to her room whenever he had company? Once in a while he asked her to stay, watching her with his owl-like gaze, daring her to ask for help. Daring her to defy him.

Fear kept her silent. Attention from his friends made her feel like his girlfriend, not his prisoner. Is that what she'd become? His lover?

He never chained her to the bed anymore. Should she thank him for that?

There was a knock at the bathroom door. "Are you alright?" he asked.

"Yes," she said. "Would you get me a clean pair of underwear, please?"

"Okay."

She cleaned herself with wet wipes and tossed them into the bloody water, covering the thing at the bottom of the bowl. She flushed, watching it all swirl together and disappear.

There was a box of pads under the sink. She got one out and had it ready to stick to the panties he brought her. When she came out of the bathroom, he was waiting, leaning against the wall with that slouch she'd thought was sexy the first time she saw him.

He was gorgeous. And he looked afraid—truly afraid. She'd never seen him look vulnerable before. It made her feel... powerful. He straightened when she walked up to him, opened his arms, and took her in.

"I'm so sorry, Hannah," he murmured against her hair. "So sorry, my sweet girl."

She melted against him, tears filling her eyes. He picked her up as she started to sob and carried her to the bedroom, laying her on the bed as though she were a child. He drew the quilt up over her, tucking her in. Then he climbed in on the other side and spooned her from behind. He wrapped his arms around her and held her close, his breath warm and soothing against the back of her neck.

Grace had warned her that she'd fall in love with him, and that was the moment that Hannah did. She fell inexplicably and helplessly in love.

But that part of her that was so connected to her twin—that Rachel part of her—still hated him, and would hate him until she was dead.

Until he killed her, or she killed him.

CHAPTER SIXTEEN

The apartment rented in Rachel's name smelled of garbage when Jordan unlocked the door. She hadn't had to bother the landlord, because there was a key to the place on the fob that had been in Carnegie's car. Obviously, Hannah had fled without getting rid of her leftover takeout on the counter.

It took up the entire second floor of a renovated old townhouse, much like the one Rachel and Naomi lived in. Most of the windows faced their house. In fact, in the apartment living room there was a telescope that Mancusi could only guess had been used to spy on the sisters. Was it possible that Rachel really hadn't known her twin was so close? If so, it said a lot for Carnegie's cruelty that he'd bring Hannah there, where she could see her family but never be with them.

Asshole.

The place was nice—expensively but comfortably furnished in a style that was similar to Carnegie's Westport house. Certainly an FBI agent couldn't afford a lot of it, not when she already had one household.

There was no telephone and no television, not even in the bedroom. A few things hung in the closet—a few pairs of designer men's trousers and shirts, and a couple of dresses, pants, and blouses on the other side. The bathroom had a minimal amount of things in the medicine cabinet and under the sink as well. And the kitchen was practically bare. It was obvious this was a place Carnegie used infrequently.

If she were a psychopath who liked to abduct a twin, Jordan would bring said twin here on the anniversary of that abduction so he could get off on her pain, and then spy on her sister's torment as well. As an extra joke, she'd make that twin rent the place in her sister's name.

As she stood in front of the living room windows, hands on her hips, Jordan's gut told her Rachel had nothing to do with this. Her surprise at learning about the apartment had been genuine. That didn't mean she was entirely innocent, however. Did Jordan want to believe her old partner was capable of being involved in any of this? No. But she had siblings herself, and she knew the lengths to which she'd go to protect them.

"Spread out and start searching," she told the unis who had accompanied her. She took the living area. The electronics they'd found in Carnegie's New York apartment were currently with the NYPD, but they shared the findings. He'd been part of a chat group on a very secure server that liked to talk about raping young women. He also sold photographs of his victims to other members. At least half of his fortune had to come from those illegal images, if not more. He had a whole network of monsters with whom he traded stories and other evidence. The New York branch of the FBI was already all over it with their Crimes Against Children division.

Fortunately, Trick had some connections there and promised to keep her in the loop.

However, she wasn't sure how much she could trust him either, she thought as she began going through the trunk near the telescope. Mostly just fuzzy throws and a few magazines. She knew Rachel had spent the previous night at his place, which confirmed her theory that something was going on between the two of them. Trick was a good agent and a good man. She wouldn't put it past him to try to do something chivalrous, like ignore evidence against Rachel or even misplace it.

Maybe Carnegie really had been just that smart. He wouldn't be the first killer that eluded capture for years, but they figured that he'd been killing for at least twenty-five years, putting him in his mid- to late twenties when he began. That was a long time to stay under the radar. Of course, keeping victims for several years helped. He could act out his urges, but not leave a trail of bodies. Smart. Evil, but smart.

She closed the lid on the trunk and moved toward a desk on the other side of the room. The floorboards beneath a Persian rug shifted and groaned as she stepped on them. She froze. She knew loose boards when she heard them. As a kid it had been the only way she could hide anything from her nosy siblings. She stepped off the rug, moved the coffee table off it as well, and then flipped it out of the way. Carefully, she poked the boards with the toe of her boot until one lifted.

Jordan got down on her knees and lifted the board out of the way. The ones immediately on either side of it moved as well. She used the flashlight on her phone to peer inside. There, covered in dust and a few cobwebs, were several large plastic folding files. She put on gloves, lifted one out, dusted it off, and unfastened it.

"Jesus Christ," she muttered when she saw the top photo. She ought to have prepared herself better. She had to look away for a second before turning her attention back to it. She'd been in law enforcement for almost fifteen years, and it sometimes still amazed her the things people could do to one another.

Not all of the photos were that nasty, but since she'd talked to Carnegie's sister the day before, they seemed even more sinister.

Everly Carnegie-Hall hadn't been particularly close to her brother, especially the last few years. She didn't approve of his "flashy" lifestyle and occasional drug use. And the sight of his "gaunt" girlfriend who hardly ever spoke made her uncomfortable—not because she was odd but because she reminded her of all the other redheads, and one redhead in particular.

According to Everly, her brother had met and fallen in love with April Rourke his sophomore year in art school. April was one of a set of twins. They dated for several months before April died of a heroin overdose at a party. Alex had been so stoned himself that he hadn't even noticed she had died, which led to police not knowing if the sex they'd engaged in had been pre- or post-mortem. Alex had passed out and woke up to the sounds of April's twin sister screaming. He'd said the pain in her face was something he'd remember forever. In fact, still high, he'd taken a photograph of her holding her sister's dead body.

And so a fetish had been born.

Had her brother always been strange? Well, Everly hadn't seemed exactly surprised to find out he was suspected of being the Gemini killer. Apparently he'd killed some neighborhood pets as a child, but the family managed to keep it quiet. His sister knew about it only because one of those pets had belonged to her best friend.

It was fairly classic, textbook behavior for a budding serial killer. Of course the family hadn't sought medical help for their son. Their mother had tried, but the father was against it, and Alex didn't seem the least bit interested. Even after the death of April, he didn't want to talk to anyone. He just retreated further and further into his art, distancing himself from his family. Everly hadn't even known he'd gotten his first job for *Vogue* until he sent her a copy of the magazine. He wanted his family to know he'd arrived. That he was important.

"To be absolutely honest with you, Detective," Everly had said, "I began avoiding my brother when my daughter turned sixteen. It wasn't that he did anything unseemly toward her, but at her party there were these lovely twins from a family we are very close to. Alex spent far too much time with them for a man his age, especially one of them. It was as though he wanted to set them against each other. It wasn't natural, and I told him to leave. When he kicked up a fuss, I knew something wasn't right. Why are we so hesitant to see the darkness in our loved ones?"

"Because we don't want to see the same darkness in our-selves," Jordan replied, a little proud of her wisdom. But as she sat on the floor of that apartment, three huge folders of evidence of Carnegie's crimes in front of her, she couldn't help but wish his family had opened their damn eyes and seen him for the monster he was. Even as she thought it, she knew there was a common blindness among those closest to some of society's most evil. People didn't want to see, so they didn't.

At least one of the folders had to be mostly all Hannah Ward, but there were shots of women she recognized as earlier victims. As Jordan looked at one of the photos, she saw something in the background. Looking at it more closely, she saw that it was a lake with a sign next to it. She couldn't quite make out what the sign said, but if she could get one of the techs to clean the image up, maybe they'd be able to figure something out. Maybe there were more clues in some of the photos. Carnegie had to take his victims somewhere private to photograph them. The scenery in a lot of the photos looked the same, even though they'd been taken years apart. Hannah Ward had been hiding here, but she was in the wind now. She'd wanted them to find this place. But Alex had more secret places. They always did. Hannah had probably gone to one of those.

"Detective?"

She looked up. One of the uniforms stood a few feet away. "Yes, Nowicki?"

"We found these in the bedroom." He held up several sets of shackles. They weren't the sexy kind either. Jordan recognized them from some of the photos. "The mattress shows signs of having been stained with bio-matter."

She winced. "I'll call CSU and have them come in. Bag the restraints, and I need one of you to help me with these file folders. They weigh a ton."

Nowicki nodded. "Right away."

Sighing, Jordan put the photos away and gave the space one more go-over before putting the boards back in place. Finding additional evidence for Carnegie was anticlimactic now that he was dead. Hannah had robbed her of the satisfaction of watching the bastard rot in prison, but now she had to find Hannah Ward, and determine just how involved she was in Carnegie's crimes. Coercion was one thing, but Jordan was beginning to suspect that Hannah had been a willing participant.

A week ago

He was going to finally kill her.

She could see it in his eyes when he looked at her—he was done. All these years of keeping her, having his way with her. Breaking her. Years that she survived, and now he was going to finish her.

It could be argued, she supposed, that he'd killed her years ago—when he kidnapped her and ended the life she'd known. He'd stolen her from her family, robbed her of her sisters and friends, denied her the dreams she had for her future.

But pain was his thing. He liked it when people were uncomfortable, disappointed. Hurt. The only thing he liked better than inflicting it himself was watching someone else do it. That was his porn. She learned that early on.

He'd already found her replacement. So many girls had come and died over the years, but this one...this one was different. She was special. Special enough to be the end of *her*. She'd always known this day would come. There had been nights she prayed for it. Remembering Grace's sweet face and her fucked-up advice, she'd wished that he'd come in and finally put an end to it all, but he never did.

Because she gave him what the others never had. He tired of them and threw them away like garbage, but not her. She was his "perfect match," he'd said. He would never, ever tire of her.

Until now.

Sitting on the bed, sweat dotting her forehead, she waited, clenching her fingers in the sheets. How would he do it? Would he drug her? Dress her up? Style her hair and paint her face? Or would he make her do it herself before putting her to sleep like an old dog? At least he had good taste.

She hoped he left her somewhere nice. It was never somewhere that there was a lot of security—he couldn't risk being seen. She never really understood why it was so important to him to leave them where they'd be found once he was done. It seemed uncharacteristically kind of him to finally give the families closure. Why not let them suffer forever? Why leave them a pretty doll of a corpse to welcome home and weep over?

Once, she'd asked him about it—about the ones before her, and why he'd kept some and not others. Why he did the things he did. He smiled and told her it all led back to a girl he'd known when he was young.

As if she hadn't been smart enough to figure that part out on her own. He'd always doubted her intelligence. He had that sort of arrogant personality that just naturally assumed he was superior to others in every possible way. Getting away with murder for as long as he had would do that, she supposed.

Would Rachel, her twin, feel her death? There had been times, over the years, when she thought she had felt things, sensed things. She'd stopped hoping they meant anything a long time ago. They were just bitter reminders that somewhere, away from him, there was someone living the life that should have been hers.

Finally, she heard his footsteps. The key turning in the lock. The door swung open, and there he was, beautiful and monstrous. He stared at her—and the girl unconscious behind her in the bed. His wide gaze locked with hers as he crossed the threshold. "What have you done?"

What had *she* done? She'd done what she had to do to make sure it finally ended. The girl had seen her face. Either the girl died, or Hannah did. And the girl wasn't the one he wanted.

She smiled.

Rachel was surprised to open the door and find Mancusi standing on her steps. She would have expected Hannah to show up before the cop.

"You have a warrant?" she asked.

Mancusi arched a brow. "Would I come alone if I planned to search the place?"

"I suppose not." Rachel waited.

Her old friend shifted uncomfortably. She obviously thought Rachel would be more welcoming. She should have known better. "I want to apologize."

Rachel crossed her arms over her chest. "For what?"

"Everything?" Her tone and expression were laughable—enough that Rachel actually smiled.

"I still think you're a piece of work, and I don't trust you anymore."

Mancusi nodded. "I am a piece of work and I don't trust anybody, so I'm good with that."

Rachel stared at her a moment, weighing her sincerity. She seemed to mean what she said. Jordan wasn't one to mince words or pull punches, and she'd always been big about owning up when she'd been wrong. "Did you find anything at the apartment?"

Mancusi nodded. "We found photographs."

"Can I—?"

"No. No, you can't. Even if you were still on the case, I'd argue against showing them to you."

Her brow pinched. They had to be bad. She didn't want to imagine what Jordan might have seen, but it was enough for her to want to reach out, even though she didn't trust Rachel.

Shit.

Rachel stepped back. "Come on in. You want a Coke or something?"

"Yeah, that would be great."

Naomi chose that moment to come down the stairs. "What's she doing here?" she demanded, glaring at Mancusi.

"She came to apologize," Rachel said.

"Or she's faking it," Naomi argued. She didn't take her gaze off the detective. "You betrayed my sister's trust and you crapped on her friendship. That makes me inclined not to like you much, Jordan."

Mancusi inclined her head. "Fair enough. I'm sorry I upset you."

"Mm," was all the younger woman said. Then, to her sister. "I'll be upstairs if you need me." She turned on her heel and went back up to her room.

"I've never seen her like that," Mancusi commented, following Rachel into the kitchen.

"She doesn't get mad very often. Congratulations."

"Did you tell her about talking to Sydney Cole?"

Rachel got glasses out of the cupboard. "Not yet. We're going over to Mom and Dad's tonight. I'm going to tell them all of it." She cringed just thinking of how her mother would probably react.

"So, what Sydney said about Hannah trying to kill her so Carnegie couldn't turn her into something like her—"

Rachel held up her hand. "I'm not talking about it with you with my sister in the house."

"Okay."

She went to the fridge and got out a bottle of Coke. She filled each glass about three-quarters full and dropped in a couple of ice cubes. She gave one of the glasses to Jordan. "Sit."

They sat at the kitchen table. That way Rachel would better see and hear Naomi if she returned.

"Do you know of any places your sister might be?"

Rachel sighed. "I've been thinking about it ever since she told me she wanted me to find her. If Carnegie had more properties, she could be at one of them."

"But she wouldn't expect you to find her there, would she?"

"I don't know. Maybe. She seemed pissed off that I never noticed she was practically across the street."

"Yeah." Mancusi took a sip of Coke. "Carnegie must have gotten off on that."

Rachel grimaced. "I don't want to think about it, the sick bastard. The only place I can think of is the cottage my grandparents owned in Chester. It's on the lake. We used to go there a lot as kids. They left it to my uncle, but he lets everyone use it. We all know where the key is."

Mancusi checked her watch. "Want to take a drive?"

She stared at her. "You're kidding, right?"

"We can be there and back in a couple of hours. Maybe we'll find her, and you can give your family closure. Worst-case scenario—you can tell Hannah you looked."

Rachel hated the fact that she was right. "Fine. Let's go."

She ran upstairs and told Naomi she was going out with Jordan for a bit. Her sister didn't look impressed. "Why?" she asked.

"We might have a lead on Hannah, okay? Keep that to yourself."

Her sister nodded. "Be careful. I don't trust Jordan anymore."

"I will, and I don't either. Not entirely." Then, before she could second-guess it, she gave Naomi a quick, hard hug. Just in case.

They took Mancusi's car. Rachel brought her gun and badge since they hadn't been officially taken away from her—yet.

It was a fifty-some-minute drive to Chester from her house if you did the speed limit, but Jordan ignored the posted speeds and pulled into the drive of Rachel's family cottage about forty minutes later.

Rachel got out of the car and pulled her jacket a little closer around her. It was a cool day for May, drizzly and gray. The lake actually looked a little choppy, not at all inviting.

The cottage was in need of a fresh coat of paint—it was peeling and there was green moss growing on some of it. T he steps had a bit of a lean to them as well, and the wharf into the lake needed to be repaired. Her grandfather would be horrified to see it looking like this. Rachel herself was horrified.

"My uncle's an ass," she said, taking out her phone so she could take photos to show her father.

"Doesn't look like there's been anyone here for a while," Mancusi remarked, glancing down at the grass that reached almost to her knees.

Rachel moved through the grass, toward the front of the cottage. The huge rock they'd always hidden the key beneath was still there, and when she lifted it, beetles and worms scurried away, revealing the key on a rusting ring. The key for the shed was there too. Rachel picked them up, shaking off the damp dirt.

The steps groaned under her weight. She took them carefully, expecting them to split, but they didn't. They didn't break when Mancusi followed her either. She lifted the latch on the screen door and slid the key into the lock. The door creaked open.

The air smelled musty and humid. Rachel was pretty sure she saw a squirrel run behind the stove.

"Shit," she said, stepping into the gloomy interior. She flicked the light switch, but nothing happened. "I can't believe Uncle Brian has let the place go like this."

"Guess your grandparents left it to the wrong son, huh?"

"They did." She looked around at the ruination of so many happy childhood memories, anger rushing through her veins. Something had to be done.

"Well, I can't imagine your sister squatting here after the kind of lifestyle she's gotten used to," Jordan remarked.

"You don't know anything about her," Rachel retorted.

The cop shrugged. "I know she's killed at least one person and tried to kill Sydney Cole. I know she's hiding, which makes me think she's well aware of the trouble she's in. Maybe you need to stop thinking of her as a victim, Rach."

Rachel ignored her. It was that or get angry, and Jordan didn't deserve to see her get emotional. Instead, she moved toward the rickety table in the center of the room, because there was a piece of paper on top of it—paper that looked far too crisp and new to have been there long.

She didn't pick it up, but bent down to read the writing on it. She could just make it out, thanks to the weak daylight filtering through the dirty window.

Dear Rachel: I figured you'd come here. I almost decided to wait for you, but I'd rather sleep on a Central Park bench. I think there's a family of squirrels in the sofa, and there are definitely skunks living beneath. Keep looking. Love, Hannah

"That's it?" Jordan had been reading over her shoulder.

"She never was long-winded." She watched as the other woman pulled a plastic evidence bag from her pocket, picked the letter up by one corner, and slipped it in. "So, she was here."

"But decided not to stay. Guess I know something about her after all, huh?"

Rachel turned her head with a glare. "You getting off on this? Because this might be just a case to you, but this is my fucking sister, Jordan. So if our friendship has meant nothing to you, keep talking. Otherwise, show me a little fucking respect."

Jordan's eyebrows rose, stretching her mouth open as well. "Sorry."

"Mm. I'm going to look and she if she left anything else." But she could already tell she hadn't. Hannah had walked in, looked at the place, left her note, and walked back out. It was a wonder she hadn't set the place on fire.

Of course they found nothing except more ruin and dust. Jordan walked out first, leaving Rachel to lock up behind them.

Jordan's phone buzzed. She looked at it while Rachel put the keys back under the rock.

"What is it?" she asked, seeing the look on the detective's face.

Jordan sighed and put her phone back in the holder on her belt. "Look, I know you want to think of your sister as a victim. I would love for her to be innocent in all of this."

"She is."

"We contacted Cassandra Lennox. She just ID'd Hannah as the woman who approached her in the mall when she was a teenager. She tried to kidnap her, Rachel. And there was evidence on Heather Montgomery that indicated she was killed by two people. You have to accept that Hannah willingly assisted Carnegie."

Rachel glared at her. "I told you, she didn't have a choice. He raped her, Jordan. He abused her mentally, physically, and emotionally. Nothing you can say will convince me otherwise. Nothing, so why don't you just take me home? Or should I call Trick?"

"You know the more time you spend with him, the more you put him in the line of fire, right?"

"You know it's none of your fucking business, right?"

They both got into the car and slammed their doors. The drive back to New Haven was even faster than their initial trip. Jordan even turned on the siren for parts of it where traffic was heavy.

Rachel didn't speak until they turned onto her block. She wouldn't have said a word at all if it wasn't for the news vans on the street and reporters clustered outside her house.

"What the hell?" she wondered out loud. Once Jordan parked, she got out of the car and started toward the house. Once the reporters caught sight of her, they rushed toward her.

"Agent Ward! Agent Ward!"

"Is it true your sister pretended to be you in order to murder the Gemini Killer?"

"Do you know where Hannah is?"

"Have you been helping your sister?"

Rachel shot a glare at Jordan. She was so mad she couldn't even see straight. Obviously, someone with the police had talked to the press, and now her parents and Naomi had probably heard about it—or they would very soon. There was no doubt in her mind she was live on some feed at the moment.

"No comment," she said, pushing her way through the crowd.

"Detective Mancusi!" one of them cried and moved on to fresh prey. Jordan followed after her. When Rachel got to the door, she unlocked it and slipped inside as fast as she could.

And then she shut it in Mancusi's face.

CHAPTER SEVENTEEN

Someone in the police had spoken to the press, but *only* after Rachel's mother had called the local news and told them that her daughter had managed to escape her abductor and kill him. She also told them that Hannah was afraid to turn herself in because she felt like she was the victim of a "witch hunt" by both federal and state law enforcement.

Rachel was so mad she could barely look at her mother, who sat in a chair in the living room of the house Rachel had grown up in, looking archly smug. Of course she was happy—Rachel was miserable.

She shouldn't have been there. Rachel ought to have let Mancusi or Trick take care of it.

"Why didn't you tell me you had heard from Hannah?" she asked.

Her mother lifted her chin. "Why didn't you tell us *you* had heard from her?"

"Because I couldn't."

Miriam Ward shrugged. "That was your choice."

"Well, at least I didn't go to the press before telling you."

The older woman looked away.

"You hate me so much for being the one who wasn't taken that you were never once thankful I was still here," Rachel said, her voice cracking. "You didn't lose one daughter that day, you know. You lost two. You turned your back on me when I needed you, and I will never forgive you for it. You want to talk to the press, you go right ahead. Tell them about your poor, misunderstood daughter. Tell them she only killed out of the kindness of her heart."

Her mother was out of the chair and in her face in a blink. "Don't you make such accusations about your sister."

"It's true," Rachel insisted. "Hannah said she didn't want Sydney or her twin, Morgan, to end up like her. And then she stabbed a sixteen-year-old girl, Mom. She stabbed her multiple times."

Miriam's nostrils flared. "Hannah would never hurt anyone."

"She hurt Sydney. And she killed Alex Carnegie."

"He deserved it."

"Yeah, but now he'll never pay for what he's done. She pretended to be me to get to him, Mom. I could have been arrested for murder because of Hannah."

Silence.

Rachel sucked in a deep breath. Her father and Naomi just sat there, watching the two of them face off, like they always had over the past eighteen years.

"Look," she began with a sigh. "I know you want her to be okay, that you want everything to be like it was, but it won't be, Mom. Hannah is not okay. She's broken and she needs help."

The slap sent her staggering backward, pain reverberating through her skull. Tears filled her eyes at the sting. God, it felt like half her face had been ripped off. She pressed her fingers to her scalding skin, making sure there was still flesh there.

"Miriam!" her father cried, jumping out of his chair. "That's enough!"

Naomi was at Rachel's side, grabbing at her hand. Rachel and her mother glared at each other.

"Don't you say that about your sister," her mother said, her voice shaking. "Hannah is *not* broken."

"We're all broken," Rachel replied quietly. "*You're* broken. And I'm done being the one you blame for it. I didn't do anything wrong."

She turned on her heel and left the room, Naomi right behind her.

"Rach, where are you going?"

"I'm not sure. Can you get home on your own?"

"I want to come with you."

She stopped and turned to her sister. "I need to be alone right now, Squirt. I love you, but I just can't be around anyone. Okay?"

Naomi nodded. She looked like she might cry, but she didn't argue.

Rachel grabbed her coat and walked out of the house. The cool night air soothed her throbbing cheek. Her mother was strong for a woman her age, and had a lot of fury behind her. Rationally, Rachel knew her mother was angriest at herself for what had happened to Hannah, but she chose to take it out on Rachel, pushing her away so it wouldn't hurt if she lost her too. Years of therapy had taught her that, but that didn't stop her from feeling like her mother would trade her for Hannah. That her mother hated her.

"Agent Ward!" a voice cried. Jesus Christ, the reporters had followed her? Of course they had. Serial killers were big news, and so were victims who had been kept a long time. People loved that shit. Loved to see people more fucked up than they were.

"No comment," she shouted back, pressing the button on the fob to unlock her car.

They kept coming, bright lights glaring. Rachel yanked open the car door and climbed inside, slamming and locking it behind her. The lights of their cameras reflected off the glass, blinding her. Their hands pounded on her window. She started the engine and put the car into reverse. Slowly she backed out onto the street—the last thing she needed was to run over a reporter.

Once she was on the street, though, she put it in drive and drove off as fast as she could on a residential street. She didn't really have a destination in mind, but somehow she ended up at the park they used to go to as kids. It had a play area for little ones, and a place where teenagers gathered to look cool. She and Hannah used to bring Naomi sometimes and played on the kiddie equipment with her. Rachel's favorite thing had been the merry-go-round. Hannah had liked the seesaws. She said going up made her feel like she was flying, and falling was just flying in reverse.

The park gates were locked, but she hopped them just the way they had twenty years ago—though with slightly less grace, she thought. It looked smaller than she remembered. Not as magical. The lights stationed along the fencing cast the place in a slightly eerie glow. Grass was dark, dirt strangely bright.

A cool breeze ruffled her hair—a reminder that summer was still a month away. Swing chains creaked as she walked by. And then she heard it—the familiar whoosh and thump of some-one seesawing solo.

Rachel walked faster. The seesaws were at the other end of the park, not that it was that far away. As she approached, she saw a shadowy figure propel themself upward, the empty board opposite striking the ground hard. The figure came back down into a squat only to push themself off the ground once again.

"Hannah!" she called, heart pounding in her throat.

The seesaw came back down. The figure dismounted and turned toward her. It waved.

"Hannah," she sobbed.

"Agent Ward!" The voice was behind her, but it was loud and it was clear. The reporters had followed her.

The figure—Hannah—heard them too. She whirled and ran away. Rachel started to chase after her, but then realized she'd be leading the wolves to the lamb, so she swerved left and ran toward the side gate. The park hadn't changed since she was a kid. She knew how to get back to the parking lot with-out being seen. If she didn't, she never would have had sex with Jaimie Deacon that summer before college. She'd known her away around that park in the pitch dark.

She sneaked along the darkened path, weaving around shrubs and bushes, skirting the parking lot. She could see a couple more reporters gathered at the gate, waiting to see if the other one had made contact. Keeping low, Rachel darted to her car. Just before she unlocked the door, she noticed something on her windshield. Tucked under one of the wiper blades was a worn old leather wristband. Pins and needles danced along her hand and up her arm as she reached for it. She recognized it instantly, because it had been hers.

Hannah had been wearing it the day she disappeared.

Six years ago

"What do you mean she wasn't interested? They're always interested."

Hannah shrugged. "I talked to her about makeup. I thought I had her, but then she changed her mind."

They were in the mall parking lot. Alex had spotted twins there that he liked the look of the week before. Now he'd done his research and was ready to take one of them. Nothing long-term, Hannah knew, because they were blond, not red-heads. He only kept the gingers. The rest died quickly. It had been almost two years since the last time he killed someone. She knew, because she had thought about that girl every day since—and the girl before her. And the one before that. She knew she was part of the reason he didn't kill more often. She did what he wanted, said what she was supposed to. She knew how to turn him on and get him off. But every once in a while, pretending wasn't enough anymore, and he needed to live the fantasy again.

"I'm sorry, baby," she said. But she wasn't. She hated sharing him, even if it was temporary. And she hated those new girls for the smile they put on his face, the way they made him happy. She hated them for being young and new, for dying for him so sweetly that he made them into works of art.

So Hannah was glad she'd denied him the pleasure of a kill. Oh, she knew she'd pay the price for it, but she could handle it. Was it her fault the girl had backed out? Maybe. Maybe Hannah tried a little too hard. Maybe she acted just a little too strange. Maybe she let the girl see what more than a decade with a monster had done to her.

Or maybe Cassandra Lennox was just fucking smarter than the others. Maybe she had enough brains to know that a chick approaching her in a mall with promises of fame and fortune was too good to be true.

"I know you're sorry," Alex said. "I'm sure you tried your best."

"I did. I really did. We can grab her later if you want." She sounded convincing even to herself.

He shook his head. "It's too risky. Her friends will remember you." His fingers tightened on the steering wheel. "God, she would have been so perfect. Did you see her cheekbones?"

"You could cut glass with them," she said. And she hated the girl for her beauty as well.

Alex shook his head. "I'm disappointed."

Disappointment meant he'd be in a bad mood, and a bad mood never worked out well for her.

Hannah reached over and put her hand between his legs. "Let's go home. I'll take a cold shower, put an ice cube in my pussy. You can pretend I'm April."

His eyes darkened, the way they always did when she offered to play dead for him. It relied on her being able to remain motionless and unresponsive while he fucked her, but it was easy enough to do. She just disappeared and let Rachel take over. She slipped into her head and fantasized about being her sister, doing something exciting—anything.

He pressed down on the accelerator as his cock strained against her palm. Hannah smiled.

He took her to the apartment. It was closer than Westport, but that wasn't the only reason. His photographs, his trophies were there. And if she was going to play dead, he'd want to photograph her too. She tried not to think about the things he would do to her body before taking his pictures.

Hannah glanced across the street when they pulled into the driveway. She had her wig and sunglasses on and there was little chance of anyone recognizing her. Still, she let herself imagine that just this once, Rachel looked out the window and saw her. Her sister would come racing out of the house with her gun drawn and shoot Alex between the eyes.

Oh, it would hurt to watch him die, but she'd stay long enough to make sure he was dead. Then Rachel would take her away and everything would be like it had been. She could forget the blood on her hands and the things Alex had made her do.

He took her hand and pulled her inside. No one tried

to rescue her. Rachel didn't pull her gun and save her. He made her go upstairs ahead of him. As soon as he unlocked the apartment door, she began removing items of clothing. It wasn't that he liked to watch her strip, but that he liked for her to be naked and vulnerable outside of the bedroom. He liked seeing the lines of her ribs, the delicate curves of her breastbone. Her breasts were smaller now than they had been, but he seemed to like that too. He liked to suck on her hip bones, trace the hollow of her clavicle.

She dropped her pants near the fridge. Her panties in the living room. Alex didn't speak, he just led her to the bathroom and turned on the cold water. She stood under it until her teeth began to chatter. When she opened the curtain, he was there with the ice cube, which she ran under the tap for a few seconds to shrink it. Then she slipped it into her body. She'd learned to breathe through discomfort, ignore pain. Sometimes she even welcomed it.

When she looked in the mirror, she saw a pale, shivering woman with lips that were almost blue. She looked like she needed a cup of tea and several dozen cookies.

Alex didn't allow her to eat sweets.

He took her back out into the living room, laid her facedown on the sofa, arranging her the way April had been. She knew because she'd seen the photos of her body, and Alex had done this to her before. She bit down on a cushion to keep her teeth still. The sound of his zipper seemed to echo inside her head. It was snowing in her mind, she was so cold. Maybe she'd make snow angels.

Or catch snowflakes on her tongue.

His cock shoved the ice deeper inside her. She almost welcomed the searing cold—it was something to focus on, lose herself in—like plunging through a frozen lake and having to push back toward the surface or be lost forever. Trying not to breathe while her lungs burned. Trying not to drown.

Her arm dangled over the side of the couch, her fingers brushing against the floor with every thrust. She knew what he was doing—he was looking out the window, at the house where Rachel lived. He was thinking about how it would hurt Rachel to know that Hannah was so close and she didn't know it. How disgusted Rachel would be by everything he did to her twin.

Her head bumped against the arm of the couch. She said nothing. He shoved a finger in her rectum—she didn't flinch. She got a kink in her hip and she had to pee, but she didn't move, didn't make a sound.

It didn't take him long to come. It never did when they played this game. He thrust hard into her—the ice was melted now. Her entire body was pinpricks of ice and fire as blood began to warm her veins once more.

He pulled out of her, but she still didn't move. He wasn't done. She remained where she was, eyes wide. She blinked only when she knew he wouldn't catch her, and kept her gaze unfocused as he posed and positioned her. The less lifelike she was, the more he liked it. The shutter of his camera clicked rapidly as he moved around, taking in her violated "corpse" at every angle.

Rachel wouldn't humiliate herself this way. She would never let a man treat her like a possession. If anyone was going to dictate her relationships, it would be Rachel herself. Meanwhile, Hannah was a sex slave to a man who liked to have sex with dead bodies. A man who had accidentally killed his first significant girlfriend with an overdose of heroin and hadn't realized she was dead until after he came inside her. Instead of being repulsed by himself, Alex had reveled in his perversion.

"I'm done," he said.

Hannah hesitated a few seconds just to be sure. Then she slowly pushed herself off the sofa. She was still chilled, but her teeth had stopped chattering.

Alex cupped her face in his hands and kissed her softly on the lips. "Thank you," he said. "You are too good to me."

Hannah smiled.

"Go warm up," he told her. "I'll order dinner."

She returned to the bathroom and emptied her bladder. It burned a little. This time when she got into the shower, the water was so hot it stung her skin and turned her bright pink. It felt so good, and it washed away what he'd done to her. The rawness he'd inflicted on her was overpowered by the burn.

Afterward, she moisturized and dressed in a pajama set he had given her for Christmas with a matching robe. She dried her hair and pinned it up on top of her head in a way that showed off the long line of her nape—what Alex said was her sexiest feature.

She walked out into the living room just a few moments before the food arrived. He'd ordered Thai—one of her favorites.

They ate at the table and talked about a play they had seen in New York the week before. And then they took their glasses of wine into the bedroom and watched a movie on Alex's computer. It was something foreign, subtitled and horribly romantic. Whenever they indulged in his fantasies, he was always extra affectionate afterward. He massaged her feet as they watched, and kissed the delicate jut of her ankles whenever something poignant happened on screen.

"Whose girl are you?" he asked softly.

Hannah looked at him from beneath heavy lids. The hot shower, the wine, and the foot rub were lulling her into a state of total relaxation. She didn't even mind the irritation between her legs anymore. It would go away eventually.

"Yours," she murmured. "Always yours." It was what he liked to hear, but it was also true.

He stretched out beside her and she laid her head on his shoulder. He stroked her hair and traced his finger along the curve of her ear.

"My beautiful Galatea," he whispered.

She smiled because she knew the reference. He'd made her read the play *Pygmalion* shortly after taking her. *My Fair Lady* was one of their favorite movies to watch together. He'd taken her to see an off-Broadway production a few years ago. She was his creation, the product of his will, his genius. Everything she was, she owed to him.

Why did she let him own her? Why didn't she try to run, or stab him in the eye with a fork? Why didn't she set him on fire in his sleep, or slit his throat from ear to ear? It wasn't just because what Grace had predicted had come true. It wasn't just because she loved him.

It was because she knew that Alex kept her alive all these years for one simple reason. Hannah was as certain of it as she was that the sun was going to rise the next morning. As she was that Alex would never replace her.

He loved her too.

Wednesday

Jordan had gone through most of Carnegie's photo stash. There were a lot of photographs—mostly glossy eight-by-tens he'd probably printed himself. No reputable company would have printed them for him. They went back a lot of years and contained more women than just those he killed. Obviously he hired models or prostitutes for some of them.

The photos of Hannah Ward were particularly upsetting—not just because of the things he'd had her do but because her face was so familiar. It was hard to remember that it wasn't Rachel.

She'd made copies of the Ward photographs and blacked out Hannah's body in many of them so she could concentrate on the background details and not the degrading image itself.

How could Hannah have survived years of that with her mind intact? Obviously, she knew that other victims had survived such horrors and managed to go on to lead productive lives, but she couldn't imagine it. Just seeing these things had left a mark on her own soul—living it would have destroyed her.

"Why am I not surprised to find you here before anyone else?"

Jordan lifted her head and gave Carl the best smile she could manage, given the task at hand. "Because I have no life, and neither do you. Whatcha got?"

He handed her a file. "COD came back on Grace O'Brien."

"And?"

"Looks like she might have slit her own throat."

Jordan puffed out her cheeks. "Well, that's just one more tragedy to add to this already-steaming pile. Anything else?"

"Yeah. CSU said the stain on the mattress at the apartment was from Hannah Ward, and that it was indicative of a miscarriage."

"Thanks. Let me know if they find anything else."

He wrinkled his nose. "I don't get it. Why keep a blood-soaked mattress? My daughter's cat had kittens on her bed and we bought her a new mattress afterward."

"Because putting it on the curb would attract attention? Hiding it was probably their only option. Or maybe he was waiting for the best time. Hardly matters now."

"Yeah, I guess not. Still." He shuddered. "Alright, that's it for me. Call if you need anything."

Jordan thanked him and went back to her photos. She'd even gotten a magnifying glass to help with the smaller details.

If Hannah hadn't stayed at the one place Rachel could think of that meant something to either of them, then maybe she'd run to a place that meant something to Carnegie. It was kind of twisted, but worth checking out. A place to hide was a place to hide.

There were a set of photos of Hannah taken at someplace rural—remote-looking. Connecticut wasn't a big state, by any stretch, but it did have a lot of countryside. She was going on the assumption that the location was either Connecticut or New York, since those were the two states she knew Carnegie preferred to live in. He might have hunted in a wider area, but if he was taking a girl out to photograph her, it made sense that he'd want to stay fairly close to home.

A search on some of the well-known pornographic websites had turned up several of the images in the collection—further proof that Carnegie supplemented his income by selling his trophies. To appease the needs of his ego, he'd even run the risk of someone figuring him out. Maybe it was the risk that had turned him on. Not like she could ask him. They'd never know how many girls there had been. Never know all their names, or who bought his work. Not unless that server they found in his apartment held records.

So, yeah, she was a little pissed at Hannah for killing Carnegie, because maybe they could have given more families closure if he were still alive. At the same time, there was no one who was going to miss the man.

In the background of one of the photos, she saw the edge of a lake through some trees. In another at the same location she spied the roofs of what looked to be cottages or cabins close together.

A resort, maybe? No, not that upscale. This was rustic. Maybe someone rented cottages on their property, or had a campground.

Then she saw it. In one of the shots, Hannah was on the steps of one of these old cabins or cottages. Now that Jordan got a better look, she realized they looked more like camp housing. There, in the background, nailed crookedly to the side of the door, was a sign. It was slightly out of focus and obscured by the breeze blowing Hannah's hair, but it looked like it said *Timber* something.

"Timber Wolf," she whispered. Immediately she got online and did a search on summer camps with cabins named Timber Wolf.

She got a lot of hits. She added *Connecticut* to the search. There were fewer results, but still too many to wade through. There had to be something else. Someone had to know where this creepy-ass place was located.

She typed in *abandoned* and then clicked on *Images*.

There it was. Someone else—someone not as talented and probably not as psychotic as Alex Carnegie—had posted photos of the same cabin. At least, it looked the same. The sign was still there, tilted to the right. She could see more of it now, more clearly. They weren't trying to hide where they were.

She clicked on the picture and was taken to a site about exploring abandoned places in Connecticut. She'd never been one for traipsing around places people had left behind. It was against the law, for one thing, but more importantly, abandoned places scared the crap out of her. Too many horror movies as a teenager.

The site listed it as a Camp Windygo in Shelton. She had to roll her eyes at the choice of name, but at least now she had a place to start. Maybe it was a stretch, but most of the photos of Hannah seemed to have been taken at that site.

Jordan picked up the phone and called Everly Carnegie-Hall. The older woman answered on the second ring. "Hello?"

"Mrs. Carnegie-Hall, this is Detective Mancusi. I hope I'm not bothering you. I just have a quick question for you. Did Alex ever attend summer camp?"

"Oh, no. He wasn't exactly a social young man, you know. He did, however, work as a camp photographer for several summers. Father thought it would be good for him to earn his own money—teach him the value of a dollar and all that. Personally, I think he also made Alex do it in the hopes that he'd give up wanting to be a photographer. It obviously didn't work."

Jordan tapped her pen against the desk. She really didn't care about their father. "Do you remember the name of the camp?"

"Oh, my. No, I don't think so. I might recognize it if I heard it. I think it began with a 'W'..."

"Windygo?"

"Why, yes! That's it exactly. Foolish name. Makes you think of that cannibal creature."

"Yes, it does. Thanks so much for confirming that for me. I appreciate it."

"My dear Detective Mancusi, if I can do anything at all to even remotely atone for what my brother has done, you only need to call."

As soon as Jordan hung up, she immediately jumped into finding out who—if anyone—owned the property where the former Camp Windygo had been located. She popped the address into the title finder and...

"Son of a bitch," she whispered.

Camp Windygo belonged to Mrs. Hannah Carnegie.

"How long has Hannah been in contact with your mother?"

Rachel shrugged at Trick's question. "I have no idea." She turned to her younger sister. The three of them were having brunch at the house. Trick had cooked—and had handled the reporters still hanging around outside.

Naomi looked caught between pissed and embarrassed. "She called Mom the same night she called here, apparently."

"And you were going to tell me this when?" Rachel demanded.

The younger woman put up her hands. "Hey, I didn't find out about this until last night after Mom flipped out. I left right after you, by the way. Where did you go?"

"For a drive." And she was the one bitching about being lied to. She took a sip of coffee. "Did Mom say anything?"

"She started crying right after you left. Dad had to get her a pill. He's the one who told me that Hannah had called them. Apparently Mom's stopped taking her meds."

That explained some of the crazy. Rachel touched her cheek. It was tender and bruised where her mother had hit her. She took her hand away when she caught both Trick and Naomi watching her. "How many times has she called?"

"Twice."

"But she didn't say where she is?"

"Not that Dad mentioned. Mom might lie about it, but you know he wouldn't. If he knew, he'd tell you."

"He didn't tell me she called," Rachel replied dryly. Naomi blushed, as if either of them had any control over their parents.

"Well, we know she's not driving the Audi anymore," Trick offered. "She sold it to a guy in Middletown."

"Middletown?" Rachel frowned. "Yeah, that's only, what, twenty minutes north of Chester? She went to our old cottage. Left me a note."

"Was the paper from a business or hotel?"

"Not that I could tell. Mancusi has the note from the cottage. All I have is this." She set the leather bracelet on the table.

Trick stared at it. "So, you're turning that over to me, right?"

"Yeah, sure." She understood being taken off the case, but it was frustrating as hell not being able to be part of it. Being expected to share her information but not being given much in return really pissed her off. "She wouldn't get far without a car," Rachel said. "She must have bought one somewhere else."

"The guy who bought the Audi said she'd called for an Uber. He doesn't know where she went, but we've reached out to the company, and hopefully the driver will be in touch soon."

"He won't have anything," she said. "She'll have had him drop her at a mall or a restaurant, then walked somewhere else and called for another car."

"How do you know that?"

"Because it's what I would do." She grabbed a leftover piece of bacon from the plate in the middle of the table. "Then she found some guy selling a car on his front lawn and paid him cash. She's not stupid, Trick. She didn't survive Carnegie for eighteen years by being dumb."

"Yeah? Then what's the endgame?" he asked, his tone sharp. "Why play hide-and-seek when she knows exactly where to find you?"

"Because she wants me to find her. She thinks I've abandoned her and she wants me to prove myself."

"Seriously?"

She nodded. "I think she's been hoping I'd rescue her for years. I let her down." The bacon caught in her throat and she coughed. Took a drink of coffee to wash it down.

Naomi reached over and caught her hand with one of her own. "It's not your fault. We thought she was gone."

Hoped she was gone, but Rachel didn't say that out loud.

"Crouse wants you to know she's friends with one of the top psychiatrists in the country. She's agreed to see Hannah when we find her."

That was code for "when we arrest her." And they had to arrest her. With the press as crazy as it was, there was no way they could do anything but. People were comparing Hannah to Karla Homolka.

Rachel's cell phone rang. It was a number from Hartford. "Hello?"

"Hey, Rach."

"Hannah." She glanced at Naomi and made a writing motion. Her sister immediately jumped up from the table. "How did you get this number?"

"Mom, of course. She gave me Naomi's too. You know I've

never owned a cell phone? Something else I need to figure out, I guess. Alex didn't let me have a lot of freedom. I tried to steal his one night, but he had it password protected. I didn't know you could make emergency calls. Stupid, huh?"

"Not knowing something and stupidity aren't the same thing," Rachel replied as her sister put pen and paper in front of her. She scribbled the name of the shop and handed it to Trick. He got up from the table, pulling his phone out of his pocket.

"Sure, if you say so. You almost found me the other night."

"Why did you run?"

"I've spent enough of my life being photographed. I wasn't going to let some asshole reporter document the first time we see each other in eighteen years. I knew you were going to Mom's, so I went to the park and waited. I hoped you'd show up."

"I know where you are. Why don't you just wait for me and I'll come get you now?"

"Mom said the police think you're helping me."

"They've asked." She ran her finger along the spine of her fork. "Han, can I come get you?"

"That Mancusi seems like a real bitch. She doesn't support you like Dason does."

"She's just doing her job." Out of the corner of her eye she could see Trick in the living room, talking on his phone. "Hannah, please."

"I have something I need to do first. Then I'll call. But I want you to find me, Rach. I need you to. Does that make sense? I need to know you still know me better than anyone. Better than him."

The lump in her throat returned. "I'll find you, I promise."

"Good." There was a breath of silence. "I love you."

"I love you too," Rachel whispered, but she was already gone.

CHAPTER EIGHTEEN

S he knew Morgan Cole was at home because she had called before driving over to West Hartford. She hadn't said anything, just called, and when the girl picked up, she'd disconnected. Then, she took her chai latte and thanked the clerk at the coffee shop for letting her use the phone before walking out into the bright sunshine.

Her next stop was a cell phone store. She really needed to get one if she was going to talk to people, but she didn't want one Mancusi could trace. She bought two "burners," as the clerk called them, and tossed the bag into the back seat of her new car. It wasn't much, but she'd bought it with the cash she'd gotten for the Audi. She had the bag of money she'd taken from the safe in the New York apartment. Alex had a "go bag" stashed there in case the police ever came after him. She didn't need the papers or the passport, but the money was good, and so was the gun. An FBI agent was expected to know how to handle a gun, and *she* knew she was out of practice.

She'd purchased a GPS device from Walmart the day before because the new car didn't have one, so she typed in the Coles' address on the screen and set it where she could see it. She'd driven more in the last few days than she had in her entire life. That was something else she needed to get better at. Alex only ever let her drive when he had to. He hated giving over his control.

She checked her reflection in the mirror and reapplied her lipstick. She wore a vintage peasant blouse with striped wide-legged trousers from Balmain, sandals, and some bangles. Her hair was down, and she'd found the most amazing wide-brimmed hat at Nordstrom. It was the most comfortable she'd been in a long time. She smiled as she slipped on her sunglasses and put the car in gear.

As she drove, she ate the two croissants she'd bought at the coffee shop. She could eat whatever she wanted now. No more cigarettes or laxatives. No more fucking salads with hardly any dressing or skinless chicken breasts.

She was getting ice cream later.

When she pulled into the Coles' driveway, she brushed the crumbs off her blouse, checked to make sure her lipstick was still good, and then grabbed her purse and got out of the car. Morgan answered when she rang the bell.

"Agent Ward?" the girl asked.

She smiled. "Hi, Morgan. I hope this isn't a bad time."

"No." The girl looked confused. "My parents aren't home."

"I actually wanted to talk to you, if that's okay."

"Sure. Come on in." She stood back to let her enter. "I thought you were taken off the case, though."

"I was. I'm not here in any official capacity. Would I be dressed like this if I was?" She laughed.

Morgan raised her brows. "I really like those pants."

"They're fabulous, aren't they? So comfortable. I saw them and fell in love. I had to have them." She put her hand over her heart as if to drive the point home.

A small frown pinched the girl's brow and then was gone. "Yeah, they're awesome. So, what did you want to talk about?"

Reaching up, she removed her sunglasses. "Maybe we could sit down?"

Shaking her head, Morgan stepped backward. "You're not Agent Ward."

Her smile was strained. "Yes, I am."

"No," the girl insisted. "You're her twin. You've been using your left hand, but Agent Ward is right-handed. And I don't think she ever fell in love with a pair of pants in her life."

Her smile melted completely. "Right-handed," she said. "I'm right-handed." But when she looked down, it was her left that was clenched into a fist.

Morgan lurched toward the door, but Hannah was ready for her. She pulled the syringe from her purse, uncapped it, and drove it into the girl's neck, slamming the door closed with her other hand. As Morgan crumpled, she whimpered. Hannah caught her in her arms, guiding her to the polished wood floor.

"It's okay," she said, looking into the girl's scared eyes. "I just want to talk."

It took Jordan three hours to get a warrant to search Camp Windygo. It would have taken longer if Judge Romano hadn't taken the afternoon off for his weekly golf game. He'd been a prosecutor when her father was a cop, so their families knew each other. She knew the warrant wouldn't be a problem—getting him to stop talking so she could get to Shelton was what would take the most time.

"You be careful," he told her when she left. "You have backup?"

She nodded. "I do." She didn't—not really. And she knew taking off to the camp on her own was stupid, so she called Trick.

"I think I found her," she said, leaning against the hood of her car. "Can you meet me?"

"Yeah," he said.

"Don't bring Rachel." She did not want to arrest Hannah in front of her—and she didn't want Rachel doing something stupid out of family loyalty. In this case she'd rather be distrusting than dead.

Trick hesitated. "I'll be there as soon as I can. Send me the address."

"I'm on my way now. See you there." She hung up, texted him details, and started her car.

Shelton wasn't far from Bridgeport. GPS put the camp near the reservoir, which meant she'd be there in twenty minutes or so. Assuming Trick was at Rachel's—and given his demeanor she'd say that's exactly where he was—he'd be about ten or fifteen minutes behind her.

It didn't take long to feel like she was in the middle of nowhere. Spring had officially arrived, and several days of rain the week before, coupled with this week's sun, had led to a growth spurt among the local flora. Trees that had been bare not long ago were now lush, their leaves forming a thick cover that was impossible to see through.

Despite her GPS, she drove past the road to the camp, and had to turn around. The entrance, with its old sign welcoming visitors, was easier to see from the opposite direction. T he rotting wood, now overtaken by vines, was creepy as hell. It looked like someone had been through there recently, and there wasn't any gate or chain blocking the way.

At one time the road had probably been wide enough for two cars to pass, but nature had reclaimed a good portion of it. Maybe another car could squeeze by if neither of them minded having branches slap against their rocker panels and tug at the side-view mirrors. At least it was still a fairly smooth path, not a lot of potholes or obstacles to maneuver around. As she drove farther in, the trees began to give way, widening her field of vision. There was still nothing but green, but at least it wasn't right up in her face.

It was probably half a mile or more back to the camp proper. When Mancusi spotted the main building, she put her foot on the brake and sat in the middle of the road for a moment, considering her options.

Protocol and common sense told her to wait for backup. She wasn't a rookie, and Hannah Ward had already killed someone. Granted, he was a man already injured and sedated, but that didn't make her any less dangerous. Still, instinct demanded she get in there and do her job. Would Trick wait for her to arrive before he went in? Not very likely. And what if he was late? What if Hannah wasn't even there?

"Fuck it," she whispered. She put the car into reverse and backed just out of the line of sight from the main building. She pulled as far off the road as she could to give Trick room to pass, and then set off on foot. She didn't want to alert anyone to her arrival if Hannah was there.

She put on her vest, just to be safe, checked her weapon and her radio, turned her phone to silent, and slipped on her sunglasses before moving toward the camp. She kept as close to the trees as she could and paid close attention to her surroundings.

At the top of the hill sat the main building, gray and somber. The roof sagged and one of the windows had been knocked out. The paint on the Welcome sign had faded and peeled away. Three of the letters had fallen off as well. *Welcome to Wino*, it said. Funny.

She peeked in the broken window, but there was nothing inside the building but old furniture and a couple of bats hanging from the eaves. She kept moving, following the tire tracks in the dirt as they led away from the main area, down a road that was marked with a sign that gave directions to the various cabins. They had names like "Sasquatch" and "Jersey Devil." Someone had tied an old boot to one of the signs—because the place needed some extra weirdness, obviously.

It would be a perfect Halloween haunt. Put a guy in a hockey mask in the middle of it and it would pay for itself.

The tracks continued down the cabin lane, so Jordan followed. The trees were so thick there that the canopy blocked out the sun for the first twenty or thirty feet. It was like twilight, then slowly the run reappeared, dappling the path with a pretty pattern of leaves and branches.

Farther in she crept, turning down the path labeled "Chupacabra." The tracks and crushed weeds led to a small cluster of cabins that weren't quite as run-down as she'd expected. Maybe they'd been sheltered from the elements, but a couple of them were still passably cute. She'd seen people living in worse.

A red Honda was parked in front of one of them. Jordan's heart gave a triumphant thump. It was Hannah, she knew it.

If she was going to wait for Trick, now was the moment to do it, just back down the path and bide the minutes until he showed up, but she'd come this far now and there was no way she could just stand around like an ass. He'd be there soon. She wouldn't make a move on Hannah without him.

If she approached through the trees, she could come around behind the cabin without being seen. It was so quiet, however, that she might have to worry about being heard more than anything else. A broken branch would sound like a gunshot. So she took each step slowly and carefully, until finally, she was at the back of the cabin. She pressed her fingers against the rough wood and raised herself up onto her toes so she could peek in the grimy window.

There was a suitcase on one of the bed frames, and an inflatable mattress on another. A sleeping bag was rolled up on top of it, along with a pillow. There was food on one of the counters—chips and crackers, that sort of thing. And a large bottle of soda.

Movement caught her eye. In the back corner of the open area, a girl was tied to a chair. Was it Morgan Cole? It was hard to tell; the girl's back was to her, and she looked to be gagged. Jordan withdrew her weapon.

She opened the back door, thrusting it open so that it bounced off the back wall. "Police!" she cried. "Hands where I can see them." She stepped inside, every nerve alive, every instinct on high alert. The open design made it easy to quickly ascertain that she and the girl were the only ones in the cabin.

Quickly she moved to Morgan. "It's okay," she said. "I'm going to get you out of here." She had to replace her gun in the holster to untie the dirty rag tied around the girl's head.

"Don't!" Morgan cried as soon as the gag was free.

Behind her a floorboard creaked. Jordan was a second too late in realizing the girl wasn't talking to her. She reached for her gun, but froze as cold, sharp metal touched her throat.

"Drop the gun," a voice commanded. It was a voice a lot like Rachel's, but different.

"Don't do this, Hannah," Jordan said. "Everyone's on your side right now. You don't want to change that."

"You don't know what I want," came the reply. "Now, drop the gun."

The blade bit into her neck just enough that she knew she'd better do what she was told. Trick would be there any minute and he'd take Hannah down. She just had to bide her time. She'd been stupid not to wait for him, but she wasn't the first cop to make that mistake. Rachel had insisted her sister wasn't a villain, that she was just scared. If that was true, she was unpredictable, but all Jordan had to do was keep her, and herself, calm.

She flicked on the safety and dropped her weapon a few feet away.

"Where's my sister?" Hannah asked.

"She's on her way," Jordan lied. "I called her on my way here." If she distracted the other woman, she might be able to get the knife. Hannah was taller than she was, but Jordan had to outweigh her by thirty pounds.

"She never helped me," Hannah informed her. "Rachel didn't know about the apartment, or anything else. It was part of Alex's game."

"I was just doing my job, okay? If the situation were reversed, Rachel would have the same suspicions of me."

"No, she wouldn't."

Something that felt like fishing line brushed against her throat—a gentle tug. Then wet warmth slipped down beneath her vest, soaking her shirt. Morgan Cole started screaming. Confused, Jordan glanced down. Blood. Her own blood.

She tried to speak, but her throat wouldn't work.

She fell to her knees.

Trick began to feel uneasy when he saw Jordan's car and realized it was empty. She wouldn't have gone in without him, would she? Yeah, she would have.

"Jesus," he swore. He drove past her vehicle, up to the main building. When he didn't see any sign of her, he parked. It only took him a few seconds to spot her footprints along with the fresh tire tracks. He set off down the road to the cabins and followed the tracks to Chupacabra.

The door to the first cabin was open, and he could see signs of someone having been inside. He withdrew his gun and moved quickly.

"FBI," he said, his back against the wall near the door.

"Help!" a woman cried. "Please help!"

Trick moved quickly, ready to act if it was a trap. As soon as he entered the cabin, he saw Morgan Cole tied to a chair. She was crying. "Please help her," she said.

Then he saw Mancusi. She was on the floor in a puddle of blood.

"Where's Hannah?" he asked as he holstered his gun.

"I don't know," Morgan replied. "She ran out. Please, you have to help Detective Mancusi."

Trick dropped to his knees beside his colleague. "Jordan?"

She made a gurgling noise. Trick ripped off the button-down he wore—he had a T-shirt beneath—and pressed the wad of cotton to Mancusi's open throat.

"It's alright," he said. "You're going to be fine." But she was already unconscious. He'd called in to let the office know where he was going, and to request backup—just in case. Still, he pressed the shirt against Mancusi's neck with one hand and grabbed his phone with the other. He dialed 911 and gave them his details and location.

He looked down at Mancusi. His heart fell. "I have an officer down," he told them. He let go of the shirt and closed her eyes with his bloody fingertips.

The operator wanted him to stay on the line, but the sound of a car approaching had caught his attention. He put the phone on speaker and set it on the floor. Then he jumped to his feet, pulled his gun, and ran outside.

A red Honda came from the direction opposite to where he'd entered. The woman behind the wheel looked like Rachel, but he knew who she really was. He raised his arms. "Stop!" he shouted, running toward the road. He'd reach it before she reached the turn. He planted his feet, aimed for the front tire, and pulled the trigger. The shot hit the front bumper, but the car didn't stop. He fired again, this time hitting the passenger mirror.

The car sped up and swerved, coming straight for him. He barely dodged out of the way in time. He landed hard on his left shoulder and felt a sharp snap. He cried out in pain and rolled onto his back. Trying to move, his left arm hurt like hell—in fact it didn't want to move at all.

Swearing, he sat up. He brought his right hand up and touched his upper chest. He sucked in a breath when he felt the bump. He'd broken his damn collarbone.

Grabbing his gun, Trick got to his feet and made his way back to the cabin as fast as he could. Morgan was still talking to the 911 operator when he returned. She had to be in shock, the poor kid, because she was far too calm for someone sitting just a few feet away from a dead woman.

"Christ, Mancusi," he whispered. How was he going to tell Rachel that Hannah had not only kidnapped Morgan but that she'd killed Rachel's former partner? There was no redemption for Hannah now. No salvation. She'd killed a fucking cop, and the law didn't go easy on people found guilty of that crime—victim or not.

He found a pair of scissors among the items Hannah had left behind and cut Morgan free of the duct tape that bound her to the chair while giving the operator a description of Hannah's car and what he had seen of the license plate. Then he hung up.

"I have to pee," Morgan said when she stood. She wavered on her feet, so Trick scooped his phone off the floor and offered her his good arm to escort her outside so she could relieve herself. While he waited with his back turned, he heard sirens in the distance. Not that they would be in time to do any good. They'd take him and Morgan to the hospital to be checked out, and Mancusi to the morgue.

Morgan fell against the cabin as she pulled up her jeans. Trick caught her with his good arm, grinding his teeth as the impact jarred his shattered collarbone. Bile rose in the back of his throat. He didn't take her back into the cabin. She didn't need to see Mancusi's body again. Instead, he drew her toward an old picnic table and sat her down on the bench.

Trick glanced down at his phone. Drawing a deep breath, he selected Rachel from his contact list and tapped the screen to dial.

She picked up on the first ring. "Trick?"

Even though it couldn't have been more than an hour since he left her, he closed his eyes at the sound of her voice. "Rachel."

"Are you okay?"

"I need you to meet me at Yale in New Haven," he said. "I'll be there in half an hour, okay?"

"What's happened?"

"I'll tell you when I see you."

"Is it Hannah?"

"No," he said, his gaze going to the cabin. He could see one of Mancusi's arms outstretched on the floor through the open back door. "It's not Hannah."

No amount of wet wipes could get rid of the sticky feeling on Hannah's hands. She wiped down the steering wheel, the door handle—everything. Still, she could feel Mancusi's blood linger.

She needed to stay hidden, but she also needed to get her hands clean before it drove her insane. She pulled into a gas station and parked around back. In the grungy bathroom she washed her hands and wiped at her face. Her blouse was ruined, so she stripped it off and shoved it in the trash. She took a fresh one from the bag she'd taken from the car, yanked off the tags, and pulled it over her head.

She stared at herself in the filmy mirror. The lighting wasn't doing her any favors, but she looked like shit regardless. She twisted her hair up onto her head in a messy bun and dug through her makeup bag for some concealer. Her hands were shaking.

She'd killed someone. On purpose and by herself. Killing Alex hadn't counted—all she'd done was push the plunger of a needle. She'd felt very little for that act, but this...This was different. She'd killed another woman of her own free will. There had been three girls whose lives she contributed to the ending of during her time with Alex, but she'd been able to excuse herself of those crimes because she hadn't been given a choice.

But there was always a choice. She'd put her own survival over theirs, telling herself that Alex would kill them anyway, so why risk her own life trying to stop him?

Rachel would never forgive her for this, even though she was the one Hannah had done it for. Mancusi hadn't been her friend.

Hannah frowned. That wasn't a good enough reason to kill someone. When had she lost respect for human life? When had Alex managed to turn her into a monster? She could just imagine him, in hell or wherever he was, laughing at her because now her transformation was complete. He'd won.

Bracing her hands on either side of the dirty sink, Hannah stared at her face in the mirror. "Rachel," she whispered. "What do I do? Help me."

She couldn't stay there—not that she wanted to. She had to find somewhere to lie low, and she was out of safe places. She couldn't go to her mother—Miriam was more broken than she was. She gathered up her things and left the bathroom, got back in the car, and drove to the nearest drive-through. She got a burger and fries, a milkshake, and chicken nuggets, and devoured all of it while she drove. This change in her diet was hell on her digestive system, but it was so worth it.

She dumped the car in Ansonia at the Metro North station—better not make it a habit—gathered up all she could take with her, including Alex's cash, fresh clothes, and makeup, into her small suitcase, and put on her hat and sunglasses. She walked up to the platform and bought a ticket to New Haven from the machine. Then she waited. She waited for half an hour—long enough to start feeling exposed and vulnerable. Every time she heard sirens, she thought they were coming for her, but they weren't.

When the train finally pulled into the station, she got on and managed to find a seat by herself. She transferred at Stratford. The train to New Haven was busier, and she couldn't sit by herself, but it was easier to get lost in the crowd.

Would the police figure out where she was going? She didn't think so. They wouldn't expect her to put herself in such high risk. She wouldn't do it for long—she just needed to be someplace that felt safe for a little while.

Had she hurt Dason? She only wanted to get away, but she saw him dive off the road when she almost hit him. Rachel would never forgive her for that either. Never forgive her for so much.

She closed her eyes for a bit. She was so tired. She ought to be ashamed of herself for feeling like she could sleep after what she'd just done, but the truth of it was, even though she knew she should feel guilty, even though she could put herself through all of the motions, she didn't really feel much of anything. Honestly? After cutting Mancusi's throat she felt like she'd just ridden the most exciting roller coaster.

Normal people didn't feel that way.

She napped until New Haven. Outside the train station she caught a cab and had it drop her off a block up from her grandparents' house. Then she walked down a side street, took another turn, and cut through a neighbor's property to reach the backyard of the apartment. She had the key to the back door, though it took a moment to find it.

Her suitcase seemed unnaturally heavy as she climbed the stairs, and she tried to lift it as high as she could to avoid making noise. Outside the door with the police tape across it, she stopped and listened. There was no sign of life elsewhere in the building. She slid the key past the tape and then into the lock. A turn of her wrist and the door opened.

When she walked into the apartment, she gasped. The police had practically torn it apart in their search. Alex would have had a stroke if he could see the mess. She took off her sunglasses and turned in a slow circle, taking it all in.

They'd found his photographs. She wasn't surprised. She'd found them once too. She remembered it had almost seemed funny how he made violence look like art. Pain like pleasure. He made degradation seductive somehow. Well, not anymore, he didn't.

She walked through the apartment, seeing it differently now that it had been violated. The shackles were gone from the bed, and so were the sheets and mattress cover. There was the stain from when she'd miscarried. It bothered Alex knowing it was there, but she pitched a fit whenever he tried to get rid of it. It was hers. She couldn't explain why it meant so much to her to keep it, but it had. Even now it meant something. She walked across the floor and placed one hand on top of the faded stain, the other on her still-concave stomach. She wouldn't have wanted the child, but she still felt its loss. One more choice that had been taken from her.

She needed a shower. There was still shampoo and body wash in the bathroom—the expensive stuff Alex liked. She used a scrub that smelled like ginger to clean her body and a rich shampoo to clean her hair. She shaved her legs and under her arms, used her glycolic-acid wash on her face, pumiced her feet. When she was done, she slathered on ginger-scented moisturizer. She felt like herself again.

Hannah froze. This wasn't her. This was Alex's version of her. He was the one who liked ginger so much. He was the one who pressured her to take care of her skin and be as hairless as a little girl. He liked her all soft and sweet smelling. The closet was a reminder of his control as well—all of the clothes on her side were things she never would have imagined herself wearing when she was a teenager. They were things she didn't want to wear now.

She took fresh underwear from the dresser—someone had pawed through the drawer—and put them on. Then, she pulled a long skirt from her suitcase and slipped that on, followed by one of Alex's shirts, knotted at her waist. She left her hair down to air dry and padded to the kitchen. There was an unopened bottle of wine in the fridge, so she opened it and poured herself a large glass. She took it into the living room.

She sat down on the edge of the sofa and looked out the

window at the house where her grandparents used to live. It wasn't fair that she'd never gotten to attend their funerals. Never got to say good-bye. She ought to be living in that house with Rachel and Naomi, or maybe married and in a house of her own. What would life have been like if Grace had never tempted her? If she never reminded Alex of a dead girl he'd become obsessed with?

A tear trickled down Hannah's cheek. She was so tired and so sorry for all of it. She just wanted it to end.

She pulled out her burner phone.

By the time Rachel got to the hospital, Trick's arm was in a sling and he'd been checked for a concussion. She found him sitting on a bed in the emergency room waiting for painkillers to kick in.

As soon as she saw him, she knew something was terribly wrong. It was in his eyes.

"Hey," he said.

He was bruised and dirty and obviously in pain. At that moment she didn't care who might see or what the ramifications were. She went to his side and put her palm against the side of his face, and then she kissed him.

"Are you okay?" she asked, pressing her forehead to his.

His right hand came up and stroked her back. "Yeah."

"Is Hannah dead?" She held her breath.

"Not Hannah."

Straightening, Rachel met his dark gaze. Her stomach fell, and the world seemed to shift with it. "Jordan?"

He nodded.

She pressed a hand to her mouth. It couldn't be true. "How?"

Trick took her hand. His thumb stroked her fingers, and he seemed to have a hard time looking her in the eye. "Hannah cut her throat."

Rachel made a noise. She didn't know what kind of noise it was. "No." She tried to pull her hand away.

He held tight. "Morgan Cole was there. She saw it."

She shook her head. "Morgan Cole?"

"Hannah abducted her. She pretended to be you."

"Oh my God." The urge to curl into herself was so strong she had to hold on to the bed to keep from sinking to the floor. "Jordan. My God."

"Hey," Trick said. "Hey, look at me." She did. "It's going to be okay."

How could he say that? Jordan was dead, and her sister had done it. There was no saving Hannah now. "Where's my sister?"

"She got away." He gestured to his sling. "That's how I got this. She almost ran me over."

Tears burned her eyes, and she knew if she let them out, she wouldn't be able to stop. She wanted to let them out, though. Wanted to let all of it out, but she knew she couldn't. Not yet.

"Where was she?"

"At an abandoned summer camp Carnegie used to work at. He took photos of her and some of his other victims there."

She nodded. "And Morgan? Why did she take her?"

"Morgan says Hannah told her she just wanted to talk. She wanted to explain to her why she tried to hurt Sydney—that she'd been trying to save her. And then she told Morgan all the things she would need to do to help Sydney get over what Carnegie did to her."

"How did she go from that to killing Jordan?"

Trick's brow furrowed. "I don't know."

But he did. She'd known him long enough to know when he was holding back. "She did it because of me, didn't she? Because I told her the police thought I was involved."

"I don't know."

He was lying—she was sure of it. She wanted to blame herself, but Jesus, wasn't it time someone blamed Hannah? Rachel nodded. "Do you need anything?"

"Just you. Sit with me. Are you okay?"

Rachel sat on the edge of his bed. Her fingers felt cold in his. "I don't know what I am, but I'm not going to lose it, if that's what you're wondering."

"No one would blame you if you freaked out. I'm pretty rattled."

Frowning, Rachel swallowed against the churning in her stomach. "Was Jordan still alive when you got there?"

"Yeah," he said with a jerky nod of his head. "Just barely. She didn't linger long."

"That's good, I guess. Someone will have to call her father."

"I think her sergeant has already taken care of it."

"Of course."

They sat there in silence for a few seconds, both unsure of

what to say. When Rachel's phone rang, they looked at each other.

"It's her," Rachel whispered. "I know it."

Trick's jaw clenched. "Better answer it, then."

She brought the phone to her ear. "Hannah?"

"I'm sorry, Sissy."

Rachel closed her eyes, fighting tears again. "That's really not good enough. You killed my friend."

"I know you thought of her that way, but she wasn't your friend."

"That's not a reason to kill her."

"It was to me."

"Jesus Christ, Hannah. This has gone on long enough. Turn yourself in."

"Why didn't you look for me, Rach? Even now, you're somewhere else when you could be looking for me. Why are you so angry that I'm alive?"

Rachel stood up, turning her back to Trick. "Because I don't want you to be alive! I haven't wanted that for years. I wanted you to be dead. I didn't want him to keep you, deform you. I would rather have found your bones than this, Han. What he's done to you..." She had to stop, because her throat was tight with tears, and then that made her think of Jordan, gasping for breath through a severed trachea. Tears and rage weren't a good combination.

"Oh," her sister said. "I understand."

"No, you don't. I love you. I would do anything to take back what happened to you. I'd even go back in time and make the stupid trip myself. I'd change it if I could, but I can't. And you have to stop. You can't just kill people because you want to."

"Alex did."

"Alex was a monster."

"And so am I," Hannah told her. "He was my Pygmalion. I was his Eliza Doolittle and he's my Henry Higgins."

Rachel clenched her left hand into a fist as the tingles started. It wasn't her heart or stress causing them—it was the fucking twin bond. The tingles were her awareness of Hannah. They had to be. That was how she'd known her sister was still alive—stupid tremors. Of all the ways they could have been connected, that had to be the most useless.

"He wasn't your Henry Higgins."

"My Dr. Frankenstein." Hannah laughed. Rachel didn't.

"I'm not coming for you, Han. I can't. You have to turn yourself in."

"If I died, all your problems would go away."

"That's not true. Don't talk like that." Rachel rubbed her forehead. "I love you. I just . . . I just can't help you. Do you understand?"

"Yeah. I do. And I love you too. Hey, remember when we used to play hide-and-seek? You always found me then."

"You kept hiding in the same places."

Soft laughter. "I thought you were good at finding me. Turns out I was just predictable. Not anymore, I guess. Goodbye, Rach."

"Hannah—"

"And I'm not sorry about Jordan. Not really." She hung up.

Rachel stared at her phone. A strange feeling of peace washed over her, as though she knew exactly what she had to do.

Only, she had no idea what she was going to do.

CHAPTER NINETEEN

Since Trick didn't have a concussion, the hospital released him into Rachel's care. She took him to the drugstore to fill his prescription, then drove him home and made him dinner while he relaxed on the couch.

"You don't need to fuss over me," he told her, his voice slightly thick from the pain meds they'd given him. "I can take care of myself."

"It's just an omelet," she said. "Relax." And it gave her something to occupy her mind so she didn't think about her sister.

"You didn't make one for yourself?" he asked when she put the plate on the coffee table in front of him.

"Nah. Not hungry. Hey, are you going to be alright if I leave?"

He looked slightly hurt, but he shook his head. "I'll be fine."

Guilt tugged at her, but she pushed it away. The farther away she was from him, the safer he was. "I'm sorry. I just...I need a little time to process all of this."

"You don't have to apologize. I get it." He reached up and caught her hand in his. "I'm here if you need me."

She kissed the top of his head. "I don't deserve you."

"I am exceptional," he joked, making her smile despite the heavy feeling in her chest.

She let herself out and made the short drive home. It was getting dark now, the day having been eaten away by pain and loss and shock.

She'd called her father and told him what Hannah had done. Better to hear it from her than on the news. He was as horrified as she was. Rachel had hung up when she heard her mother start screaming. It was too close to what she wanted to do, but couldn't let herself. She'd called Naomi too, who offered to come home from the overnight trip she and her girlfriend had taken. Rachel told her to stay and have a good time. It would be nice to have the house all to herself. She could cry as much as she wanted and no one would be bothered by it.

And she intended to cry. She needed to cry.

In the house, she turned on the lights and kicked off her shoes. She put her badge and gun away, and cracked her neck on the way to the kitchen. It was always easier to bawl after a glass or two of wine, so she poured a glass and took it into the living room. She stood at the window that looked out onto the street and stared over at the building where Hannah had spent so many nights, unknown to her. The bottom- and top-floor apartments had lights on, but the middle floor was completely dark.

Was her sister there? Sitting in the darkness, watching her?

"Come and get me," she whispered. "I've been chasing you for eighteen fucking years. It's your turn."

The detail Mancusi had put on her house was gone. Did

they blame her for Jordan's death? She might, if she were one of them. As it was, she did feel guilty, but only because some stupid part of her refused to give up responsibility for Hannah, the sister who'd been gone longer than she'd been home. The sister who had her own mind and obviously made her own fucked-up decisions. So how was Rachel responsible for that?

What had Jordan been thinking going after Hannah by herself? She'd probably thought Hannah wasn't dangerous. Rachel had made the same mistake. She'd assumed that there was something of her sister left in Hannah, and she'd been wrong. Her Hannah wouldn't kidnap someone to talk to them, and she certainly wouldn't have been able to cut someone's throat. No, that was all "Anne."

Poor Jordan. She'd have to see if there was going to be a memorial service for her.

She was just about to turn away from the window when she caught a reflection behind her in the glass. Her heart froze when she saw who it was.

"Hi, Sissy," Hannah said.

Rachel didn't ask her how she got in. As children they'd known every way to sneak into that house—which windows to use, how to get in through the basement. There was no need to ask. In fact, Rachel didn't say anything, she just walked toward her, tears running down her face.

Hannah began to cry as well. She opened her arms and Rachel opened hers. For the first time in eighteen years, Hannah hugged her sister. She was whole again. Rachel held her tight.

"You're so thin," she whispered.

Hannah laughed. "I'm working on it." She ran her hands over her sister's hair, down her shoulders and back. She might be thin, but Rachel had a lot of muscle. Her sister was strong—capable. Hannah wanted to be that. She *would* be that.

"It's so good to see you," she said, wiping at her eyes. She pulled back and looked at Rachel's face, lifting her fingers to the slight welt left by their mother's hand. "Does it hurt?" she asked when her sister winced.

Rachel shrugged. "A little. It's like a sunburn." She hugged Hannah again. "Honey, we have to call the police and let them know you're here."

Hannah nodded. "In a minute. Can we just sit for a bit? I want to talk to you before we're pulled apart again."

Her sister hesitated, but then took her hand and led her to the couch.

"You've changed the place," Hannah commented. "Got rid of the wallpaper."

"I'm not a cabbage-rose kind of person."

Hannah chuckled. "You've never fallen in love with a pair of pants either."

Rachel blinked. "No, I don't think so. You haven't changed." She pointed at Hannah's long, flowy skirt.

"For years he told me what to wear. I'd forgotten how comfortable these are. Don't look at me like that."

"Like what?"

"Like you're going to cry." She blinked back tears of her own. "He's dead and I'm not. The rest is history."

Rachel took both of Hannah's hands in her own and held them on her knees. "I'm going to make sure you have whatever therapy you need—whatever it takes for you to get beyond what he did to you."

"Okay," Hannah agreed. "I have to ask, how's Dason? I need you to know I never meant to hurt him."

"He's fine. A broken collarbone."

"And Morgan?"

"She's in shock." Rachel looked her in the eye. "You killed Jordan in front of her."

"Yeah, seeing someone die for the first time *is* difficult," Hannah admitted. Her sister made a choked sound. "I'm sorry, that's not a normal response, is it? I've seen people die, Rachel. And I've seen photographs of as many corpses as you have, probably, if not more. For more than half my life I lived with a man who saw death as a means to an end. I think...I think that changed me."

Sympathy shone in Rachel's gaze. Hannah didn't like it. It made her uneasy. "It would change anyone, Han."

"Killing Alex set me free." She meant it. For all the moving around and stress of the last few days, she felt like a butterfly emerging from its cocoon. She needed to flex her wings and fly.

"He'll never hurt you again," Rachel said.

"No one will," Hannah added. "No one will ever hurt either of us."

"I can't believe you were across the street sometimes and I never saw you."

"Alex thought it was a great joke." Hannah couldn't keep the bitterness from her voice. "He'd tease me and say that you and I were sorry examples of the twin connection. I guess we were."

"Any time I thought I felt something, I told myself it wasn't real. I thought you were dead."

"Hoped I was dead," Hannah reminded her. "I'm not sure how I feel about that."

"The idea of him keeping you alive, torturing you, wasn't something I could handle."

Hannah stared at her. All these years thinking Rachel was the stronger of the two of them, and now she realized she was wrong. *She* was the strong one. Rachel wouldn't have survived under Alex's hand. She wouldn't have been able to adapt and change.

"They'll put me in prison, won't they?" she asked.

"I don't know," her sister answered. "I think they'll want to put you in a hospital for a while first."

"I don't want to be a prisoner again, Rach."

Warm fingers squeezed hers. "I know, honey. I don't want you to be one either, but you killed a cop. The law is going to want you to answer for that."

Alex never answered for any of his crimes, Hannah thought. But then, that was her fault too. He'd be going to jail too if she hadn't killed him. She frowned as she looked down at their joined hands. Hers looked like claws next to Rachel's. She pulled them away, curling them into fists in her lap.

"I know what I am," she confessed. "I was with Alex longer than I was with you. I changed in order to survive. Locking me in a box won't make me sorry for what I've done, because I'm not sorry. I'm not…anything. I didn't escape one prison to go to another. I won't."

"What are you going to do?" Rachel asked. "Spend the rest of your life running? That's no way to live either."

"No," Hannah said, shaking her head. "I want my life back."

"That's not possible. You know that."

"Then I want the life I should have had."

"And you will. But first we have to call the police."

"There's only one way to fix this," Hannah told her. "Only one way I can be free. I have to die." And then she reached underneath the couch cushion and shoved the knife she'd hidden there between Rachel's ribs. "It's your turn to be me."

Oh, sweet Jesus, it hurt.

Rachel looked down in shock at the knife hilt sticking out of the left side of her chest. She was pretty sure it had punctured her lung.

But not her heart, which was the intended target.

Her mind screamed for her to pull it out, but a little voice told her not to. The last thing she needed was a sucking chest wound.

She looked at her sister. "Why?" she rasped.

Hannah didn't even look worried or regretful. She looked curious. Impatient, maybe. Carnegie had completely destroyed the person she was, leaving behind a shell that was…what? Criminally insane? A sociopath?

"Whenever he hurt me, I pretended I was you," Hannah told her. "I was good at pretending to be you, remember?"

Rachel nodded. Sweat beaded on her brow as she fumbled for her phone. She had set it up a long time ago to be voice activated.

"Call Trick," she commanded.

Her twin shook her head. "Not yet. I'll call him when you're dead, Hannah."

Rachel gritted her teeth against the pain as she drew a breath. "You're not me and he'll know it."

"No, he won't. I've been practicing using my right hand more, and I'll wear loose clothes until I put on some weight. I will be you, and then I won't have to be me anymore. Hannah will be dead and I won't have to live with what I've done."

Rachel stared at her. "That's fucking crazy and you know it."

"I deserve a life!" Hannah shouted, jumping up from the couch. "My life was taken from me because of you—you! You owe me!"

"Your life was taken because Alex Carnegie was a predator and he chose you."

Hannah started laughing. "He didn't choose me. He chose *you*. He'd been watching you. He knew about the school trip. He thought he was sending Grace after you. Once he realized the truth, he decided to keep me anyway."

Ice crept up the back of Rachel's neck into her brain. Oh, God, it was true. No, it didn't matter which one of them he'd stalked. "I wouldn't have gone with him," Rachel told her. "I would have been too suspicious."

"I know." Her sister gave her an apprehensive look. "How are you still alive, Hannah?"

Rolling her eyes, Rachel pushed herself up into a sitting position. She put her left hand to the entry point of the knife, in an effort to keep it from moving too much. "I'm alive because you missed my heart."

"That's impossible. I looked it up."

Rachel laughed. It turned into a gasp for air that felt like a thousand knives in the chest instead of just one. "My heart's in the opposite spot."

Hannah frowned. "You're lying."

Lifting her left arm, Rachel offered her the Medic Alert bracelet. "Look."

Her sister came closer, taking her arm in her hand and turning it so she could see the wording on the back of the bracelet. *Situs Inversus.*

"That's me."

"Then I have to try again." Just as Hannah reached for the knife, Rachel wrapped her fingers around her sister's wrist and lurched forward, yanking up her pant leg and grabbing the small pistol she kept holstered there. She was licensed to carry concealed, and both she and every agent she knew made sure they had a backup piece. She didn't even think, she clicked the safety off and pulled the trigger.

Hannah fell.

By the time Trick arrived at Rachel's, he could hear sirens approaching. He ran up the front steps and tried the door—locked. Without hesitation, he pulled out his gun and used it to smash one of the small glass panels at the side. Then he reached in between the shards of broken glass and turned the dead bolt.

Once he was inside, he tapped the keypad for the alarm. "Rachel?"

"In here," she called in a faint voice.

She was in the living room, on the sofa, a knife sticking out of her chest and a pistol in her hand. Her sister was on the floor, clutching at her left shoulder and crying.

"Don't freak out," Rachel said. "I have fucked-up organs, remember?"

He did. Still, that didn't stop him from going to his knees on the floor beside the sofa. "Don't speak. Don't move. The ambulance is on its way. I didn't know what was going on when you called, and then I heard the two of you. I didn't think I'd get here in time."

She smiled at him. "Even with a broken collarbone you're still saving my ass."

"Shh." He glanced over his shoulder at Hannah. She hadn't moved, but she didn't really seem to notice that he was there. "You're going to be okay," he said to Rachel.

She nodded, then set down her pistol and reached for his hand. He let her take his left, the one in the sling. He wasn't about to give up his gun in case Hannah made a move.

Not even a minute later, paramedics and police came through the door. Trick didn't care what they did with Hannah—she didn't even try to fight them—his focus was on Rachel.

"It's okay," she told Hannah as paramedics looked after both of them. "I've got you." She reached out and took her sister's hand, only to be separated when they were carried outside.

He told them about her medical condition, which one of the EMTs had actually seen before.

"Be careful with her," he told them as they lifted her onto the stretcher.

"She's in good hands, man," the EMT assured him. "You riding with us?"

He'd shoot anyone who tried to stop him.

In the ambulance he called Naomi and told her to meet them at the hospital. He also asked her to inform her parents. But if Rachel's mother showed up acting like a crazy bitch, he'd lock her in a closet.

He held Rachel's hand all the way to the hospital. She just kept looking at him as though she'd never seen him before, her features partially obscured by an oxygen mask.

"When you're better, we're going on a date," he told her. "A real one. No more sneaking around. Got it?"

He thought maybe she smiled, but he couldn't be sure. She nodded.

The EMT looked at him. "Aren't you guys already together? I mean, you seem like you're pretty into her."

"I am," Trick replied, meeting Rachel's gaze. "I am pretty into her. And she's into me—she's just a little slow."

Two weeks later

June had arrived with a vengeance, bringing with it hot, humid weather that made air-conditioning a necessity. Rachel was at home on her new sofa watching a movie on Netflix. She was still sore, but healing well, according to her surgeon. She was also very fortunate that her organs weren't where they ought to be, otherwise she'd be dead. Score one for being a freak.

She still couldn't believe Hannah had planned to take her place—take her life. Would she have gotten away with it? Probably not. It wouldn't be as easy as it had been when they were kids. She couldn't fake being an agent—or sane.

"Are you ready to go?" Naomi asked as she entered the room.

Rachel hit the Off button on the remote and rose to her feet. The new sofa was nice—really big and overstuffed. Her favorite thing lately had been just lying on it and napping or reading, or vegging out. Thinking about her future. Cleaning out the boxes in her head. It was time to throw that stuff out, and she had a great new therapist helping her do just that. They had family-therapy sessions as well, which had been her father's idea. Rachel wasn't holding her breath waiting to have a relationship with her mother, but she supposed Miriam deserved points for trying.

Naomi handed Rachel her sunglasses and purse. "I'm driving."

Rachel shrugged, wincing slightly at the pull in her chest. "I have no objection to being chauffeured." Plus, she'd overdone it with physical activity the day before and had to take a Perc that morning. She shouldn't be operating anything larger than a toaster.

"Mr. Mancusi called earlier," Naomi told her as they left the house. The glass pane Trick had broken to save her had been replaced and new locks installed—just to be safe. The back door had been done too.

"I spoke to him. I'm taking him to lunch next week. He's still pretty broken up."

"Jesus." Naomi sighed. "I can't imagine what that's like."

Rachel glanced at her as she fastened her seatbelt. "Yes, you can. You lived with it. And now they have to go through it all over again."

"At least Mom is back on her meds."

"Yeah," was all Rachel could bring herself to say on the topic.

Naomi put the car in gear and they pulled out onto the street.

The hospital where Hannah was being kept was a facility for dangerous mentally ill people. Rachel hated going to it, but she needed to see her sister. She had gone at least once a week, sometimes more, but it was painful and she didn't stay long. Saturday was family day, so they all met up for a visit there in the afternoon.

It was particularly weird for Rachel because...well, because she couldn't be herself when they were there.

She and Naomi met with her parents in the lobby, and together the four of them went through security and put their belongings in lockers. They met with one of the doctors on duty first to be given an update on Hannah's condition.

"She's doing well," Dr. Drake told them with a hopeful smile. She was a blond woman in her fifties with a gentle voice and pale green eyes. "No altercations with other clients. She's always very eager to help others, and ready to participate in group sessions. She's become something of a den mother to some of the other women, who have come from rather tragic backgrounds."

"Is she still insisting that she's me?" Rachel asked. Her mother gave her a sharp look, which she ignored.

Dr. Drake looked uncomfortable. "Yes, but I have every confidence that will stop once she's come to terms with what's she's been through."

Rachel didn't have that same confidence, but then she didn't need to, she supposed.

After the meeting they were taken into one of the private family rooms. A few minutes later an orderly brought Hannah—"Rachel"—in to join them.

She looked good. She'd gained weight and her skin and eyes were bright. She was still favoring her left arm, but other than that, she looked healthy. She hugged their parents and Naomi, and then turned to Rachel. "Haha," she said, tears filling her eyes.

Rachel didn't stiffen when her sister hugged her, which she supposed was an improvement. The first few times, she actually expected Hannah to attack her or do something violent. She hadn't, but that was probably only because she wasn't Hannah anymore.

The worst part about the visits was that the whole family went along with the delusion—at the advice of the doctors on staff. They agreed it was what was best for Hannah's recovery, and Rachel supposed she couldn't deny her sister that. But that meant she had to sit through the visit pretending that she was the one who had killed people.

"How are you?" Hannah asked. "Have they set a date for your trial?"

"No," Rachel replied. "Not yet. And I'm good, Rach. How are you?"

"Oh, you know," she said with an airy wave of her hand. "Hanging in there. I can't wait until this undercover job is over and I can go home."

That's what the fantasy was—that she was undercover in the hospital and only pretending to be ill. She had the whole story worked out the first time Rachel came to visit.

During family time Rachel let the others do most of the talking. She was content to sit and watch her twin interact with the family she'd been denied for so many years. Regardless of the circumstances, it was good to have her back. Rachel had missed her like a limb, and even though there was nerve damage...well, at least the limb still worked.

About an hour of listening to Hannah pretending to be her—and their mother indulging her—was about all Rachel could take. Her mother was far kinder to Hannah's version of her than she'd been in a long time to Rachel herself. It was hard to witness.

"I'm sorry," she said to Hannah. "I have to go."

"Do you have an appointment?"

She smiled at her. "I have a date."

Hannah's eyes grew wide. "With Trick? I'm so glad the two of you have gotten together." In Hannah's version of events she'd broken up with Trick because of their professional relationship, leaving him open to date her twin.

"Thanks," Rachel said. What else could she say? There was no telling her sister the world she had created wasn't true—not when the delusion had helped her survive hell for eighteen years.

"Give me a hug," Hannah commanded. "Will I see you again this week?"

"Yeah. I'll come by Wednesday maybe. We'll watch that show you like together."

And that was all it took to make her sister's eyes light up. Hannah grabbed her in a fierce hug that hurt her healing chest—and had to hurt Hannah's shoulder.

"I'm so happy to have you back," Hannah whispered against her ear. "I never want to lose you again."

"You won't," Rachel assured her. "No matter what happens, you'll never lose me. Ever." And she meant it. She didn't like the game, but she'd play it for as long as she had to. She'd do whatever she had to. If Hannah wanted to be the queen of England, Rachel would go along with it. Having her back broken was better than not having her at all.

She said good-bye to the others—it was still strained with her mother—and left the hospital. Trick was waiting for her out front when she stepped outside. She climbed into his SUV and leaned into the kiss he immediately offered.

"How'd it go?" he asked.

"The usual," she said. "She's still me and I'm still her and it's weird and awful, but good too. As long as I don't think about her being Mancusi's killer, or that she tried to kill me, I can be okay. It's when I forget that she's ill and think of her as a criminal that I get in trouble."

Trick squeezed her hand. "You'll get through it."

"Yeah, we will. So where are we going?"

"You mean on our date?" he asked with a teasing grin.

Rachel rolled her eyes. "It's not like it's our first date, you know."

"Actually, it is. Officially we've never gone on a date before."

"If you say so." She kept her tone casual, but her heart was pounding. She was nervous. Nervous about going on a date with a man she'd already seen naked.

"I'm not going to tell you where we're going," he said, steering with his right hand—his left was still in a sling. "Does that scare you? Not knowing what I've got planned?"

She smiled at him and leaned back against the seat. "No," she replied honestly. And it didn't. She wasn't afraid of anything with him. So many terrible things had already happened that there wasn't anything to be afraid of anymore.

"Let's go," she said.

He flashed her a smile and they drove away. Rachel glanced back at the hospital as they pulled out onto the main road.

Her left arm tingled. And she smiled.

Ready or not...

ACKNOWLEDGMENTS

I need to thank a couple of people for helping make this book happen. First of all, a big thanks to Lindsey Hall for taking a chance on the story, and to Bradley Englert for making it better. Thank you to Hollie Overton for talking to me about being a twin and for being such an all-around sweetheart. I'm so glad we got to spend Thrillerfest together!

Also thank you to Detective Tanya Compagnone for answering my questions about police procedure. Any mistakes are mine alone.

Love and hugs to my husband, Steve, who put up with me while I tried to work out the plot, and who didn't complain about all the takeout! I couldn't do this without you.

And finally, thanks to the readers out there who have taken the time to review my books and let me know you've enjoyed them (or haven't!). Your feedback is invaluable, as is your support.

MEET THE AUTHOR

Photo Credit: Kathryn Smith

As a child KATE KESSLER seemed to have a knack for finding trouble, and for it finding her. Kate now prefers to write about trouble rather than cause it, and spends her days writing about why people do the things they do. She lives in New England with her husband.

if you enjoyed
DEAD RINGER
look out for
IT TAKES ONE
by
Kate Kessler

"Deliciously twisted... Kate Kessler's positively riveting
It Takes One *boasts a knockout concept and a thoroughly
unique and exciting protagonist, a savvy criminal psychologist
with murderous skeletons in her own closet."*
—Sara Blaedel, #1 internationally bestselling author

*Criminal psychologist Audrey Harte is returning home after
seven years.
Less than twenty-four hours later, her best friend is murdered.
Now Audrey is both the prime suspect and the only person who
can solve the case...*

It Takes One *is the opening to a thriller series where a
criminal psychologist uses her own dark past to help law
enforcement catch dangerous killers.*

CHAPTER ONE

Would you kill for someone you love?"

Audrey Harte went still under the hot studio lights. Sweat licked her hairline with an icy, oily tongue. "Excuse me?"

Miranda Mason, host of *When Kids Kill*, didn't seem to notice Audrey's discomfort. The attractive blonde—whose heavy makeup was starting to cake in the lines around her eyes—leaned forward over her thin legs, which were so tightly crossed she could have wound her foot around the opposite calf. She wore pantyhose. Who wore pantyhose anymore? Especially in Los Angeles in late June? "It's something most of us have said we'd do, isn't it?"

"Sure," Audrey replied, the word forcing its way out of her dry mouth. "I think we as humans like to believe that we're capable of almost anything to protect our loved ones." Did she sound defensive? She felt defensive.

A practiced smile tilted the blonde's sharply defined red lips. "Only most of us are never faced with the decision."

"No." That chilly damp crept down Audrey's neck. *Don't squirm.* "Most of us are not."

Miranda wore her "I'm a serious journalist, damn it" expression. The crew called it her Oprah face. "But David Solomon was. He made his decision with terrible violence that left two boys dead and one severely wounded."

It was almost as though the world, which had gone slightly askew, suddenly clicked into place. They were talking about a case—a rather famous and recent one that occurred in L.A. County. Her mentor, Angeline, had testified for the defense.

It's not always about you, she reminded herself. "David Solomon believed his boyfriend's life was in danger, as well as his own. The boys had been victims of constant, and often extreme, bullying at school. We know that Adam Sanchez had suffered broken ribs and a broken nose, and David himself had to be hospitalized after a similar attack."

Miranda frowned compassionately—as much as anyone with a brow paralyzed by botulism could. "Did the school take any sort of action against the students bullying the boys?"

Audrey shook her head. She was on the edge of her groove now. Talking about the kids—especially the ones driven to protect themselves when no one else would—was the one place she felt totally confident.

"A teacher suggested that the attacks would end if the boys refrained from provoking the bullies with their homosexuality." *Asshole.* "The principal stated that there would hardly be any students left in the school if she suspended everyone who picked on someone else." *Cow.*

"Why didn't the boys leave the school?"

Why did people always ask those questions? Why didn't they run? Why didn't they tell someone? Why didn't they just curl into a ball and die?

"These boys had been raised to believe that you didn't run away from your problems. You faced them. You fought."

"David Solomon did more than fight."

Audrey stiffened at the vaguely patronizing, coy tone that seemed synonymous with all tabloid television. She hadn't signed on to do the show just to sit there and let some Barbara Walters wannabe mock what these kids had been through.

Maybe she should thank Miranda for reminding her of why she'd dedicated so much of her life to earning the "doctor" in front of her name.

"David Solomon felt he had been let down by his school, his community, and the law." Audrey kept her tone carefully neutral. "He believed he was the only one who would protect himself and Adam." What she didn't add was that David Solomon had been right. No one else in their community had stood up for them.

Miranda's expression turned pained. She was about to deliver a line steeped in gravitas. "And now two boys are dead and David Solomon has been sentenced to twenty years in prison."

"A sentence he says is worth it, knowing Adam is safe." David Solomon wasn't going to serve the full twenty. He'd be out before that, provided someone didn't turn around and kill him in prison.

Miranda shot her an arch look for trying to steal the last word, and then turned to the camera and began spouting her usual dramatic babble that she used in every show about senseless tragedies, good kids gone bad, and lives irreparably altered.

This was the tenth episode of the second season of *When Kids Kill*. Audrey was the resident criminal psychologist— only because she was friends with the producer's sister and owed her a couple of favors. Big favors. Normally, Audrey avoided the spotlight, but the extra money from the show paid her credit card bills. And it upped her professional profile, which helped sell her boss's books and seminars.

She'd studied criminal psychology with the intention of helping kids. In between research and writing papers, she'd started assisting her mentor with work on criminal cases, which led to more research and more papers, and a fair amount of time talking to kids who, more often than not, didn't want her help. She never gave up, which was odd, because she considered herself a champion giver-upper.

Thirty minutes later, the interview was over. Miranda had had to do some extra takes when she felt her questions "lacked the proper gravity," which Audrey took to mean drama. Audrey dragged her heels getting out of the chair. It was already late morning and she had to get going.

"Don't you have a flight to catch?" Grant, the producer, asked. He was a couple of years older than her, with long hipster sideburns and rockabilly hair. His sister, Carrie, was Audrey's best friend.

Only friend.

"Yeah," she replied, pulling the black elastic from her wrist and wrapping it around her hair. She wrestled the hairspray-stiff strands into submission. "I'm going home for a few days."

His brow lifted. "You don't seem too happy about it."

She slipped her purse over her shoulder with a shrug. "Family."

Grant chuckled. "Say no more. Thanks for working around the schedule. Carrie's been harping on me to be more social. Dinner when you get back?"

"Sounds good." There was no more use in stalling. If she missed her flight, she'd only have to book another. There wasn't any getting out of the trip. Audrey gathered up her luggage and wheeled the suitcase toward the exit.

"See you later, Miranda," she said as she passed the older woman, who was looking at herself in the mirror of a compact, tissuing some of the heavy makeup off her face. Audrey would take hers off at the airport. She hated falling asleep on planes and waking up with raccoon eyes.

"See ya, Audrey. Oh, hey"—she peered around the compact—"you never answered my question."

Audrey frowned. "I'm pretty sure I answered them all."

Miranda smiled, blue eyes twinkling. "Would you kill for someone you love?"

"Of course not." Huh. That came out smoother than it should have.

Miranda looked contemplative, but then, too much plastic surgery could do that. "I'd like to think I would, but I doubt I could."

"Hopefully you'll never have to find out. Have a good day, Miranda."

The woman replied, but Audrey didn't quite make out the words—she was too busy thinking about that question.

No, she wouldn't kill for someone she loved.

Not again.

It was an eight-and-a-half-hour flight from L.A. to Bangor, with a stopover in Philly. It was an additional two hours and change from Bangor International to Audrey's hometown of Edgeport, on the southeast shore of Maine. She was still fifteen minutes away, driving as fast as she dared on the barren and dark 1A, when her cell phone rang.

It was her mother.

Audrey adjusted her earpiece before answering. She preferred to have both hands on the wheel in case wildlife decided to leap in front of her rented Mini Cooper. It was dark as hell this far out in the middle of nowhere; the streetlights did little more than punch pinpricks in the night, which made it next to impossible to spot wildlife before you were practically on top of it. The little car would not survive an encounter with a moose, and neither would she.

"Hey, Mum. I'll be there by midnight."

"I need you to pick up your father."

Something hard dropped in Audrey's gut, sending a sour taste up her throat that coated her tongue. Could this day become any more of a cosmic bitch-slap? First the show, then she ended up sitting next to a guy who spent the entire flight talking or snoring—to the point that she contemplated rupturing her own eardrums—and now this. The cherry on top. "You're fucking kidding me."

"Audrey!"

She sucked a hard breath through her nose and held it for a second. *Let it go.* "Sorry."

"I can't do it, I have the kids." That was an excuse and they both knew it, though Audrey wouldn't dare call her mother on it. In the course of Audrey's knowledge of her father's love affair with alcohol, never once had she heard of, nor witnessed, Anne Hart leaving the house to bring her husband home.

"Where's Jessica?"

"She and Greg are away. They won't be home until tomorrow." Silence followed as Audrey stewed and her mother waited—probably with a long-suffering, pained expression on her face. Christ, she wasn't even home yet and already everything revolved around her father. She glared at the road through the windshield. She'd take that collision with a moose now.

"Please, babe?"

Her mother knew exactly what to say—and how to say it. And they both knew that as much as Audrey would love to leave her father wherever he was, she'd never forgive herself if he decided to get behind the wheel and hurt someone. She didn't care if he wrapped himself around a tree. She *didn't*. But she couldn't refuse her mother.

Audrey sighed—no stranger to long-suffering herself. "Where is he?"

"Gracie's."

It used to be a takeout and pool hall when she was a kid, but her brother, David, told her it had been turned into a tavern a few years ago. Their father probably single-handedly kept it in business.

"I'll get him, but if he pukes in my rental, you're cleaning it up."

"Of course, dear." Translation: "Not a chance."

Audrey swore as she hung up, yanking the buds out of her ears by the cord. Her mother knew this kind of shit was part of the reason she never came home, but she didn't seem to care. After all these years, Anne Harte still put her drunken husband first. What did it matter anymore if people saw him passed out, or if he got into a fight? Everyone knew what he was. Her mother was the only one who pretended it was still a secret, and everyone let her. Classic.

Rationally, she understood the psychology behind her parents' marriage. What pissed her off was that she couldn't change it. Edgeport was like a time capsule in the twilight zone—nothing in it ever changed, even if it gave the appearance of having been altered in some way. When she crossed that invisible town line, would she revert to being that same angry young woman who couldn't wait to escape?

"I already have," she muttered, then sighed. Between Audrey and her husband, Anne Harte had made a lot of excuses in the course of her life.

Although seven years had passed since she was last home, Audrey drove the nearly desolate road on autopilot. If she closed her eyes she could keep the car between the lines from memory. Each bump and curve was imprinted somewhere she could never erase, the narrow, patched lanes—scarred from decades of abusive frost—and faded yellow lines as ingrained as her own face. The small towns along that stretch bled into one another with little more notice than a weathered sign with a hazardous lean to it. Long stretches of trees gave way to the odd residence, then slowly, the houses became more clustered together, though even the nearest neighbors could host at least two or three rusted-out old cars, or a collapsing barn, between them. Very few of the homes had lights on inside, even though it was Friday night and there were cars parked outside.

You can tell how old a town is by how close its oldest buildings are to the main road, and Ryme—the town west of Edgeport— had places that were separated from the asphalt by only a narrow gravel shoulder, and maybe a shallow ditch. Edgeport was the same. Only the main road was paved, though several dirt roads snaked off into the woods, or out toward the bay. Her grandmother on her mother's side had grown up on Ridge Road. There wasn't much back there anymore—a few hunting camps, some wild blueberries, and an old cemetery that looked like something out of a Stephen King movie. When *Pet Sematary* came out there'd been all kinds of rumors that he'd actually used the one back "the Ridge" for inspiration, though Audrey was fairly certain King had never set foot in her mud puddle of a town in his entire life.

She turned up the radio for the remainder of the trip, forcing herself to sing along to eighties power ballads in an attempt to lighten her mood. Dealing with her father was never easy, and she hadn't seen him since that last trip home, years earlier. God only knew how it was going to go down. He might get belligerent.

Or she might. If they both did there was going to be a party.

Gracie's was located almost exactly at the halfway point on the main road through town. It used to be an ugly-ass building—an old house with awkward additions constructed by people devoid of a sense of form or beauty. The new owner had put some work into the old girl, and now it looked like Audrey imagined a roadhouse ought to look. Raw wooden beams formed the veranda where a half dozen people stood smoking, drinks in hand. Liquor signs in various shades of neon hung along the front, winking lazily.

She had to park out back because the rest of the gravel lot was full. She hadn't seen this kind of crowd gathered in Edgeport since Gracie Tripp's funeral. Gracie and her husband, Mathias, had owned this place—and other businesses in town—for as long as Audrey could remember. Gracie had been a hard woman—the sort who would hit you with a tire iron if necessary, and then sew your stitches and make you a sandwich. She and Mathias dealt with some shady people on occasion, and you could always tell the stupid ones because they were the ones who thought Mathias was the one in charge.

Or stupider still, that Mathias was the one to be afraid of.

Audrey hadn't feared Gracie, but she'd respected her. Loved her, even. If not for that woman, Audrey's life might have turned out very differently.

She opened the car door and stepped out into the summer night, shivering as the ocean-cooled air brushed against her skin. Late June in Maine was a fair bit cooler than in Los Angeles. It was actually refreshing. Tilting her head back, she took a moment there on the gravel, as music drifted out the open back door of the tavern, and drew a deep breath.

Beer. Deep-fryer fat. Grass. Salt water. God, she'd *missed* that smell. The taste of air so pure it made her head swim with every breath.

Something released inside her, like an old latch finally giving way. Edgeport was the place where practically everything awful in her life had taken place, and yet it was home. An invisible anchor, old and rusted from time and neglect, tethered her to this place. The ground felt truly solid beneath her feet. And even though she'd rather give a blow job to a leper than walk through that front door, she didn't hesitate. Her stride was strong and quick, gravel crunching beneath the wedges of her heels.

The people on the veranda barely glanced at her as she walked up the steps. She thought she heard someone whisper her name, but she ignored it. There would be a lot of whispers over the next week, and acknowledging them could be considered a sign of weakness—or rudeness—depending on who did the whispering.

She pushed the door open and crossed the threshold. No turning back now. Inside, a country song played at a volume that discouraged talking but invited drinking and caterwauling along. There were four women on the dance floor, drunkenly swaying their hips while they hoisted their beer bottles into the air. Most of the tables were full and there was a small crowd gathered at the bar. Whoever owned this place had to be making a killing. Why hadn't someone thought of putting a bar in Edgeport before this? Drinking in these parts was like the tide coming in—inevitable.

Audrey turned away from the dancing and laughter. If her father was drunk enough that someone needed to fetch him, then he was going to be in a corner somewhere. She didn't doubt that he'd provided quite a bit of entertainment for Gracie's patrons a couple of hours before. He thrived on attention, the narcissistic bastard. How many songs had he shouted and slurred his way through? How raw was the skin of his knuckles?

She found him slumped in a chair in the back corner, denim-clad legs splayed out in front of him, a scarf of toilet paper—unused—draped over his shoulders and wrapped around his neck like a feather boa. He reeked of rum but luckily not of piss. He'd better keep it that way too. She'd toss him out on the side of the fucking road if his bladder let loose in her rental.

John "Rusty" Harte wasn't a terribly big man, but he was solid and strong. He had a thick head of gray hair that used to be auburn and mismatched eyes that he'd passed on to only one of his children—Audrey. Thankfully she'd gotten her mother's dark hair and looks.

Audrey approached her father without fear or trepidation. Her lip itched to curve into a sneer, but she caught the inside of it in her teeth instead. Give nothing away—that was a lesson she learned from her mother and from Gracie. Show nothing but strength; anything else could be used against you.

She stretched out her foot and gave his a nudge with the toe of her shoe. He rocked in the chair but didn't stir. Great, he was out cold. That never ended well.

She reached out to shake his shoulder when someone came up on her left side. "Dree?"

Audrey froze. Only one person ever called her that—because she never allowed anyone else to do so since.

She bit her lip hard. The pain cut through the panic that gripped at her chest as years of memories, both good and terrible, rushed up from the place where she'd buried them.

Not deep enough.

She turned. Standing before her was Maggie Jones—McGann now—grinning like the damn Joker. She looked truly happy to see Audrey—almost as happy as she had the night the two of them had killed Clint.

Maggie's father.